Prai

LAUR

"*The Good Li*

sudden, swift, precise, deadly. Here is a taut international thriller certain to keep readers breathless and awake until the wee hours of the morning. Not to be missed."
—James Rollins, *New York Times* bestselling author of *Map of Bones*

"[Caldwell's] most exciting book yet, with a plot that begins with an extramarital affair and develops into a tale of betrayal that makes an affair seem like the least of one's worries. It's a summer must-read."
—*Chicago Sun-Times* on *The Rome Affair*

"This book blew me away. *The Rome Affair* is a fabulous, hypnotic psychological thriller. Not only did I wait for the other shoe to drop, but then the next shoe, and the next... Laura Caldwell is a force we can't ignore."
—*New York Times* bestselling author Stella Cameron

"Riveting. Laura Caldwell has weaved a haunting story of suspense and family secrets. If you pick up *Look Closely,* you won't want to put it down."
—*New York Times* bestselling author Mary Jane Clark

"An excellent suspense that kept me turning all night."
—*Mystery Scene* on *Look Closely*

"*Look Closely* is an action-packed thriller of surprising emotional depth. Caldwell mixes the ingredients—an unexplained death, family secrets and foggy memories—into a compelling story you won't want to end."
—Edgar Award winner David Ellis

Also by LAURA CALDWELL

THE ROME AFFAIR
LOOK CLOSELY

LAURA CALDWELL

THE GOOD LIAR

ISBN-13: 978-0-7783-2501-7
ISBN-10: 0-7783-2501-6

THE GOOD LIAR

www.MIRABooks.com

Printed in U.S.A.

ACKNOWLEDGMENTS

My deepest appreciation to Margaret O'Neill Marbury, Maureen Walters and Amy Moore-Benson. Thank you to everyone at MIRA Books, including Donna Hayes, Dianne Moggy, Loriana Sacilotto, Craig Swinwood, Laura Morris, Stacy Widdrington, Pamela Laycock, Katherine Orr, Marleah Stout, Don Lucey, Gordy Goihl, Dave Carley, Erica Mohr, Darren Lizotte, Andi Richman, Kathy Lodge and Carolyn Flear.

Thanks also to everyone who read the book or offered counsel on it, especially Jason Billups, Dustin O'Regan, Clare Toohey, Trisha Woodson, Pam Carroll, Mary Jennings Dean, Morgan Hogerty, Ted McNabola, Joan Posch, Elizabeth Kaveny, Margaret Caldwell, William Caldwell, Kelly Harden, Karen Uhlman, Rob Kovell and Les Klinger.

Lastly, thanks to my panel of experts–Dr. Stuart Rice and Dr. Richard Feely for their medical counsel, Maria Fernanda Mazzuco for her Rio de Janeiro expertise, Dr. Roman Voytsekhovskiy and Peter Zavialoff for their insight into Russia, Gary LaVerne Crowell for his knowledge about the Phoenix Program and Vietnam and Rob Seibert for his special ops and weapons guidance.

"Only you can save your own life."

Everyone told me this in one version or another, during the very bleak days after Scott and I fell apart. I took the advice to heart. I did everything I could to rescue myself.

I prayed to a divinity I couldn't see or feel. I logged hours on the couch. I cleansed. I twisted my body into awkward positions intended to purify. I scribbled and scrawled in journals. I read Goethe. I slept and wept. I watched comedies and dramas. I swore off TV. I ate organically. I drank toxically. I took up gardening. I ran until my legs could hardly hold me.

Nothing helped. The problem was I no longer really wanted to save my own life. Someone had to do it for me. That someone was Liza.

But even Liza had no idea what it would take to save me.

1

Rio de Janeiro, Brazil

Roger Leiland both hated and loved Brazil. On one hand, he'd grown up there professionally. The Trust, the organization he worked for, the one he was now in charge of, had planted him in Rio many years ago. He'd lived there under his alias, Paul Costa, posing as an American businessman selling vaccinations to the Brazilian government. Paul Costa had fallen in love with a woman named Marta and consequently had fallen in love with Brazil itself. But then Marta was gone, dead after a drive-by shooting on the Rodovia dos Lagos Highway. The shooting had left Paul Costa all but dead, too. The Trust had realized he was slipping and pulled him out. Sent him to Chicago, where he was like a walking corpse slowly coming back to life, strangely paralleling his research there—the Juliet Project. Eventually, he'd moved to New York where he took solace in the resilience of power instead of the tenuous comforts of love. He climbed the ladder at the Trust until he'd forged an entirely new existence at the top, all the while keeping his thumb squarely on the Juliet Project.

Now, his expertise was needed in Rio again. Technically, he could have sent someone else, but he wanted to prove to himself that he was at the apex of his game, that Rio no longer touched him. He had been back in Brazil for a few weeks, and while he had felt a flicker of longing for his old life, it was only that—a flicker. He was a different person now.

He had done his job while here. He'd gotten all the intel he required, and now he was meeting with Elena Mistow. Usually members of the Trust knew each other only by their aliases, and they'd been strictly trained to look no further. But even before he was a board member of the Trust, he knew Elena Mistow's real name. Everyone did. Because Elena Mistow was royalty. Her father had founded the entire organization.

Now, he and the woman called Elena sat at an outdoor café in Santa Terese, a charming area set on a hillside in Old Rio. He tried not to be impressed by Elena. She was younger than he, after all, and his subordinate. But there was her lineage. And her beauty.

Elena was all business. "What do we know about Luiz Gustavo de Jardim? Will he show himself anytime soon?"

"Gustavo will appear in public in the next six months. He has to. He's talking about running for office again, and he needs to thwart rumors that he's already dead."

"Wouldn't that be convenient?"

They both laughed. Nothing was ever easy or convenient with the Trust. They were silent for a minute, sipping coffee that tasted nutty and somewhat ashy. To the many on the street, they probably looked like a couple enjoying a break from the day.

"He'll pull the same stunt he always does," Roger continued. "He'll make his kids and wife surround him."

"The bastard uses them as human shields," Elena said bitterly, which amazed Roger. She still cared about who got hurt.

"It works for him," Roger said. "He's a small man. His wife is the same height. By now one of his sons will probably be taller."

"Audacious," she murmured. "And evil."

"We might have to take out the shields."

They exchanged a long look.

Roger broke the stare first, taking another sip of his coffee and gazing at passersby.

"We've never done that," Elena said. "We've sworn not to."

"It's impossible to infiltrate Gustavo's inner circle...so other measures have to be taken to eliminate him. And times are changing. You know that as well as I."

"No collateral damage. That's always been our rule."

"Everything changes. Don't hold on too tight. Just hold on to our mission. Taking out Gustavo, no matter what the cost, advances our end, and that's still pure."

Elena Mistow peered up at the gray-blue sky. She seemed to study something in the atmosphere. A minute passed, then another. "Jesus," Elena said.

Roger stayed silent. He sensed the searching of her mind, the processing, the emotion. He hoped she would draw the conclusion he'd already made.

Finally, she nodded. “So we take out the shields as a last resort.”

Roger permitted himself the faintest of smiles before he raised his cup and took another sip.

2

One week later
Oakbrook, Illinois

I looked out my kitchen window. The Saturday afternoon sun was lighting the empty swing set and the bare winter ground. Another endless Saturday lay before me. I could remember, in a distant way, a time when my weekends were packed with activity and bursting with possibility.

I picked up the phone and called Liza's cell phone. "It's your sad, pathetic friend Kate," I said when she answered.

"Don't call yourself sad," said Liza.

"Can I still call myself pathetic?"

"Absolutely."

I laughed. Talking to Liza was about the only thing that got me laughing anymore.

"Are you back?" I asked.

"I was back, and I left again."

"Where were you last week?"

"Montreal. And I got something for you."

Liza Kingsley was always finding gifts for me on her

travels. In Tokyo, she bought me a handbag in taupe-colored silk. I carried it for years until the lining began to shred. When Liza was in Budapest, she sent back a handwoven rug swirled with gold and celadon green. She was always going to London and bringing me packets of sweets from Harrods and, once, a cocktail dress in a chocolate brown, which she said would complement my eyes.

She was that kind of a friend. A great friend. Her friendship went beyond thoughtful gifts and a shared history. It was her phone calls and her visits and her cheerleading and her love that had propped me up and sustained me since Scott left.

And now this souvenir from Montreal.

"Tell me," I said.

"I found you a man."

I coughed. "What?"

"He's amazing," Liza said.

"I'm not ready to date."

"Kate, it's been ten months since he left. It's time to dip your toe in the waters." A pause. "And look, you're not going to *date*. You'd just go on *a* date."

Wind forced one of the swings into the air. A second later, it listed to a halt. "I don't think so."

"His name is Michael Waller." She paused. "And he's French." Now she had a little goad in her voice.

"Don't kid."

"It's true. Well, he's American, but he's of French descent, and he speaks the language fluently."

"You're taunting me." Liza knew that French men, or at least men who could speak French, were my downfall. It was a trait uniquely embarrassing, because everyone I knew hated French men. Such men were thought pompous. Affected. Liza and I had grown up in Evanston, Illinois, but I'd spent six months after high school in a small town outside Paris, where I fell in love with a boy named Jacques. It was tragic. It was ridiculous. But I was hooked on the accent and the hooded eyes and the utter disdain French men carried for everyone, including themselves.

"It's true," Liza said again. "Of course, it's just one of the six languages he knows."

"Stop." I turned away from the window and leaned against the stainless steel fridge.

"All true."

"How old is he?"

She cleared her throat. "He's a little older than you."

"Spill it, Liza."

"Michael is a very young fifty-five."

"That's seventeen years *older* than me!"

"I know, I know, but I wouldn't recommend him if I didn't think he was the perfect rebound man. Remember, this is just for fun."

"But seventeen years?"

"Hey, Scott was our age, and that didn't make a damn bit of difference, did it?"

I squeezed my eyes closed. It stung, yet Liza was absolutely right. The only thing that had made a difference was that I couldn't have a child. Oh, I could get pregnant with a little medical assistance—and I did three times, in fact—but such pregnancies always ended in miscarriages. My body rejected the babies, and in return, Scott rejected me. Having a family was the most important thing in the world to him, even more important than his wife. And he was fiercely opposed to adoption. He wanted a baby who was *his,* he'd said over and over. Strangely, I didn't think I even wanted children anymore. The quest had sucked me dry, left me with little maternal desire. So Michael's age didn't matter in that respect.

"You there?" Liza said.

"Unfortunately. I'm stuck in the house that Scott built."

"Sell it."

"I will. Soon. I just can't take any more changes for a while."

"What you need is a good night out with a nice, attractive man."

"And that's it? A night out?"

"That's it. He lives in Vermont but he visits Chicago for business. It's perfect."

"How do you know him?"

"Work. He used to be at Presario. I haven't seen him in years, but I ran into him in Montreal. And how fantastic is this? He's opening a restaurant called the Twilight Club in St. Marabel. It's outside Montreal."

"Exactly how am I supposed to date a man who lives in Vermont and is opening a business in Canada?"

"Have you not heard me? I'm just talking about one date."

"Why don't *you* date him?"

She made a snorting sound. "He's not my type, and I have no interest in the French thing, unlike you. So can I have him call you? He's coming to Chicago to meet with investors for his restaurant. He's staying at the Peninsula."

"Expensive."

"Well, he's got money. I'm telling you, this guy has everything, Kate—looks, smarts, money, sense of humor."

I stood away from the fridge and walked into the powder room just outside the kitchen. I flicked on the light and looked at myself in the mirror. "I'd need a haircut," I said. My blond hair, which I normally wore to my chin, had become unruly over the past few months. The too-long bangs had to be pushed aside now and the ends were in desperate need of a trim.

"So get a haircut, for Christ's sake," Liza said. "Get some new clothes, get a massage, treat yourself. Head down to Michigan Avenue and do some Christmas shopping."

"Maybe," I said in a noncommittal way.

The truth was, I'd lacked motivation of any kind since Scott took off. For the first time in my adult life, I hadn't even put up a Christmas tree. All I could manage was to drive to work every day, which was tough since I'd come to despise my job as an accountant at a medical-supply company. Before Scott and I got married, I used to work downtown at a big accounting agency, where we had major clients with interesting portfolios. Most people consider accounting boring, but I've always loved the order of it. My job seemed a challenging puzzle. But once I began working in medical supplies there were very few puzzles. Instead, I was crunching numbers about bedpans and catheters. The job was easier than my old one—and it was just a ten-minute drive from the house—but these things mattered only when Scott and I assumed we'd be having children. At least I hadn't changed my name. My family's name, Greenwood, was the one thing about my life that still felt like mine.

"God, I wish I was there to get you out of that house," Liza said.

"Where are you now?"

"Copenhagen."

Liza had an apartment in Chicago overlooking Lake Michigan, but as the head of international sales for Presario Pharmaceuticals, she was often globe-trotting.

"Your cell phone works in Copenhagen?"

"My cell phone works everywhere. And if it doesn't I forward it to one that does."

"How is Copenhagen?" I asked.

"Freaking freezing."

"Are you having any fun?"

"When do I have time for fun?"

"Liza, you can't work all the time."

"Shut up, we're talking about your pathetic life, remember? Let him take you to dinner."

"You're relentless."

"Someone's got to be. So what do you say?"

I groaned. And yet I felt buoyed just by talking to Liza. She had that effect on me. I glanced out the powder-room window at the lonely swing set. "All right. Have him call me."

3

Thirty-seven years earlier
Fort Benning, Georgia

At fifteen thousand feet, the door of the DC-47 was unceremoniously yanked open, letting in a roar Michael Waller could compare to nothing he'd heard before. A piercing, silvery morning light flooded the plane, and fierce winds stung his eyes.

"This is it!" his team leader shouted. "Hook up, check down, stand in the door."

Michael adjusted the pack straps on his parachute, tightening them past the point that had been recommended.

"Waller! You're up!" he heard, sending his heart rate into full gallop.

He walked toward the door, crouched low and hunched forward like a turtle with too heavy a shell on its back. He'd endured much in his specialized army training—jungle school at Holabird, where his group was forced to walk for days in jungle-like conditions, and enemy captivity training at Fort Polk, where they were put into metal lockers and buried underground—but nothing was as intense or terrifying for Michael as having to dive out of a plane.

He knew this was considered fun for most, and he'd told no one how scared he was. His fear of heights embarrassed him, almost as much as the reason for that fear. As the yawning door of the plane came closer, he saw his father's face—handsome but cruel —as he stood on the high dive of their local pool, right before he picked up his five-year-old son and dangled him, headfirst, above the water, the glints of yellow sunlight thankfully blinding Michael's eyes. His father had thought this stunt would make Michael tough. Unfortunately, it had had the opposite effect where heights were concerned, and that too mortified Michael. He'd always told his father in later years that the high-dive trick had worked. He wasn't afraid of heights at all. But he'd lied.

If Michael's son-of-a-bitch father could see him now, he'd be proud. Finally. The problem was, Michael hadn't been able to tell anyone about the training they'd been put through. He'd volunteered for the army for the same reason a lot of guys did—boredom, literally a lack of anything better to do. He had checked Intelligence as his desired field, mostly because it sounded very James Bond.

He'd been put through testing and accepted for agent training and the intelligence corps. At Holabird, his schooling had been fun at first, as had the after-hours trips to downtown Baltimore. But the training had become more intense, and agents were weeded out. Michael knew he must have shown an aptitude for something to have been allowed to continue. Yet it was confusing, because no one knew what kind of program they were being brought into, or what, exactly, they were being trained to do.

And now this. Now he had to throw himself out of a goddamn plane.

"Waller, ready!" his team leader yelled as Michael reached the door.

He stood paralyzed, feeling the sting and scream of the wind on his face. He looked down and saw the land fifteen thousand feet beneath him, resembling a patchwork of emerald and dirt brown, while the sky's powdery blue spread around him. *No way,* he said to himself. He turned his head, ready to call it off for the sake of survival, when again he saw his father's face.

"Waller, ready!" his team leader yelled again.

This time he shouted back, "Waller, ready!" surprised at the heartiness of his voice.

He grasped the sides of the door, rocked himself three times and flung himself out. His body flipped head over toes. Over and over again. His brain fought every instinct and warning that his frantic nerves sent. He arched his chest and hips to the point of pain, forming a U shape, the way he'd been taught. Finally, the position of the body worked, and he was hovering facedown, flying through the blue, his cheeks flapping. There was no sensation of falling. He'd been told that but hadn't believed it. He was simply suspended there, bouncing in the sky, above everything, above reason or fear now.

Too soon, he checked his altimeter and it was time to activate the chute.

In the hangar, as other unit members landed, Michael clapped them on the back and accepted their congratulations. They were all giddy and high. Michael marveled at the capacity of his mind to move from sheer fear to exuberant joy. It was a lesson he was grateful to learn.

The team leader walked up, and the unit automatically went silent.

"We have a special guest," the team leader said. "Colonel Coleman Kingsley."

He and the rest of his unit snapped to attention in full salute.

An arresting figure stepped through the doors of the hangar and paused. The sunlight flooded behind him so that Michael couldn't see his face.

"At ease," the colonel said, stepping closer. His voice was deep and calm, so different from the terse barks of Michael's commanding officer.

Michael felt a thrill race through him. He'd never met someone of such high rank. And then there was the man's imposing presence—the way he stood with a calm confidence that spoke of battle, and the way his eyes, the color of an exotic sea, assessed the unit with an all-knowing gaze.

"Gentlemen," Colonel Kingsley said, "congratulations on your first jump. There will be others, I assure you, and there will be more training. Training that will test every fiber of your body, every cell of your mind. You will succeed in this training. You will do so because we have selected you carefully. When you complete this, you will join me."

Colonel Kingsley paused then, his blue, blue eyes

landing for a moment on Michael. And in that moment, Michael wanted to make the man proud. He wanted to succeed for him, in a way he'd never wanted to for his father. Michael raised his chin at the colonel, hoping the gesture would show he'd do anything, *anything,* he was asked to do.

4

Oakbrook, Illinois

The goal of babymaking had sapped all my energy and focus for the last few years. It had taken all of Scott and me. And since he left, my goal had been to get some peace in my life, less focus, less intensity, more freedom. No more hormone shots. No more doctor visits or blood tests. And I got that peace, I suppose. It had been *very* peaceful in the house that Scott built. But I was ready for some excitement. So when Michael left a message five days after my talk with Liza, I didn't play coy and count the prescribed, recommended amount of days to reply. I called him immediately. I was geared up for something new, some craziness perhaps, maybe just a touch of chaos.

"How did Liza convince you to call me?" I asked him.

"Liza is very persuasive."

"That's the truth."

We both chuckled.

We launched into a long get-to-know-you discussion. The next night, he called again. And again a few days after that. They were easy conversations, filled with stories that required a new audience to be fresh and entertaining, stories my old friends had heard way too often.

Michael was charming and interesting. He talked of jazz and art and restaurants all over the world. His conversations were filled with anecdotes from the numerous jobs he'd held throughout his life—a photographer in Washington, D.C., a pharmaceuticals salesman in Boston, a winery owner in Napa.

"How did you get from taking pictures all the way to stomping grapes?" I asked.

"Well, let's see. The winery thing happened because I was having a midlife crisis, and I wanted a legitimate reason to drink a lot."

"That makes no sense."

"Hey, it was a rough time. My thinking wasn't entirely clear."

I laughed and listened to Michael talk about going from photographing senators to selling vaccinations to testing soil. He could be serious as well, mentioning the tough years in Vietnam, and his marriage afterward to a woman named Honey.

"Her name was Honey?" I said, a wry tone to my voice.

Michael wouldn't take the bait. "She was Southern. And a lovely woman."

I was silent for a moment. I liked how he wouldn't engage in the usual divorcé pastime of ex-bashing.

"What about you?" he asked.

"His name was Scott. It's still pretty raw."

"Want to talk about it?" Michael had a smooth, melodic voice, and now there was a kindness in his tone that touched me.

I told him I wasn't quite ready. Not yet anyway. But I had a strange inkling that Michael might soon be someone I could talk to about anything.

When he asked me out, a week and a half after our first conversation, I said, "Took you long enough."

"Yes, well. I'm not as good at this as I used to be. So, what do you say? I'm in town on Friday. I'd love to take you to dinner."

"Great." My voice went a little high despite myself. "That would be wonderful."

He called a few days later to say he was on his way. It was a moment I'd been thinking about all week, and I was nervous. There were the usual first date jitters, but they were multiplied exponentially because I hadn't dated since I ran into Scott at our high-school reunion five years ago. Also, I was anxious about the age difference. I had forgotten about it during our conversations, but soon he would be on my doorstep—a fifty-five-year-old man. I was drawn to him on the phone, but what about when I saw him? Could I be attracted to someone so much older?

I flitted around the house, trying to apply lip gloss while straightening the crap that had accumulated during my self-imposed seclusion. I scooped up stacks of newspapers and shoved them in the recycle bin. I pitched old iced-tea bottles and rinsed a couple of crusty plates sitting in the sink. I wished I'd had the sense to get a Christmas tree this week, or at the very least a wreath, something to cheer up the place. But maybe it was just me who saw the house as gloomy, a mere receptacle of what-could-have-been.

I darted into my bedroom, and stood still a moment, gazing at the bay window with its padded silk bench and olive-colored pillows, and at the corner bookshelf filled with mementos. Finally, I let my eyes move to the bed. I hadn't made up the linens before work this morning, and I debated whether to do so now. Wasn't making the bed akin to wearing brand-new, skimpy underwear on a date? Weren't you jinxing yourself? I reminded myself that I didn't actually want to sleep with Michael. The thought of having sex with someone new was mortifying. Yet I did want the date to go well. Was there some kind of bad karma in making the bed?

I decided I was being ridiculous and quickly pulled the sheets straight, yanked the comforter up and plumped the pillows. I hurried back to the kitchen and opened a bottle of Merlot. It was a good bottle that Scott and I had splurged on last year when we were trying to get over the third miscarriage. We never did drink the wine. We never did get over it.

As I took glasses from the cabinet, the doorbell rang. I froze for a second. No one—save the UPS man—had come to my door in a very long time. I glanced down at myself. Presentable enough—slim black pants, a cream silk blouse, ridiculously high heels. And I'd gotten my hair cut and highlighted. But what was I doing going on a date? My divorce wasn't even final for three more weeks. I thought of the rumors around town that Scott was dating a twenty-five-year-old law student, someone young and fresh, someone who could probably give him the children he wanted. The thought put my feet into motion.

When I opened the door, I saw a slim man nearly six

feet tall, wearing a camel-hair sport coat. He smiled, showing white teeth. A light snow had started, dropping flakes on his brown hair, which had only a few shots of gray at the temples. In his hands, he held a small copper pot covered in cellophane. Inside was a white and purple orchid.

"Kate," he said, his voice stirring something inside me to life. "This is for you."

He handed the orchid to me, then leaned forward and kissed me lightly on the cheek. His skin smelled warm, like he'd been in the sun, and it reminded me of getting off a plane in Florida after a long Chicago winter.

I'd lived in or around Chicago for most of my life, and yet Michael took me to a place I'd never been before. It was called Cucina Carrissima, and it was far west on Grand Avenue.

We got a parking spot in front, a bad omen to my mind. In Chicago, the enjoyment of a restaurant seemed inversely related to how far away you had to park. To me, walking a few blocks or more usually meant good food and service.

"How do you know this place?" I asked Michael. He opened my door and helped me from the car. Scott had never done such a thing.

"The owner is an old friend. In fact, he might invest in my restaurant."

"So, I better be on good behavior?"

Michael grinned, his hand still light on my arm. "You don't have to impress anyone, Kate. You're already marvelous."

I flushed deeply. In my recent existence, compliments were as rare as a solar eclipse.

The door was a black industrial thing, scarred and nicked. The hallway was dark with low-hanging ceilings, the kind you might see in a tenement house. But when we reached the end of the hall and Michael threw open the inside door for me, the world opened up. The space was small and looked like a moonlit courtyard. The ceiling was painted with vines and a half moon and decorated with strings of tiny lights. The tables were covered with crisp white linen. Spotless silverware and vases of vivid blue irises adorned the tables. Violin music twisted elegantly through the room.

A man in a black suit approached us. "*Benvenuto,* Michael!" he said loudly.

He and Michael kissed on both cheeks. "Tomaso," Michael said. "How are you?" Michael's words seemed strangely overenunciated.

They exchanged a few words, and I noted the man had an odd way of speaking, as if he had something in his mouth, but then he was clearly Italian, so possibly it was a language thing.

Michael turned to me and introduced me as "A new but very dear friend."

I smiled and shook Tomaso's hand. "So nice to meet you."

As I commented on the restaurant, Tomaso bent his head slightly, his eyes intent on my mouth, his face close to mine. I almost pulled back in surprise.

Tomaso caught my expression. "I am sorry," he said. "I read lips."

"Oh, you're…" I stopped short of uttering the word *deaf,* afraid such a term might not be PC somehow.

Tomaso and Michael both broke into laughs. "I don't hear so good," Tomaso said. He pointed to his ears, making Michael laugh harder.

"He's one hundred percent deaf," Michael said. "But be careful, because he'll read your lips across the room."

"Only with friends who I suspect might say something unkind about me."

Tomaso led us to a table near the center of the room and pulled out a chair for me. "Champagne to start?" he said.

Michael looked at me. I nodded.

Michael and I began with champagne and moved to Chianti. After the glass of Merlot we'd already had at home, I immediately caught a wine buzz. I enjoyed the slight fuzziness of my brain and the electric stars over my head. Michael told me how he'd met Tomaso in Italy when he was still working in the pharmaceutical business.

"That's how you met Liza, too, isn't it?" I asked.

Michael nodded, pouring me more Chianti. "Liza is an exceptional young woman."

I chuckled. "She's not so young anymore. Neither of us is."

"Well, you're both young to me."

There was a moment of silence. This was the first time we'd acknowledged our age disparity.

"I'm sorry," Michael said. "Is that not appropriate first-date banter? I have no idea anymore." He gave me a shy smile that melted me.

I laughed. "I can't remember either."

"Vive la différence?"

"I'll toast to that." When I thought about it, I really didn't mind being younger than Michael. In fact, I was enjoying it. He'd already introduced me to a new person and a new place, all within the span of half a date. And I could tell that Michael was filled with such people and places—he had an air of worldly experience that appealed immensely.

"So, you and Liza have known each other since you were kids?" Michael asked.

"Seventh grade."

"You two must have made quite the pair."

"Yes, hormones and the power of a new best friend will make you do just about anything when you're thirteen." I told Michael of the time I'd dyed Liza's normally auburn hair jet-black because she wanted to try out for the role of Velma in the school's production of *Chicago,* and the time we stole her brother's bike and accidentally rode it into a pond.

"Her brother, Colby," Michael said. "He's no longer around, right?"

I shook my head. "Colby died when Liza and I were seniors in high school. Car accident. Drunk driving on the part of the other guy. I've always hated that, aside from the obvious reasons, because it seems almost a clichéd way to die, and Colby was so special."

I thought of Liza's older brother—a tall, big guy. He'd shared Liza's smattering of freckles, but his hair had been a darker auburn, and he had a crooked way of smiling, one side up. His eyes were devious and fun. We both adored him, looked up to him. He was a few years older than us, while all my own brothers were much older and long gone from the house.

After Colby died, something crumpled in Liza. I didn't know how to help her, and this failing of mine was one of the reasons I grabbed the opportunity to participate in an exchange program in France for six months. I left Liza alone, hoping that when I came back she might be better and we could return to the way we'd been for years. It was a coward's way out, and I still feel guilty about it, particularly when Liza was the one who got me through my divorce. But we had been young when Colby died, and my time away seemed to have worked. Liza was never exactly the same—how could she be?—yet by the time I returned, she had lost the sad tinge to her eyes and the slow way of moving.

I took a sip of Chianti and looked at Michael. He was studying me, almost the way Tomaso might if he was trying to read my lips.

"*You're* special, Kate," he said.

I opened my mouth to protest, to say I certainly hadn't felt special for a very long time. But I stopped, because I realized that something had shifted over the last week since I'd met Michael. Instead of protesting, instead of telling this man that there was nothing unique about me at all, I smiled.

"Thank you," I said. And then before I could think twice, I leaned across the table and kissed him.

5

Moscow, Russia

The day after his date with Kate, Michael Waller entered the passport control area of the Sheremetyevo airport. He reached into his carry-on bag and removed a Russian passport, then he got in the line marked for Russian citizens. It was only minutely shorter than the massive, slow-moving line for foreigners. Some things about Russia would never change.

Michael lifted and dropped his shoulders to release the muscle tension and rolled his neck to try to shake away the headache he felt coming. He simply wasn't the traveler he used to be. Rarely had he noticed his age all these years crisscrossing continents, but now he felt all of his fifty-five years.

He thought then of Kate. God, how unlikely that he should be thinking of her. That he should be thinking of any woman. He'd learned from his divorce that his life did not lend itself to marriage. While secrecy was everything in his business, he simply couldn't stomach it in a romantic relationship. It made everything feel false, even the parts that were true. And yet now he'd found himself here, easing out of his business. He was pulling away, forcing the Trust to make him one of the outsiders, one of the support staff.

This mission to Russia would hopefully be his last. Thank God. Because age made it harder to stomach the missions, too. Or maybe it wasn't age. Maybe it was the Trust's recent descent toward the ruthless and the careless. That wasn't how they used to operate. Luckily—if you could call it that—his mission in Moscow was absolutely necessary for the good of the organization, and most importantly for the good of the United States. And so he would do his job, no matter how distasteful, and then he would go home, and he would try to start living a more normal existence. And he would call Kate. Because if he was no longer playing the same role he used to, there might be room in his life for a partner. And he might have found her.

He moved forward in the line. He would be next to give his documentation to the agent. A flicker of anxiety hit him—a slight increase of his pulse, a knotty feeling in his stomach. Even though the Soviet Union had died and the cold war was over, Michael still felt nervous every time he arrived in Russia. The truth was, "Michael Waller" would have serious problems getting through the passport check. The U.S. government had placed restrictions on his passport for travel into any country once considered communist because he had, technically, worked for the CIA in the past. His presence in a post-communist country might be taken as an act of espionage. But Michael wasn't "Michael Waller" today.

He took a full breath into the lower lobes of his lungs. He forced his pulse to slow. His anxiety calmed quicker than usual. He wondered if the speedy calm was because he'd done this so many damn times. Then another possibility came to him. Maybe it was because of Kate. She made him feel younger, and somehow cleansed of the sins he'd committed, although she knew nothing about those sins, nor would she ever. That thought stalled him for a moment—no matter how present he was now with Kate, no matter what the future held, she could never know his past. Michael felt a wave of sadness, but he let that emotion evaporate from his body. He focused instead on how Kate made him feel—virile and youthful, yes, but more than anything optimistic, actually looking forward to his future.

The customs agent signaled to Michael. He stepped up to the man and handed him the passport he was holding. The man flipped it open and read it.

"Sergei Kovalev?" the agent said.

"Da," he said. *Yes.*

"What countries did you visit?" the agent asked in Russian.

"Italy. France."

"How long were you gone?"

Michael continued to answer the man's questions in Russian, all the while giving the air of a wearied traveler eager for his trip to be over.

The agent paused then, his eyes flicking from Michael to Sergei's passport photo.

Michael felt his breath become shallow, but he continued to give the agent a bored look.

Finally, the agent lifted his head and stamped the passport with a hearty thud. "Welcome home."

"Thank you," Michael said. But really, his trip had just begun.

6

Five hours later, Michael walked through the lobby of his Moscow hotel, a once shabby place that was now grand again, the gold ceilings sparkling like new. The combination of the shabby memory and the new gold made him think of Vegas. Like Vegas, Moscow now had its glamorous sides, its historically seedy sides and its always dangerous sides. Yet Moscow was still much, much tougher.

Michael stepped outside the hotel and walked to Red Square, where gray snow edged itself along the perimeter. He walked through the square, admiring, as he always had, the brightly colored, funhouse cupolas of St. Basil's. The square was different now than it used to be. In the past, the cathedral and the Kremlin stood stark against the bleakness that used to permeate Moscow, making the square almost eerie, sinister. Now the square boasted a skating rink and a new mall filled with designer stores. Michael preferred the old Red Square, but it remained an excellent place to stroll and to search for a tail.

He crossed the square twice, stopping to gaze occasionally at the star atop the Kremlin tower. Yet he was always aware of all the people around him, most of them tourists, along with stylish Russian youths and a few babushkas seeking alms. Each person who came into his sightline turned away in time. He wasn't being tailed. At least not right now.

Michael walked to the metro station with its arched marble doorways, bronze sculptures, ornate chandeliers and vaulted, chrome ceilings. Michael had always been intrigued by the stations. They'd been Stalin's pride, built in the thirties, forties and fifties, and they were intended to display preeminent Soviet architecture and art, to show the privilege of the Russian lifestyle. Whether the opulent stations were optimistic, delusional or simply deceiving, he had never been able to decide, but he could certainly see their beauty.

He took one of the long, long escalators downward, studying the mosaic walls while methodically glancing over his shoulder, memorizing the faces of the other commuters. At the landing, he looked at a portrait of Stalin receiving flowers from a group of children. He walked to another lengthy escalator and took it farther into the bowels of Moscow. The landing boasted a mosaic of Yuri Gagarin, a Russian cosmonaut, made of colored glass.

The Muscovites pushed past Michael, no one stopping to notice the art, much less him. Two minutes later, he boarded a train, rode two stops and disembarked. Once street side again, he held out his hand and waited for a car to stop. Muscovites didn't take cabs, they simply waited until a driver headed in their direction pulled over. A fare would be negotiated, usually a few hundred rubles, and off they went. It was sort of an elevated level of hitchhiking.

A car pulled over. Inside, it was cramped and smelled of cigarettes. The driver was a grim woman in her sixties who wanted no talk, only cash, which was fine for Michael.

After a mile, Michael asked her to stop. He took a minibus in the opposite direction. He got out after a few miles and took another metro ride on a different line, all the while calmly watching anyone he came into casual contact with. There was no indication that he was being tailed. Even if he was, the Moscow Metro was the best place in the world to lose a tail because there were so many levels in the stations, so many trains.

Finally, he disembarked again and went to the street level. Using an international cell phone he'd rented at the airport, he dialed a man he knew as Sebastian Bagley, a Trust operative stationed in Seattle. Sebastian, a man about ten years his junior, was probably the smartest person Michael had ever met, and one of the most humble. Sebastian and Roger Leiland were his two best friends at the Trust, and Sebastian, like Roger, had a medical background. But a long time ago, Sebastian became enthralled with computers and technology. Once he was a member of the Trust, Sebastian had willingly become backup staff, running things behind the scenes. He had never suffered dreams of glory, he just wanted to do an exceptional job, and as such he was a preeminent Trust staffer. Luckily, Michael had enough seniority that he got to work with Sebastian whenever he requested.

"It's Andrew Marson," he said when Sebastian answered, giving one of the aliases he used in the field.

"You're ready," Sebastian said calmly.

"Trotsky in his office?"

"Yes."

"His usual staff in place?"

"Yes. How do you feel?"

Michael smiled. No other backup ever asked an operative how they felt. And he wasn't sure if Sebastian did this for anyone else but him, but he liked it. It was nice to have someone give some small measure of appreciation for what he now had to do.

And so finally, he walked a half a mile to the squat concrete office building where he was to meet Radimir Trotsky.

Radimir Trotsky was a high-ranking member of the Mafiya, the Russian mob, and he was one of the most dangerous. Since the Soviet collapse, Michael had shifted his focus to the Mafiya, and he had not been satisfied with that shift. In days past, he'd felt his work made him an honorable warrior. Now he felt like a beat cop chasing gangsters. And these gangsters were even more brutal than the KGB had been. It was part of the reason why he wanted out of the game. But the Trust didn't let people out, and it was only as a favor to him that they were letting him step down. Or they were *trying* to let him step down. The fact was, no one knew the Mafiya like he did, and Radimir Trotsky needed to be dealt with. Now.

Trotsky had seemingly come out of nowhere six years ago. They knew little about his early years. From what they could tell, he'd been raised in a small town in Siberia, and eventually became a hockey star for one of Russia's many pro teams. A knee injury sidelined him for good, but he used his star power to get into business with Boris Petrov. Trotsky took easily to Petrov's petroleum and cigarette running, the prescription-drug counterfeiting. But it was in the back office—with the skull bashing, the threats, the physical intimidation—that Trotsky's hockey skills really came in handy. Brutality was highly praised and rewarded in the Russian Mafiya, leading Trotsky right to the top of Boris Petrov's organization, where he became Petrov's right-hand man.

Then Trotsky turned his sights on the U.S. He'd always had exceptional language skills and a particular affinity for English. So when Boris started looking toward the lucrative streets of New York, Trotsky was the man he sent. In the last few years, Trotsky was believed to have ordered the killings of at least twenty-nine men and five women who had crossed him in one way or another. And that was what the Trust cared about—the loss of American life, the potential for much greater loss. They cared even more when Trotsky stepped on the wrong toes, those of the oil and cigarette companies, many of whom had representatives in the Trust.

Michael hadn't been watching the Mafiya for a while, but had been told by the Trust that Trotsky was still the poster boy for everything that was so keenly dangerous about the Russian mob—they had no code of ethics, and they were unbelievably ambitious. They would stop at nothing to get what they wanted, and what they wanted was money, power and control in the United States. Their kill-or-be-killed tactics worked, and they always carried out their threats. So the people who dealt with them gave them anything they wanted. But Michael was about to stop that. Or at least a piece of it. The Trust had asked Michael to get back in the game for this one mission because of his expertise. Michael had accepted because, from what he'd learned in the past, it was the right thing to do.

He entered the building through the glass-and-steel doors. He gave the name of Sergei Kovalev to the young man at the front desk who had feral eyes and, Michael could tell from the way he sat, a pistol tucked in the back of his jeans. Sergei Kovalev, thanks to Michael's painstaking work in creating him over the last few decades, had a reputation as a quiet but very wealthy and respectable Russian businessman. A few phone calls to Trotsky's people indicating Sergei wanted to join forces had led to this meeting while Trotsky was in the country. To get within even a block of Trotsky would have been impossible but for Sergei.

The young man with the feral eyes squinted into a computer screen. After a minute, he said something into a handheld radio. A door behind the man clicked open and a large, bald guy stepped into the lobby. He instructed Michael to take off his coat and to spread his arms and legs. He ran a wand over Michael's body, covering every inch in a slow, meticulous fashion. He patted down Michael's arms, chest, back, crotch, ass, legs and feet, then asked Michael to open his mouth and peered inside. He ran Michael's coat through a gunpowder sensor. Finally, he stepped back, pointed to the elevator and said, "Four," in Russian.

Inside the elevator was another young man with cold

eyes, dressed in jeans. Michael asked for the fourth floor. The man eyed him and hit the button.

When they reached the floor, the man escorted Michael down an unadorned concrete hallway to a set of double steel doors. He pressed a bell. They both looked up at a security camera above the doors. Soon the doors clicked open. Inside, the man walked Michael down another concrete hall, past closed doors, until they reached the last door on the left. He knocked, then stepped back.

Radimir Trotsky opened the door and shook Michael's hand. He was a pleasant-looking man with short brown hair, gray eyes and a blue wool sweater. He could have passed for a Midwestern, suburban father. But then, Michael had found benign appearances common to many heartless people.

Trotsky shook his hand, led him into the office and closed the door behind him. To steel his nerves against what he was about to do, Michael reminded himself of the man's laundry list of crimes. He reminded himself of how much danger this man posed to the United States, should he continue his climb to power.

"Thank you for meeting me," Michael said in Russian. "I won't keep you long."

Michael launched into his spiel about his business of making petroleum products, his exportation of his products, his contacts in the U.S., and how he thought their joining forces with Trotsky would benefit them both. When Trotsky turned his head to get a document off the credenza behind him, Michael leaped forward and over the desk, his body falling easily into a maneuver he'd performed too many times now. He locked Trotsky's head with one arm, the other one covering his mouth and holding tightly to his chin. The Russian's arm shot toward an emergency call button, but Michael anticipated the move and pivoted his body away. Michael knew he had to do this fast. The former hockey player was bigger than him, younger than him. If given even a second, Trotsky would gather his wits and make this a real fight, which would no doubt alert the guards. But Michael's knowledge and experience trumped Trotsky's brawn.

So Michael stopped reminding himself why this was necessary. He allowed himself no prayer for the soon-to-be-dead, no prayer for forgiveness for himself. He pushed down on Trotsky's head and, at the same time, wrenched it to the left, then the right, then once back again, snapping the vertebrae, ensuring death.

Trotsky's body slumped and Michael froze, listening for any sounds from outside. The breaking of a neck was a noisy maneuver, but it was the best alternative under the circumstances. His body was tingling with adrenaline and sick with the knowledge of what he'd done. He listened in fear for the sound of running feet. But Michael heard nothing.

Michael draped Trotsky's torso over his desk. He took a tiny digital recorder from the lining of the waistband of his pants. It was nearly as thin as a business card and had escaped detection from the guard downstairs, as Michael knew it would. Pulling his sleeve over one hand, he lifted the phone off Trotsky's desk and dialed the number for the security personnel outside Trotsky's office.

When he answered, Michael pressed play on the digital recorder. The Trust had been watching and, more importantly, listening to Trotsky for over a year and had been able to splice together words they'd recorded.

Michael averted his eyes from the body, as he heard Trotsky's voice shoot from the recorder. "He is coming out. And I want to be left alone for an hour."

The security guard confirmed he understood. Michael slipped the recorder back in his belt, left the office and nodded to the guard on the way out.

Trotsky had been his last job, he reminded himself. It *had* to be his last, because Michael knew what would happen now. He would return to his hotel, check himself out and head for the airport. He would fly home in a comfortable first-class seat that folded out into a bed, but he wouldn't sleep. He could never sleep for days after a job like this. During those days, he would remind himself why the Trust existed, why he had done what he had done.

Yet this time, he didn't dread the next few days like he normally did, because he would insist that this be his final job, and that thought filled up the usually empty well where his optimism was to be stored. But it wasn't just the thought of his diminishing role in the Trust that was filling the well. There was Kate. Thoughts of Kate. Kate's quick, deep laugh. Kate's vulnerability. Kate's luminous brown eyes that gazed at him with wonder, seeing only the good in him. Kate was like water, clear and cool, rushing into his well. And he couldn't wait to see her again.

Time to leave Moscow. Time to leave this world. Time for Kate.

7

Oakbrook, Illinois

"I can't take it," I said, holding the phone. "I can't take this anymore."

"God, I can't either," I heard Michael say. His voice was low and rough, his breathing ragged.

I turned over in my bed and lay on my stomach, still holding the phone. "Jesus, Michael."

"I know, I know. This is the best sex I've had, and I haven't even touched you yet."

Since our date two weeks ago, Michael and I had been on the phone every night. We talked about our work, our comings and goings, our marriages, our dreams—those that had failed us and those we still had—but we also talked about how we would kiss each other if we were together; how we would do all sorts of things.

Technically, this was phone sex, a practice that had mystified me before. I mean, *what's the point?* I used to think. Why not simply wait for the real deal? I hadn't realized how much imagination was involved with phone sex. I hadn't realized how it forced you to talk about *pre-*

cisely how you liked your body to be handled, your thighs to be stroked, your ear to be whispered in. And you learned from the other person what they liked as well.

While at work, as I analyzed the company's quarterly earnings or talked to the office manager, I could not stop hearing Michael's voice. I could not stop seeing us in bed together. Because, of all the explicit details we'd discussed, these images were as vivid as if we'd actually made love.

But now it had gone too far. Now I was mad for him.

"I don't know if I can wait two weeks." Michael was supposed to return to Chicago in two weeks and we would have our official second date.

"I know. I can't wait either."

"I'll get a flight tomorrow morning," Michael said.

"Thank God."

The next night, we had dinner at Merlo, an eclectic Italian place on Maple Avenue. Our conversation never waned, nor did our intense looks across the table. Later, I walked out of the place with Michael's arm around my back, and I was electric from just that touch.

The Gold Coast was awash with lights, but it was quiet with the post-holiday lull. A light sprinkling of snow covered the sidewalk.

"Careful," Michael said as we walked down the restaurant's front steps.

I stopped. Michael, who was one step below me, did the same.

"I'm sick of being careful," I said. I grabbed his face, his warm, smooth-shaven face, and I kissed him hard. Within seconds, our bodies were pushed against each other, our arms wrapped around each other tight. I could feel my body temperature shooting high until I wanted to tear off my cashmere coat.

"Let's go to your hotel," I said.

"You're sure?"

"Shut up."

In his hotel bed, Michael held himself up on his arms, gazing down at Kate. Gorgeous, smart, sexy Kate.

They were stripped of their clothes, and in fact, he felt they were both stripped of *everything*—every pretense or artifice. His body felt as lean and hard as it ever had, and yet his core was somehow liquid and alive. They were right on the brink, about to consummate this intangible chemistry.

He stared into Kate's eyes—neither of them had closed their eyes tonight, even while they were kissing—and he felt the momentousness of the instant. Sex had never been like this for him. He almost laughed because they still hadn't technically had sex yet, but this was it. *This was it.* That phrase kept returning to his mind. His life was different now. He was taking a step back from the Trust into a normal existence, and yet he was taking a step forward with Kate.

"Ready?" he asked Kate.

Her brown eyes stared into his—into his soul, it felt like. She didn't say anything. Not a word. Instead, never letting her eyes stray from his, she reached for his hips. Slowly, slowly, she drew him into her.

8

Four months later
St. Marabel, Canada

"Kate, my girl, it's your wedding!" Liza yelled, bursting through the door of the church's anteroom. "I can't believe you're shameless enough to wear white." The sides of her auburn hair were pulled back, a few wavy tendrils escaping. She wore a soft pink dress that draped over her shoulders and exposed her collarbones.

My mother shot Liza a disapproving look.

"Liza, stop," I said, laughing. I loved when Liza was like this—funny and over-the-top—and the fact was, she was like this ninety percent of the time. The other was a serious, soulful Liza, moody and hard to reach. She rarely let anyone see that Liza.

My mom scurried around me, fluffing my dress, and pinching off a few bouquet flowers she saw as less than ideal. We were in a tiny church tucked on an angled alley street of St. Marabel. The church was where Michael came to Mass the few times a year he did so while summering in this town. Despite the fact that I hadn't gone to Mass in years, I found the church cozy and comforting. I needed that because now that Michael was opening a restaurant here, and Michael was about to become my new husband, and all of this meant that my life was entirely new and different and unknown. Fitting that it was spring.

"I need one minute alone with my friend," Liza said, drawing me away from my mother and against a stone wall. Her smile waned. She looked contemplative. "Are you sure you want to do this?" she said, her voice low.

"Liza. We've been through this."

Liza had seemed pleased when my first date with Michael had gone so well. She seemed delighted when he came to see me again in Chicago. She sounded cautious when I went to visit him for a weekend. And when we got engaged, she was alarmed. I understood. Our relationship had progressed so rapidly, I hardly knew how to process it myself.

Long-distance relationships are the toughest breed. Michael and I fell for each other—hard—aided by the phone sex and the long weekends and the painful goodbyes that often brought me to tears. And then I couldn't stand being away from him. It literally wrenched something inside me that I couldn't see him, that I was forced to only hear him at night on the phone. And so our relationship had moved with electric speed. It was either that or pretend I didn't care and try to let it grow with a slow build. But Michael wasn't slow, at least when it came to me. He told me the first weekend I visited him that he loved me. We were in Vermont, riding horses down the back trail of his property and watching the sun sink fast over a small mountain ridge. His horse nudged up to mine. I tightened my gloved hands on the reins, surprised. Then I relaxed when I looked into his face, a face so familiar somehow.

"I can't believe I'm going to say this after such a short time," he said. "But I have to." He paused.

I heard a branch break somewhere in the woods, then the hum of a distant plane.

"I love you." He said this with certainty. And certainty was a concept I hadn't been familiar with for a long time. I'd been living with Scott, wondering and wondering and wondering— Would we have a baby? Would we last without one?

I didn't return the sentiment that cold day in Vermont. I wanted to. But I also wanted to be smart. I wanted to take Michael's words home and roll around in them. I wanted to see if they fit.

Yet the next day, when I was about to leave him at the ticket counter of the little airport, I felt a clutch in my chest. I would miss this man so much. And I didn't want to miss him. I wanted to see him every morning, and every night. Before I'd met Michael, I'd honestly believed I would never feel like this again. Scott—like a thief who carries off valuables in the night—had stolen from me trust, hope, innocence, belief, all the components of first love. I had assumed the theft was complete and that I would never possess those things again. But now I had this surge in my chest, the return of feelings lost.

I dropped my bag on the concrete sidewalk. I stood on tiptoe and grabbed Michael's face in my hands. "I love you, too."

"Well, it's about time."

We kissed, laughing.

I went back to Vermont the next weekend. The week after I visited his summer place in St. Marabel, where he was moving to permanently open his restaurant. The weekend after that when he returned to Chicago, I walked into Michael's room at the Peninsula to find it wasn't a room, it was a suite, and it was filled with peonies, my favorite flower. A table was set up under the window, laden with a meal made of my favorite Chicago dishes—a cheese flight from Avec, endive salad from Bistrot Margot, sea bass from Spring and chocolate truffles from Vosges called Black Pearls.

"If you were to leave Chicago," Michael said, "I know you'd miss the city. But I promise to try and bring Chicago to you whenever I can. My home is wherever we're together."

In that instant, I saw where this was going and I started to tremble.

"Kate." He cupped one cheek with his big hand and kissed my eyes, my forehead, then, slowly, my mouth. "I want to do that every day. Will you marry me?"

I didn't hesitate a second before I said yes.

I put my house on the market within a week. I won't say that I didn't sob—great, gulping sobs—when I left. But once I was in my mother's car, on the way to the airport and away from Chicago for good, I felt like I was lifting off.

And now I was in St. Marabel, about to be married again.

"Liza," I said. "Remember, it was *you* who set us up."

"I know, I know." She tucked a tendril of auburn hair behind her ears and peered into my eyes. "I just didn't think…"

"You just didn't think what?"

"That you'd get *married.* He was supposed to be a transition guy."

"Well, he turned out to be *my* guy."

She breathed out hard.

"What?" I said. "What is it?"

"It's just so soon."

"Liza, you like Michael, right?"

"Of course."

"Why do you like him?"

She shrugged. "Because he's an honorable guy. He's a great man."

"Right. And you know that just from meeting him at work. You should see his personal side. You should see him at home with me. He's amazing."

I watched Liza's face as I said this. It had occurred to me early on that maybe Liza and Michael had had a fling. Sometimes the way they spoke of each other made them seem more familiar than just two old colleagues. But Liza had flatly denied this when I asked her, and Michael had laughed.

"I'm in love with him," I said. "Can't you be happy for me?"

Liza stood straighter. She kissed me softly on the cheek. "Of course. I am happy for you."

Behind us, my mother cleared her throat. I turned to her. "You okay, Mom?"

My mother, Geri Greenwood, was a worrier at heart.

My brothers, seven and eight years older than me, had created enough trouble that she worried her weight away, leaving her a diminutive sixty-six-year-old, whose designer clothes were a size zero. She had on a beige chiffon dress today, and although I knew she was happy for me, the lines at the corners of her mouth looked deeper than usual.

She smiled, then went about fluffing the hem of my dress. "I just want what's best for you."

"*This* is what's best for me!" My voice rose, despite myself. "C'mon, you guys! It's my wedding day, and I'd like a little support, and—"

My mother's hand reached out and touched my arm, stopping my words. She looked at me. The lines of her face softened. "I know you're in love. And I'm thrilled for you."

"Me, too," Liza said. "So let's do it, ladies."

Liza turned and threw open the door of the anteroom. I could see the small cobblestone foyer of the church and, beyond that, the open, arched doors leading to the aisle.

I took a few steps and peeked my head forward, peering down that ivory-covered aisle, and I caught a glimpse of Michael—tall and beautiful, hands clasped, rocking back and forth on his heels. Michael smiled at Roger Leiland, his best man, whom he'd met while married to his first wife. Michael's marriage had split up years ago, but he said he'd never split from Roger, even though Roger had changed a lot. Apparently, the love of Roger's life died many years ago, and he'd become hardened and callous in many ways. But Michael said he'd never give up on a friend, and I loved his unabashed loyalty. Roger was shorter than Michael, more powerfully built, and probably five or six years younger, but they had a camaraderie that could always be felt when they were together.

I took in the rest of the tiny church, mostly empty, although Tomaso, the restaurateur from Chicago, was there with his wife. My brothers and their wives were in attendance, too. They were all grinning big, no doubt relieved that their little sister wasn't the depressed creature she'd been for a year now. And there was my dad, nervously twisting around in his seat. I'd told him that I wanted to walk down the aisle by myself this time. It felt more adult somehow, more honest and real, that I and only I would walk toward my new husband.

I felt a rising of something through me—a vision of a new husband, a new town, new friends, a new life.

"Ready?" Liza said, bumping her hip into mine.

I threw back my shoulders. "Absolutely."

Michael and Roger stood at the bar of Jameson Place, a small, charming pub in St. Marabel where the reception was being held. There were only twenty people, but the mood was as ebullient as if hundreds were in attendance.

St. Marabel was the place where Trust members from around the world had been meeting for years, and so Michael had spent a lot of time there. But now, newly married to Kate, it felt like home for the first time.

Michael ordered a glass of Lagavulin scotch from the bartender. Roger asked for red wine.

"No, no," Michael said, "he'll have a Beychevelle Bordeaux." He turned to Roger. "I've told you, my friend, you can't just ask for red wine or they'll give you some Cabernet swill."

Roger accepted his glass from the bartender and sipped. "Delicious. You became such a wine snob when you ran that winery. That was the best cover the Trust has ever given someone."

Michael laughed. "Now what will I become? A restaurant snob?"

"No, from the way you're staring at Kate, I'd say you're about to become one of those insufferable people who believes everyone can find true love. If they just look in the right place."

Michael dragged his eyes away from Kate's incandescent face and met the gaze of his best friend. "Guilty as charged."

Roger turned to face the bar. Michael's scotch was delivered, and they sipped in silence.

"So," Roger said, "I haven't had a chance to tell you personally—good work in Moscow."

Michael's body tensed ever so slightly. No one would have noticed, but he knew Roger did. They were friends, after all, but they were also trained to look for such physical clues in everyone.

"That has to be the last job," Michael said. "Now that I'm here running the Twilight Club for the Trust."

"Now that you've got Kate."

"Yeah, that's right. Are you going to give me hell for wanting to be a good husband? A normal husband?"

Roger held his hands up in mock self-defense.

"Jesus, Michael, Moscow was just something you had to finish."

Michael sighed. "I don't *want* that anymore. I want to give Kate a great life. I want to make her happy."

"You can't tell her anything about the Trust."

Michael gave him a withering look. "I would never. You know that."

Roger nodded. "I gotta tell you, buddy…" He trailed off, shaking his head, and Michael readied himself for more ribbing about true love. "I'm jealous," Roger said simply. "I miss feeling like that."

Michael looked at him. "I thought you never wanted another relationship after Marta."

Roger shrugged. "You never know."

They shared a silence during which Michael gave his friend an opportunity to elaborate. He didn't.

"I'm telling you, I'm fine running the Twilight Club," Michael said. "I'm excited that the Trust will have a meeting place, and I like being in on the ground floor of it. But that's it for me. That's my involvement now, and that's all."

"You're repeating yourself."

"Well, I just want you to know. You're a member of the board."

"You used to be as well."

"That's right. *Used* to be."

Roger took another sip. "Fine, I've gotten the message, for what it's worth."

"It better be worth something. I've given my whole life to this."

"Who hasn't?"

"Michael!" Kate's voice rang out. She and Liza were holding on to each other, cracking up. "You have to hear this story."

Michael could feel the grin stretch across his face. Genuine, spontaneous smiles still felt foreign to him.

"Go," Roger said.

The two men looked at each other.

"Thanks," Michael said.

Roger gave him a clap on the back, and as Michael walked toward his wife, he let that smile take over his face again.

9

A few hours later, after most of the wine had been drunk and the bride and groom had waved goodbye, Roger Leiland approached the bar and the one person he'd wanted to talk to all night.

She stood with her back to him, one strap of her pink dress falling over a lightly freckled shoulder. Roger felt himself stirring, turned on by the sight of her. But that wasn't the only reason he wanted to talk.

There were only a few people left at the pub. Kate's brothers and their wives were tucked in at the end of the bar, completely blotto and shrieking with laughter. At one of the tables, Michael's contractor from the Twilight Club plied his date with a bottle of champagne.

"Hello, Elena," Roger said, stepping up to her, using her alias.

She turned to him. In her eyes, he saw a look of worry. She quickly cleared her expression. He was surprised she'd let any emotion show, even for that fraction of a second, since she was notoriously stoic. He wondered what it was that troubled her.

"Hello, Paul," she said, using his alias as well.

"Fancy meeting you here."

"Cut the bullshit," she said, although not harshly. He liked how she talked simply and sometimes crudely, like a man, but how when you looked at her—with that body and that red hair and those intense green eyes—you were always very aware that Liza was a woman.

He looked around to make sure no one was listening. The bartender was taking care of Kate's brothers. "So why did you introduce them?"

She gave him a hard stare, then picked up her glass of white wine and took a sip. "I didn't think they would get *married.* Jesus, I just thought they could go on a date or two. I mean, Kate is my best friend, and she'd been moping around for almost a year since her marriage fell apart. And you know Michael. He hadn't been out with someone in forever."

"That's because he didn't want to bring anyone into this world."

"Give me a break. He's settling down here in St. Marabel. Why shouldn't he be with someone who makes him happy?"

"Because it's dangerous. It's dangerous for your friend."

She swallowed more wine, her brows knitting. "They'll be fine. Michael has a totally different role now, right?"

He nodded. "That's right. He's requested step-down status, and running the Twilight Club is the assignment we've given him."

"But you won't let him out."

"He can't be out entirely. You know the rules."

Liza sighed and turned to face the bar. "God, do I."

He stepped closer. He could smell the lotion on her skin—scented with vanilla and something a little darker—and he felt himself grow hard. He could have stopped it. Like her, Roger had gotten very good at concealing emotion when he wanted to. But he didn't want to. Just for tonight, and with someone exactly like Liza, he wanted to let sensation get the better of him. Although she was his subordinate, she was a star in his world. The thought of capturing that star, consuming her, was intoxicating.

"It's not so bad, is it?" he said.

She stared at her wineglass. "It's tough. You know how it is."

"This is your legacy."

"Sometimes I don't care."

"If it helps, I can tell you that the research we're doing in Chicago is going well. Incredibly well, actually. I'd love to show you sometime."

Liza gave him a confused look. "I know nothing about that research, and since I'm not involved, you shouldn't be telling me. That's protocol."

He shook his head. "Rules can be bent." If she only knew how he'd bent the rules.

"Since when?" Liza said.

He stepped even closer, to the side of her now. "I want to make you feel better."

She looked up at him, and her face shifted to one of surprise. She'd seen his open desire.

"Roger," she said sternly, dropping the alias, and taking a step back. "Don't."

He stepped closer. He could smell that scent again, and it made him want to pin her arms down and bite the side of her long, white neck. "Why not? Why should Michael and Kate get everything?"

"No fraternization. Those are the rules. And you helped *make* those rules."

"I'll break them."

She gave a short laugh. "Have some respect for yourself. Stop while you're ahead."

"Let me make you feel better."

"Roger, get the fuck away from me."

The word *fuck* coming from her mouth made him angry and yet it turned him on even more. He was losing a little bit of control. He saw that. But he liked it. It had been a long, long time.

He grabbed her arm and pulled her toward him. "C'mon. Come back to my hotel."

"Roger, maybe you're not understanding. I have no interest in you, I have no interest in your body, and I'd rather spend six months in solitary confinement than go to your hotel room."

He tightened his grip on her arm. Now she was pissing him off.

She dropped her voice. "If you don't get your hand off me, I'll break it. I will break every phalanx and every joint and every metacarpal."

Just then, one of Kate's brothers yelled "Liza!" from the end of the bar.

She yanked her arm away and shot them a smile. "Be right there," she called.

She turned her attention back to him, her features growing stern again. "I'm going to pretend this didn't happen. And it will *not* happen again. Do you get that?"

He felt the urge to smash her face with his fist. He was embarrassed now that he'd let her get the better of him, but he would never show her that. He merely gave her a smirk.

Liza tossed her shoulders back and walked to the end of the bar. She accepted a beer from one of Kate's sisters-in-law and pecked one of the brothers on the cheek.

A minute later, she glanced over her shoulder to see if Roger was still there. He stood, trying to let his anger sift away. She was a star in their world, yes, but the way she treated him, as if he were some commoner, as if he weren't *someone,* was inexcusable.

Finally, Roger turned and left the bar. The cobblestone streets of St. Marabel were slick. It must have rained. Roger put his hands in his pockets and headed for his hotel. He'd been able to clear most of his emotions and leave them at the pub—he'd left behind his desire and his momentary lack of control. But he was still carrying one emotion with him. His anger. He was having a very hard time getting rid of that.

10

Chicago, Illinois

Liza Kingsley crossed LaSalle Street at Madison and entered one of the block's smaller buildings, which bore brass plates by the entrance. Nine of those plates proclaimed the names of local law firms. The other plate read simply, Presario Pharmaceuticals.

"Morning, Ed," she called to the security guard, as she did every morning she came to the office.

"Morning, miss."

Liza walked to the elevator and got in with two lawyer types who hit the button for a firm called Toffer and Brodley. She nodded at them and smiled.

"Hey," one guy said to her, allowing his eyes to linger on her face. Those eyes had also darted down Liza's body when she stepped inside the elevator. He probably thought she hadn't noticed. She had.

Liza wore a sleek, black pantsuit, as she did many days at work, but today she'd added a low-cut, salmon-colored silk blouse. Something about seeing Kate and Michael at their wedding last week had made her think that it was about time she found someone to date. Or at least someone to sleep with. She'd spent her weekend deciding that it had been entirely too long.

"How was your weekend?" the guy asked Liza, as if they knew each other.

She turned to face the lawyers. The one who had spoken wore khakis and a blue button-down shirt that matched his eyes precisely. He had brown hair, cut short—typical lawyer fashion—but he had a wicked grin. Liza knew his type. Full of confidence. Full of bravado. Full of himself. And usually very good in bed.

"A little lonely," she answered.

His grin deepened. "Yeah, me too."

They stood, their eyes not leaving the other's face.

"So you work at Presario Pharmaceuticals, huh?"

She nodded.

"What kind of pharmaceuticals do you specialize in?"

The elevator dinged and the door opened to the spacious, ivory-painted foyer of Toffer and Brodley. The other lawyer got out and took off down the hallway.

Her guy stood in front of the doors so they couldn't close. "I'm Rich Macklin," he said, holding out his hand.

She shook it. "Liza Kingsley."

"I'm from Boston, but I work out of this office part-time. Maybe I'll stop up at Presario and say hi someday."

"Oh, no, don't do that."

His cocky grin faded.

"It's a zoo, and the receptionist can never find anybody." She rolled her eyes at the imagined craziness of her office.

He pulled a card out of his pocket. "Well, then, call

me when you're heading downstairs for a coffee sometime, okay? Or whenever. My cell phone number is on there, too."

"Sure," she said, taking it from him, liking the tiny race of her pulse.

Even though the number for her floor was already lit, she hit it again. "I'll see you then."

"Yeah, I'll see you." He gave her that grin again and stepped back.

Liza held Rich Macklin's card as the elevator climbed. She liked the feel of it—light but with sharp edges. She stepped out when the elevator reached her floor. A large, glass block sign hung in the foyer with heavy, steel letters spelling out Presario Pharmaceuticals. Below that were two visitors' chairs with an end table between them and a single black phone atop the table.

Liza lifted the phone, which was a STU-III, a secure telephone device designed to take audio signals, mix them digitally into a serial data stream and encrypt the voice. She rattled off a series of letters and numbers. "X68BTY233BR5Y780."

A door in the side wall, barely perceptible, clicked twice. Liza pushed it open and entered a hallway with thick beige carpeting, the kind that might be seen in Rich Macklin's law office downstairs. But the offices here weren't filled with open doors and chatting lawyers. Every door was locked. No sound filtered into the hall.

Liza walked to her office door and held her thumb to the fingerprint pad. When prompted, she punched a different series of numbers and letters into the keypad. She stepped into her office. Its plain white walls surrounded a scruffy but beloved pine desk that had been handed down from her father. Her only adornments were an Oriental rug—plum and olive green—that she'd picked up in China, and two pictures frames, an oval one showing her and Kate at college graduation and one of her family taken in the mid-eighties. In it, her father stood behind Liza, Colby and her mom, his arms stretched out, trying to encircle them. She still thought of her dad that way—trying to hold all of them close, keep all of them safe. It was hard to believe she and her mom were the only ones left.

The phone on the desk made a single buzzing sound. Liza picked it up and held it to her ear without a word.

"Good morning, Liza," said a female voice.

The voice belonged to a woman who was one of the analysts for the Trust. Her job was to monitor and interpret world events and to notify Trust operatives, like Liza, when those events might be of the slightest interest. But there was usually no "good morning" or "how are you doing" involved in these discussions. Why the formality? Liza wondered.

"Morning," Liza replied cautiously.

"A small plane went down at the Moscow airport about half an hour ago."

Liza furrowed her brow, still confused. "Was it carrying any cargo?" Moscow was one of the few Russian cities where Presario actually sold product.

"No."

"Casualties?"

"Seven. The crew. Four passengers."

"Anyone we know?"

There was a pause. An odd, surreal pause when the walls of her office seemed to close in one minute and then expand like a balloon the next. Liza swallowed hard. She closed her eyes and opened them.

"Aleksei Ivanov," the woman answered.

Liza let her weight fall against the chair behind her. She felt as if a cannon had been shot at her insides. "Aleksei?"

Why was she having such a reaction? She hadn't laid eyes on him in a few years. She sat immobilized then, unable to speak.

But Liza knew why—because Aleksei was different than anyone she had ever known or would ever allow herself to know.

She could imagine him as clearly as the first time they'd met in Rio. She could see those deep green eyes that went from shrewd to laughing in a split second, the perpetually mussed sand-colored hair, the thin, worn leather jacket. And those reporter's notebooks he was always carrying around. He tried to get her to carry them, too. "For memory," he said, tapping her gently on the forehead, his green eyes laughing then. She told him she didn't need help with her memory. But now Aleksei was gone, and she wished she'd filled a notebook with the other details she remembered of him.

Liza struggled to take a breath. "Do we know why the plane went down?"

"No, but the other passengers were journalists, too."

"Thanks for the call," she managed to say.

"Of course."

Liza hung up the phone and left her office just as quickly as she had entered it.

11

Five years earlier
Rio de Janeiro, Brazil

As a warm blanket of darkness settled over the city, Liza Kingsley drew away from the spotting scope she'd been peering into. She took off the headphones. She stood and stretched, then allowed herself to slump onto the polished wood floor of the apartment. With her back against the outside wall, she stared at the place. Recently, this apartment had been owned by a wealthy Brazilian couple. It was in the Gávea neighborhood—a gentrified area in a city of *favelas* or shanty towns—but the couple hadn't been wealthy enough to pass up the insane amount of money Liza offered them through a broker. The couple might have known that they lived directly across the street from João Pedro Franco, a business partner of Luiz Gustavo de Jardim. They would have undoubtedly followed Gustavo's push for power and occasional threats to run for the presidency. They probably didn't know that their apartment would be used solely to study and listen to Franco, Gustavo's main confidant.

Gustavo, along with all of his close associates, was being watched. If ever reelected to the political realm, Gustavo would be in charge of many things other than the value of the real, the Brazilian currency, and the arms dealing he already controlled. Gustavo could eventually control the country's vast oil resources and its production of fighter jets. It was not a power to be taken lightly. Gustavo was also known for being as corrupt as they come. When he'd been in office once before, it was widely suspected that he'd funneled significant funds meant for AIDS research to dummy companies in his control. Worse, they now had intel that he was taking meetings with different terrorist organizations and promising under-the-table sales of fighter jets, along with private aircraft. These terrorist organizations had been quietly searching for such jets for years, hoping to fill them with explosives and use them as flying bombs to attack the United States.

The Trust was attempting to determine whether such intel was correct, and if Gustavo meant to keep his promises once in office or if he was just shooting off his mouth. And so somewhere across the city, Gustavo's house and office were under surveillance, while Liza watched his buddy, Franco (and his wife, kids, housekeeper and cook). In reality, Liza mostly listened to the conversations of all these people through the bugs they'd placed in Franco's house. Like many of Rio's nicest homes, Franco's was built around an internal courtyard, invisible to the front, with only one window facing the street.

And so now across the street from Franco the newly purchased apartment had been bled dry of personal effects, and family memories and color, and it was filled with the cool blacks and silvers of surveillance equipment. Liza felt this apartment was somehow a metaphor of her own life, the way it was taken up with work and work only.

Before the light completely disappeared, Liza roused herself, packed away her scope and replaced it with an ATN night-vision scope. She returned the headphones to her ears. As she focused the scope across the street, watching for any visitors to Franco's home, she saw a man approach the house, stop briefly to adjust his shoe, then move on down the street.

Liza refocused the scope and watched his retreating figure. The man had hair that was messy, as if he'd just roused himself from bed. He wore jeans and a lightweight leather jacket, despite the sticky heat. She'd seen this guy before, sometime yesterday. She remembered because of the jacket. Was he simply a neighbor? But he didn't look Brazilian, nor did he look like he could afford the neighborhood.

Liza brought the scope back to the house and stared at the spot where the man had squatted to adjust his shoe. A knowing smile took over her face.

She left the apartment, locking the four double-cylinder dead-bolts and punching in the numbers on the keypad to arm the fingerprint-ID lock, all of which had been installed after the purchase of the apartment. She left the building and crossed the street, walking quickly past Franco's house, then turned at the end of the block and walked back the same way. On the second pass, she saw what she was looking for—a rock in the tiny front lawn, right by a post of the black iron fence. She bent slightly and scooped up the rock. She took it upstairs with her and settled into an interior room with no windows, where she flicked on the lights.

She studied the rock, then turned it over and saw the false bottom. She smiled again as she removed it. A tiny camera had been installed, no doubt to take photos of guests arriving at Franco's house. The rock was simple in design, the color too uniform to look real. If Gustavo and his crew were already in power, with a large security detail in place, the device would have been discovered easily.

She switched off the lights, left the apartment again and walked one block away. She hid herself in a dark corner of an alley where she had a half view of the street. She waited for an hour, then another. It was a Friday night, and a few couples strolled home from dinner, tipsy and laughing. She disappeared deeper into the alley at those times. Sometimes it made her feel too lonely to see couples. She hadn't been a part of one in a long time. Not ever in her adult years, if she admitted it.

Her loneliness had been hammered home a few weeks ago when Kate had married Scott, who was a friend of theirs from high school. Scott was a decent enough guy, both in looks and personality, but in Liza's opinion he wasn't a match for Kate's wit and smarts. Maybe Liza was just being protective, or maybe she simply felt the sting of still being single—and very much alone—while her best friend charged into marriage and family.

After another hour from her vantage point in the alley, Liza saw what she was looking for, the man in the leather jacket. She'd had a feeling he'd be back sometime tonight. Franco often had people over for drinks on

Fridays, and the man probably expected his little rock to have taken a few snapshots of the guests. She watched, amused, as the man ambled by Franco's place, then did his bend-and-adjust-shoe technique. But this time, he didn't rise as quickly. She saw his hand dart onto the lawn, grasping for an object that was no longer there.

He had the sense not to linger and was soon walking the other way. Liza tailed him until he reached a busy *avenida.* She came closer to him. The noise from the restaurants and bars hid the sound of her footfalls. Soon they were shoulder to shoulder.

He stopped abruptly and turned to her. "May I help you?" he said in Portuguese, but with a very distinct accent. Russian.

"I think you may have lost something," she answered in English. She paused to make sure he understood the language and saw from his eyes that he did.

"I think you are mistaken," he said in English. But there was anxiety in his green eyes.

She flashed the rock at him, then closed her fist and crossed her arms. "You need to come with me."

He hesitated. His eyes darted toward her arms. He wanted that rock back.

"A few questions, then I give you back what you've lost."

The man glanced around. Liza scanned the crowd with him. Did he have backup? She pulled up her shirt slightly, just enough to show him the pocket Glock tucked in the waistband of her jeans. It was one of the smallest Glocks available, one that could only be handled by the sharpest of shots. Which she was.

At the sight of it, the man's shoulders drooped and he pressed his lips together. He wasn't armed.

"I will give you back what is yours," she said.

"Yes, okay," he answered.

It turns out, Aleksei Ivanov was a terrible spy. Actually, he wasn't a spy at all, just a journalist who'd been convinced he could become one.

Ordering him to walk ahead of her, Liza directed the man from the streets of Gávea, into the neighboring *favela* of Rocinha. The vertical streets were winding and barely shoulder width, lined with shanty-style houses. The sheer volume of people and sounds and smells was overwhelming. The man had clearly never been in Rocinha before, she could tell from the way he flinched at the shouts from the children, many smiling despite their plight.

He looked back at her once, and she could see he was analyzing his chances of bolting. "Keep going," she said, flashing her Glock again.

The man looked from the pistol to her face, then continued his trudge through Rocinha. They were openly stared at by the residents of the *favela.* The adults looked wary, the children shouted for money or cameras.

At one point, Liza saw the man reach for his pocket.

"Don't," she said in a sharp bark.

The man turned to her with a slightly pained expression. "I don't have a weapon. I just thought I would give them some money."

Liza felt herself soften, but she shook her head. "They'll mob you if you do." She gestured at him to keep walking.

When they reached the top of one of the coiling streets, Liza stopped the man and nodded at a shanty. The walls were covered by haphazardly placed tiles, most of which were crumbling or discolored with soot. A young man stepped outside the structure. He wore a red cloth tied around his head. His eyes were black, and to Liza, they appeared dead. He was the kind of man who scared her most—one with nothing to lose—but he was her contact in this neighborhood, someone who took money for information or accommodation or just about anything. His name was Faustino, and despite his meager standard of living, he knew lots of people in this corrupt town. Liza had found that he could get nearly anything accomplished for the right price.

"Faustino," Liza said.

He nodded.

Surreptitiously, she took some réis out of her pocket and passed it to the man.

"May I use your residence?" she said in Portuguese.

He nodded again.

Liza directed the Russian inside. The house was just a room, really, with three dingy, uncovered mattresses shoved against the far wall. A sink and toilet, rarities in this part of town, stood unceremoniously against another wall, next to mildewed cardboard boxes filled with clothes. One wood chair, old and battered, sat in the middle of the room. Liza directed the man to sit. She turned over an empty plastic milk crate and sat across from him.

"Who are you working for?" she asked.

The man looked less frightened now, more weary. "I don't know what you mean."

"Why were you surveying the home of João Pedro Franco?"

"I don't know what you mean," he repeated.

"Why were you taking photographs of Franco's home?"

He shook his head. Same answer.

They went on like this for an hour. Liza could have gone long into the night and through the next day. She'd been trained that way. But this man had not, and he soon became exhausted. Liza could see it in the way he kept searching the room, looking for an out. There were many, but apparently he hadn't been educated in how to run. More than anything, she could tell he wanted the rock back. It was tucked in the pocket of her jeans, and Liza could see his glance continually coming back to that area of her body. The gun was there, too—in her waistband. He might have been staring at that, but Liza also wanted to think that his glances had something to do with her looks. Surprisingly, she hoped this hapless man found her attractive. There was something about him that appealed to her, an air of having seen too much, incongruously combined with the fear of having something to protect. That fear, she decided, meant there was still newness in him. She imagined that he had not been beaten down by his profession the way Liza had.

Into the third hour, almost midnight, he broke. "Please," he said. "Please just give it back to me."

She scooted the milk crate closer. "What will happen if I don't?"

He looked on the verge of tears. He blinked, and the

expression disappeared, but Liza had seen it. "What will happen?" she said again.

"I am a writer." He named a well-known newspaper in Moscow.

"You're an international journalist?"

"Yes."

It was easy enough for Liza to guess the rest, for this was an old story. "They recruited you to provide intelligence while you traveled for your writing."

"Yes."

"And you did it because you needed the money."

"No!" His green eyes slitted into anger.

"Why then?"

He looked away. "I said I would not be a part of it. I would never compromise my career. And I thought they went away."

"Who? Who approached you?"

He exhaled loudly. "I do not know. I believed it was the F.S.B., although I couldn't be sure. I only know that two weeks later I was visited by a man I did know. You see, I had covered this man for a story on the Russian Mafiya."

Liza raised her eyebrows and sat back. The F.S.B., the successor to the K.G.B., could be nasty. But the Russian Mafiya was even worse. She nodded at him to continue.

"I believe this man had been asked to help the F.S.B. convince me. And this man had also been waiting for the right time to punish me for the article I'd written."

He had a scar on his cheekbone, the only mark on his pale skin, and he rubbed at it with his forefinger.

"Did they do that to you?" Liza pointed at the scar.

He laughed. “No. My brother did this to me when I was six.” Then the laughter in his face died away, replaced by anguish. “My brother is a priest. My sisters are married. One has five kids, another four. My mother is…how do you say?…handicapped. My father takes care of her.”

“Ah,” Liza said, understanding now. “They threatened your family.”

“Yes.”

“They said they would kill them all unless you provided intelligence.”

“Yes.”

Liza reached out and touched his knee. He almost pulled away from her, she saw that. But then he simply met her gaze. “You’re terrible at it,” she said.

He laughed again, this time for a long time. A cleansing, relief-filled laugh. “I know! I told them I would be terrible. I have no mind for secrecy.”

“What happens if I don’t give you the rock? What happens if you don’t return it to them with photos?”

He stopped short. “Please don’t let me find out.”

“What is your name?”

He paused, then shrugged. “Aleksei Ivanov.”

Liza took the rock out of her jeans. She handed it to him. “I can help you, you know.”

“How? Who are you?”

She thought of the words she’d heard many times from the person who’d pulled her into this world. Her father. “I’m an American who loves my country,” she replied. It was a rather cheesy thing to say, but it was the truth. One of the only truths in her life.

"I cannot be seen with you," he said. "I may have already risked my safety and my family's by being here."

"That's not a problem," Liza said. "I know how to keep a secret."

12

Manhattan, New York

Roger Leiland stood in front of the floor-to-ceiling windows of his loft office on Fifteenth Street. In his hand was his secure phone, ready for the call he'd been waiting for all afternoon. The windows in front of him had been professionally coated with a darkening solution to prevent anyone from seeing inside his office, day or night, whether he had the lights on or not. And so he stood, legs apart, knowing he was invisible and dreaming of invincibility.

This was not the only unit Roger owned in the building. His home was an even bigger condo one floor down, filled with the trappings that would make most New Yorkers happy—incredible space, hardwood floors, exposed brick. When the upstairs unit had come up for sale seven years ago, Roger had purchased it. He was proud that he could afford it. He loved that, as a member of the Trust whose stock was rising, he no longer had to go into the New York office every day.

But desires, once met, tend to evolve and grow. And

Roger had begun to believe that he wasn't destined to be just a cog in the wheel of the Trust, but rather a driving force. He began to crave—in a hungry, insatiable, almost voracious way—wealth and greatness. His own personal brand of greatness.

As Roger watched the traffic stream by on Fifteenth Street, he wondered where those desires had come from. Raised in a suburb of Pittsburgh, with a teacher mother and a veterinarian father, his family was comfortable but not exactly ambitious. He went to Penn for undergrad, where he got a joint major in biology and Spanish. And when he was recruited for the Trust two years out of Penn medical school, he was thrilled. His surgical residency had made him question whether he really wanted to practice medicine. The malpractice premiums were going up and fellowships tougher to land than ever. There was too much gore and not enough upside.

In his early years with the Trust, it had never occurred to him that someday he might want to take over the organization, that someday he might want to take the group in a very different direction. He was in Brazil then, and he had Marta. But then Marta died. And that gave him an incredible toughness. The Trust had also given him confidence. Really, the Trust *required* confidence from its operatives in order to do their jobs. To compensate for the loss of Marta, he worked harder and harder. Eventually, over the years, which had taken him from Brazil to Chicago and then New York, his confidence grew to a point where he sensed he might assert his own vision, rather than that of his superiors.

And now, his loft office and his loft apartment no longer

satisfied him. The view of the inelegant Fifteenth Street frustrated him. He wanted a palace with a rooftop garden and twenty-four-hour staff and mural-painted ceilings. He wanted a driver outside, always at the ready. He wanted two other homes—one mountainside in Aspen, one ocean-side in St. Barts. He wanted a private jet to take him to these homes, and he wanted to own that jet.

But the Trust, at least the way it had always been, was not going to bring him those things. And so Roger had been biding his time while his stock slowly rose. He'd helped spearhead the Juliet Project in Chicago, becoming an integral part of the process, and finally he'd become an integral part of the Trust. He cultivated relationships with members and contacts around the world, even when he didn't need to do so for a particular mission. Now that he was a ranking board member, now that purist members like Michael were stepping down, and others had been helped in that direction, he was going to take the Trust toward his vision and his desires. The Juliet Project was just the beginning.

The phone rang. Roger glanced at the display, which scrambled incoming numbers according to a code developed by the Trust and further personalized by each individual member. It was the call he'd been waiting for.

He answered it with a polite, "Yes."

"The apartment has been searched," said a man's voice.

Roger checked his watch. "It's 11:00 p.m. there. What took so long?"

"A dinner party in the building. We wanted to make sure no one saw us entering."

"And?"

"Nothing."

"You're certain?"

"Of course."

"I want it cleaned out, just to be sure."

"Not a problem. We'll have it done within two hours."

"Thank you."

Roger turned, walked to his desk in the corner and hung up the phone. The desk was merely a maple table, minimally adorned with a few stacks of papers, all of which would be placed back in the safe when he was finished for the day. And then what would he do with his evening? he wondered. Maybe he would call one of the women he dated (and slept with) who knew little about him?

He had hoped the phone call would give him reason to celebrate. He hoped the evidence they were searching for would have been discovered in the apartment and that anything that could shed light on the Trust and its role in certain events would have been destroyed. Trust only worked if it worked in secret. That was true whether it operated his way or the way it had for decades. And so he would always protect the secrecy of the Trust. No matter what it took.

But there was no reason to celebrate right now. That would come. Roger walked around his desk, took a seat and continued working.

13

St. Marabel, Canada

"Tell me about the first boy you kissed." Michael said as we strolled St. Marabel's long main promenade on a Tuesday evening.

"What?" I punched him lightly on the arm. "You don't want to hear about that."

"I do. I want to know everything." Michael tucked my other hand tighter into the crook of his arm, and I nuzzled against his shoulder, unbelievably content.

It was June, when the days were getting longer and the summer had only begun to show itself, just like my new life, my new marriage, my new home of St. Marabel. St. Marabel, so far, had not disappointed. I adored its main street with its steep mansard roofs and brightly painted shutters over dormered windows. I loved the bistros protected by striped awnings, the little boutiques that stayed open until eleven at night, the *galeries d'art.* I liked the sight of vacationers moving languidly from store to bistro and back again. I loved the sound of French being spoken around me, buffeting me.

"Michael, I can't tell you about my first kiss," I said. "That's the kind of thing people tell each other when they're dating, not when they're married."

He made a stern face. "What kind of ridiculous statement is that? And besides, I will always be dating *you.*"

"We're married." I loved the sound of it.

"But still courting." Michael steered me onto a side street that curved its way around an old stone building. The scent of chocolate and pastry permeated the air. "So tell me about the first boy you kissed."

I inhaled deeply, breathing the scent of the pastries and the cool, earthy smell that came from the cobblestones. "Maybe my first kiss was with you."

"You were married before, my dear."

I waited for the pain in my abdomen that always came when I was reminded of my relationship with Scott. But it didn't hit. Not even a pinch. "Just because I was married doesn't mean I kissed him." I said this teasingly and felt a burst of relief that I could make a joke about my first marriage.

"Hmm, excellent. So *I'm* the first."

"Yes."

"I like it," Michael said.

Suddenly, there was a rapid staccato sound from somewhere up the alley.

Michael swung me around and shoved me hard against the side of the building.

"Ouch! Michael, what—"

"Get down," he barked in a low but insistent tone.

I did as he said and dropped to a squat, my heart thumping fast.

Michael spun around and faced the alley, one arm reaching behind to protect me, the other reaching toward his waist.

Two teenage girls ran past, their high heels clicking on the stone. Michael sighed, heavy with exasperation.

"I'm sorry," he said, turning to me. "Sorry. I got jumpy."

"Jesus," I said, standing up. "What was that about?"

He stared in the direction of the girls. He blinked fast. "Sorry."

"Are you all right?"

"I'm fine."

"What did you think was happening there?"

"I don't know. I got startled, I guess." He lowered his head to kiss my neck and then whisper in my ear. "So where were we?"

I pulled his face to mine, so I could see his expression. The calm demeanor he usually wore had returned. "You're okay?"

"I'm with you, aren't I?" He grabbed me around the waist and nuzzled my collarbone.

"Yes."

"Then I'm good."

I wrapped my arms around him. "You're sure?"

"I'm fine," he said, but under his shirt, I could feel his heart beating fast.

14

Anguilla, West Indies

Liza sat on her balcony at Cap Juluca resort. Below her, the white sand was combed smooth and the morning sun glittered like diamonds on the aqua of the Caribbean Sea. She turned her attention to the table in front of her. Like many vacationers at the resort, Liza's table bore coffee, rolls and the mini version of the *New York Times.* But Liza was not a vacationer, and so she pushed away the rolls, took a sip of her black coffee and opened up the complete version of the *Times* on her BlackBerry.

It was hard to focus on the articles. Normally, when she was on a job like this, focus was never a problem. But now Aleksei was gone, and she hadn't been able to find out a damn thing about the crash. The Trust, which knew all about her and Aleksei and also knew that she might be distracted by his death, had sent her on this mission to Anguilla. She'd been grateful, but now she was finding that *she* was the distraction.

Normally, Liza would conduct surveillance and collect intel, and if an elimination was necessary, and only then, would she design the job based on what she'd found. In this situation, she hadn't performed the legwork, she'd just been asked to take care of the end result. The piecemeal approach was the way the Trust seemed to work these days, which made Liza uncomfortable. She liked to know everything about a project and a target. Today's mission was a simple one, at least for her, but seemingly simple jobs could turn into chaos if the operative wasn't completely attentive and alert.

So Liza tried to put aside thoughts of Aleksei and questions about his death. *Later,* she told herself. *Later.* Yet she found it impossible not to remember.

15

Five years earlier
Rio de Janeiro, Brazil

The Trust called it a safe house, but really it was just a different apartment, bought the same way the place in Gávea across the street from Franco's house had been purchased—quickly and with a lot of money. Similarly, the safe house had been stripped of the remnants of its previous owners, and then it had been decorated in what Liza liked to call Twentieth-Century Hotel. It was clean and decently appointed in lots of beige. Spending any amount of time there had always reminded Liza of the starkness in her life. But now Aleksei was with her. And the safe house seemed bursting with light and chock-full of something very new and very exciting.

It had been three days since she'd accosted the poor man and made him tell his story. After they'd left Rocinha, she'd placed the rock for him in a better spot, one which would catch the faces of those entering Franco's house instead of their profiles. She had no interest in stopping the Russians from gaining information about Franco and Gustavo. The photos were easy, the kind of surveillance anyone could get, and Liza's organization wouldn't compete. They left other countries, other groups, to their own devices unless it appeared those countries or groups could compromise the United States and its citizens. Then they could get highly competitive. The results weren't pretty, but they were necessary. That's what Liza had always believed—would always have to believe if she were to keep her sanity.

One of the things Liza taught Aleksei was how to perform without emotion. It was never lost on her that she'd done the exact opposite when she'd met him. But she kept trying to teach him this nonetheless, because he also had to do his job without being particularly successful at it. He didn't believe in what he was doing, not like Liza did, but for the safety of his friends and family he had to appear as if he cared very much. His handlers had instructed him in a rudimentary way on how to spot a tail and how to make a drop and various other tactics, but he was awful at them. Liza taught him the way she'd been taught.

They made sure it appeared as if Aleksei was living in the small hotel room where he'd been told to stay, and they made sure he checked in with his handler and turned over the photos that his sad little rock acquired every day. Once those things were done, no one seemed to care much about Aleksei. Except for Liza.

Every day, Liza conducted lessons with him, breaking the rules in a whopping way by letting him into the apartment in Gávea. She showed him the scopes and the listening devices and the alarms and bugs. She was reckless; she felt literally out of control. She had at first entertained the idea that Aleksei's facade was just that—a facade—and that he might be a much better spy than she was, one who had quickly and easily wormed his way into her world.

And yet, for once, Liza trusted someone. She felt pulled toward him by an undercurrent she'd never seen coming and didn't totally understand. She was attracted to him, but there was also something intangible that made her feel deeply connected to him. Throwing caution to the wind was intoxicating.

He never asked who she worked for, and she never told him. If an outsider learned about the Trust's existence, there was a serious possibility that outsider would be eliminated. So Aleksei didn't know her employer, but he knew everything else. She told him everything about her life, and she felt like he had grown to know all of her.

"You're so lucky I'm teaching you all these things," she said one night.

They were stationed in front of the window in Gávea, peering through night scopes at Franco's front door and the one window that faced the street. Because of a party Franco was having, the window was open and the drapery pulled back.

Aleksei had been trying to quit smoking, he said, but Liza could smell the scent of a cigarette on his jacket. She hated cigarettes, and yet with him she didn't mind. She even liked it. She liked everything about the man—his book-smarts, the way his thick hair was colicky and hard to tame, the way his green eyes filled with pain when he saw children barely clothed and nearly starving on the Rio streets.

"I am lucky," he said, and then he was silent. His silences were different than that day in Rocinha. They were comfortable silences now.

"You probably would have been killed sooner rather than later if it wasn't for me." She had no idea why she was doing this bragging. "I could be killed for teaching you what I know."

Aleksei remained quiet, then out of the corner of her eye, she saw him sit back from the scope. He gazed at his hands. He gazed at her.

In the moonlight filling the apartment, he appeared larger, the scar on his cheek almost white.

He moved toward her. It was a quick, clumsy rush of physical movement, and Liza almost blocked him. She could have easily defended herself if he were trying to harm her. But in a fraction of a second, in that moonlight, she caught the look in his eyes, and it was not the look she'd seen when she'd been attacked by someone before. This was a gentler look, and Liza thought, *Is he going to* kiss *me?* Then she thought, *Finally.*

Aleksei's body met hers, his weight pushed her off her stool and the two of them tumbled to the hardwood floor. And then he was kissing her, and then his hands were on her shoulders, on her breasts, on her back, her waist. He was all over her. Liza felt enveloped by his eager touch. And she was happier than she ever remembered.

16

Anguilla, West Indies

Liza shook the thoughts of Aleksei from her brain. *Enough,* she said to herself. She checked her watch: 10:45 a.m. She looked at the villa to her right. She had fifteen minutes.

She stood, readjusted her black tank bathing suit and opened the straw bag on the chair next to her. She checked that the yellow tube that read Caprilano Sunscreen was tucked in the inside pocket.

Caprilano Sunscreen was sold only in two places—Barneys New York and a store in the Galleria Alberto Sordi in Rome. This tube, however, had not been purchased at either store. Instead, it was a replica. Likewise, the contents inside looked exactly like the white Caprilano sunblock and had been designed to bear its faint, citrusy scent.

Liza adjusted her earbud and put on her large, floppy beach hat. One side of the hat drooped almost to Liza's jaw and had a tiny mike sewn into its cotton folds.

"Tucker," she said into the mike. "Ready?"

"Confirmed," came the reply in her earbud.

She went to the edge of her balcony and leaned over the railing. A hundred feet off shore, the multicolored sails of a Hobie Cat flapped prettily as it tacked back and forth across the water.

Liza called the front desk, gave the name Elena Mistow and checked out of her room over the phone. She asked for a bellman to collect her bags, which she put outside her front door, and requested that a cab be called. She left the room, walked downstairs and made her way to the beach's edge.

Once there, she didn't step into the sand immediately. Instead, she looked at the villa to her right. She glanced at her watch again. Any minute now. She waited patiently in her bathing suit, her straw bag in one hand, her hat firmly on her head, hiding her auburn hair. As she stood there, some of the resort's guests began to filter down to the beach, throwing towels over the plush chaise longues and settling in with books or stacks of magazines.

Liza envied those people. She couldn't remember the last time she'd gone on a real vacation or simply sat on a beach and read.

She turned her attention back to the villa. Five minutes later, she saw the French doors open and, as they had every morning for the last five days, the members of the Naponi family began to make their way to the beach. As usual, Angelo Naponi was the last to cross the threshold.

Angelo Naponi was the president of a wealthy family company that owned waste-disposal facilities around the world. Liza and the Trust had no problem with

Naponi's company and the work they did. What they had a problem with was how he spent some of his money. Lately, Naponi had been funding a militant Muslim organization that had its sights on a large-scale bombing in Vilnius, the capital of Lithuania. Naponi himself was Roman Catholic, and was unsympathetic to the Muslims, but such a bombing would wreak havoc in Vilnius where Naponi had been trying to get a foothold for years. Once such havoc occurred, outside companies, just like Naponi's, would be called upon to help clear the wreckage.

From the perspective of the Trust, Liza had been informed, the problem with this whole scenario was that Vilnius wasn't the only city the Muslim terrorist group was targeting. The other was Washington, D.C. Naponi knew this, but he didn't care. And the Muslim organization was so large, and its members so adept at evasion, that eliminating all of them was a difficult task. It had been decided that taking out Naponi, their largest capital contributor, would be an easier way to marginalize them.

As he did every other morning, Naponi stretched his short arms to the sky. He yawned and rubbed his ample belly. Then, wearing only his purple Speedo bathing suit, he followed his family to the beach.

"You're up, Tucker," Liza said into her mic.

The Hobie Cat turned its sails and headed for the waters in front of Naponi's villa.

Naponi reached the beach and greeted a resort worker who was setting up buckets of sparkling water next to the chaise longues. He settled on the chair next to his wife, Lana, a slim woman six inches taller than him and twenty years his junior. Lana took out a yellow tube of Caprilano Sunscreen and put it next to her husband's chair.

From their intel, they knew that Naponi had recently been diagnosed with a basal cell carcinoma on his shoulder. As a result, his wife was insistent that he cover every inch of his exposed skin with Caprilano Sunscreen, while the rest of the family would use oil and continue tanning themselves.

Liza hesitated a moment, saying a silent *I'm sorry* to Lana Naponi. Liza did not like to operate like this, with someone's family surrounding them, but this had been the simplest alternative and the one guaranteed to produce the result the Trust needed.

Liza cleared her mind of the guilt. "Go, Tucker," she said into her mic.

"Got it," she heard in her ear.

Just then, as the Hobie Cat sailed right in front of the Naponi family, its starboard hull burst into flames. Exactly as they had planned it.

A shout went up from the Naponi family. They all raced to the water's edge, staring at the catamaran and yelling to the resort staff to get help. Down the shoreline, other resort guests were doing the same.

In the midst of the commotion, Liza calmly began walking toward the Naponis' chaise longues. When she reached Naponi's chair, she made sure the Naponi family still had their backs to her, then she reached down, took the Caprilano Sunscreen and replaced it with the tube from her bag. It took only a second. Liza then continued her stroll.

"Show's over, Tucker," she said into her mic.

She glanced out at sea and saw Tucker put out the flames with a fire extinguisher. Liza turned away and kept walking down the beach. She knew exactly what would happen next. Tucker would turn on the motor they'd installed on the Hobie Cat, and he would disappear before the local Coast Guard could reach him. And the Naponis would return to the chaise longues. Angelo Naponi would sit on the edge of his chair and slather himself with sunscreen.

The only problem for Naponi was that the tube Liza had swapped no longer contained sunscreen but nitroglycerine cream. The tiniest dab could be applied to the skin to lower blood pressure in case of an impending heart attack.

Liza knew that Angelo Naponi would not sense anything awry as he rubbed the cream over his body. Not at first. But within a minute, because of the large amount he would have applied, Naponi's blood pressure would not just lower, it would tank. Angelo Naponi would go into immediate shock, and he would be dead within a minute. Naponi's medical history included two heart attacks, and his death would mimic another one. There was a decent chance no autopsy would be performed. Even if an autopsy did happen and the nitroglycerine cream was discovered, Liza would be gone, and there was no way she, or the Trust, would be tied to Naponi.

Liza made her way to the lobby of the resort and entered the public bathrooms. In a stall, she pulled on khaki linen pants and a pink tank top. She put on large sunglasses and a white baseball cap, tucking her hair inside. She removed the mic from the straw hat and tossed the hat in the garbage.

Forty seconds later, Elena Mistow was on her way to the airport.

17

St. Marabel, Canada

Liza had "gone missing." That's what I called it when she got too busy with work, when she traveled constantly and we didn't talk for weeks. I knew that such was the fate of friendships today, with everyone having so much to do, but I worried about her. I wanted my friend to enjoy her life, not run herself into the ground, and I feared she was doing just that.

I also missed her. It had been three weeks since the wedding, and for some reason I'd imagined talking to Liza every day, maybe mentioning the hammered-silver salad tongs we'd been given by my cousins, telling her about the honeymoon we were finally getting this weekend in Montreal, and the opening of the Twilight Club—what the residents called *Le Brunante*—only a week or so away now.

Instead, finally on the phone with Liza, I sensed a vague distance between us.

"How was your trip?" I asked. "Where were you?"

"New York. And then L.A. Travel these days is the worst."

Her voice was a little abrupt. Or was it me? Was I the only one who felt this tension and noticed some sadness she was trying to mask with efficient chat?

"Why was the trip so hard?" I meant to sound supportive, understanding, but somehow it came out as if I could never understand why traveling to fabulous places was a hardship.

"It's just such a drill. Same thing. Over and over, you know?"

"Can you get Presario to lighten up on your travel schedule?"

I stood and started pacing around Michael's kitchen—*my* kitchen, I corrected myself. There were so many things I enjoyed about the place, like the windows,which were white and coated with paint but had thick, solid sills that easily held vases of flowers from the tiny garden out back.

"It's just the nature of the beast," Liza said.

"They have to give you downtime." I felt us falling back into a familiar conversation, with me asserting Liza worked too hard and Liza telling me this was just the way her job was. I wished I could help her the way she'd helped me. Her support, her advice, her just *being* there had pulled me out of deep hole after my divorce, and I wanted, even in some small way, to be able to return the favor.

"You know how it is," she said. "I like my job. I do. It's just that the travel is the hard part." She groaned. "God, listen to me. Stop me. Shoot me. I have a great life."

"You do, but you've got to slow down, too. You know I'm right."

A pause.

"Are you seeing anyone?" I asked. Now that I'd found Michael who had brought such vitality and wonder to my life, I wanted love for Liza, too.

"C'mon," she said.

"Well, are you?"

"I met a cute lawyer on the elevator, does that count?"

"Have you given him your number?"

"No, but I have his."

"Have you called him?"

"No."

"Then unfortunately, my friend, it doesn't count."

Liza was quiet. I could almost feel her stillness across the phone.

"What's going on, Liza?" I asked.

She breathed in deeply, but didn't respond. This was how she got when she had something on her mind, when she wasn't sure whether she should share it with me. I'd taken off for France after her brother, Colby, died, and although we stayed best friends, I felt awful about leaving her. I'd made her deal with her sadness alone. Sometimes she continued to do that—sometimes she wouldn't let me in.

Still nothing from Liza.

"Are you okay?" I asked.

"I don't know."

"Tell me," I said.

She cleared her throat. "Someone died."

Alarm leaped through my body. "Who?"

"Aleksei."

"Oh, Liza." I knew about Aleksei. He was a Russian

guy Liza had met through work and had a fling with. One of her very few flings, or at least one of the few she'd told me about. "What happened?"

"He died in a plane crash." Liza made a choking sound, and I wondered if she was going to cry. Something she didn't do often.

"What? When?"

"A few weeks ago."

"What happened?"

"They don't know. Pilot error, maybe."

"How many people were in the plane?"

"Seven."

"And?"

"And they all died."

"Oh, my God. I'm so sorry. How are you doing?"

A pause. I could almost hear her wrestling with her emotions. "Terrible."

"Do you want me to come to Chicago?"

"No, I've got too much to do. And I'll probably have to travel again for work."

"Do you want to come here?"

"No, seriously, I'm okay. It's just a shock."

"Well, of course it is. Look, don't push this away. Let yourself be upset if you're upset."

She laughed, but it sounded strangled. "I am! God, I am."

"Oh, honey, I feel so bad for you," I said.

She clucked her tongue, and I knew in that instant I'd given her too much sympathy. Liza did not take well to large doses of sympathy.

"I'll be okay," Liza said. "New topic. How's Michael?"

"Liza."

"Seriously. Tell me something."

"You can talk to me, you know. Whenever you need to."

"I know. I know. Now, get my mind off this. Tell me how Michael is."

"Well, he's amazing. I can't believe I'm married again."

"I can't either, and I introduced you. Where is he?"

"The restaurant."

"How's it coming?"

"Fantastic—from what I hear. He won't let me see it until it's done. He wants to surprise me with the completed version. The opening is next weekend."

"I wish I could be there."

"Any chance? This might be the perfect time to visit."

"Nah. I've got work to do. And you guys don't need me anymore."

"Don't say that."

"Well, it's true."

"It's not."

"I'm leaving you alone for now. Be happy and prosper."

I laughed. "I'll try."

"I love you, sister girl." *Sister girl.* That was what we had called each other since high school. Neither of us had a sister.

Michael walked in then, the sun pouring behind him, diffusing into a gold ring around him.

"Love *you,* sister girl," I said.

18

Montreal, Canada

My hands were bound together and tied to a bedpost. My eyes were covered with a blindfold, and I could only make out a thin horizon of light below it.

I listened for a sound, a sense of what was coming next. Silence answered me. My heart began beating harder, louder. A pulsing heat filled my lower body.

I twisted myself back and forth on the bed. The stiff white cotton of the bedsheets made a gentle *shush, shush* sound.

I stretched my body down, feeling the material cut into my wrists.

"They're tight," I said.

"They're supposed to be" came the reply.

I felt the tingle of something cool on my big toe. The sensation kept moving—the tingle drizzled over the front of my foot, around the skin of my ankle, up the muscle of my calf, around my kneecap. As it traveled up my thigh, I tensed.

"Relax" I heard. "Relax. Let go."

I listened to the voice and let the tension slide away. I let the warmth in my body continue to build.

"That's right. That's it."

The drizzle stopped at the very top of my thigh. I could feel my pulse in my hips.

Silence. An anticipatory pause.

Then something different touched my toe, then the top of my foot.

A nervous giggle escaped my mouth.

A deep chuckle came in return. "Kahlúa tastes delicious on you."

I felt Michael's tongue lap the cool string of Kahlúa, following it to my inner thighs. I gasped when his mouth finally found the place that had been waiting.

"Baby, this is exactly how a honeymoon is supposed to be," I said. It was an hour later, and we'd showered, called housekeeping for a change of linens and gotten promptly back in bed. I hadn't seen much of Montreal other than our room, and I didn't mind one bit.

I thought of my honeymoon with Scott, spent in Costa Rica and filled with activity—scuba, hiking, parasailing.

Michael flopped onto the sheets next to me. "I'm here to please."

"Then will you please get me a glass of wine?"

He lifted his head off the bed. "You're insatiable."

"It's past happy hour." I pointed to the window, where we could see the sun sinking, replaced by a purplish glow. "It's time, don't you think?"

Michael kissed me. "It's time for whatever you want. Anything at all."

"Thank you." I felt satisfied with the pampering and the sex. Especially the sex. I had never been so adventurous before, unencumbered by thoughts of how I looked or what was right or wrong.

Michael stood and found a white terry robe on the floor. He slipped it on and turned on the bedside lamp. On the credenza was a black lacquer ice bucket with the hotel's gold logo on the side. Michael lifted a bottle of white wine, the ice crackling and shifting. He wrapped it in a hand towel and looked around for the opener.

Michael's cell phone was on the dresser, too, and although it didn't ring, I waited for him to pick it up and look at the display. I felt a flicker of anticipation, wholly different from that I'd had an hour ago. Now I was waiting for him to lift that phone, and then disappear. Again.

There was one thing that hadn't been perfect about our honeymoon—we'd been in Montreal for two days, and Michael had been preoccupied with the phone. It never rang—it didn't even vibrate—but Michael always seemed to sense when a call was coming in or when messages had been left. And then he would slip away, sometimes only for a minute or so, but I noticed his absence. Work calls, he told me. Details about the restaurant to be dealt with.

But I wondered why he couldn't take those calls in front of me.

I watched Michael hunt for the corkscrew. I waited for him to glance at the phone. But this time he didn't. Instead, he muttered, "Where in the hell is it?"

Finally, he turned to me. "The corkscrew has pulled a disappearing act. You take a nap while I use the facilities and then I'll hunt for it."

"I'll be here," I said.

I waited for him to take the phone and disappear into the bathroom. But he turned and walked away, just a man in a terry robe, a man on his honeymoon, a man going to the bathroom.

I couldn't help but eye the phone on the credenza. *Leave it alone,* I told myself. Without listening to that rational inner voice, I scampered off the bed and picked up the phone.

One missed call, the display said.

I flipped open the phone and clicked on *View last number called.*

A familiar number appeared. Or maybe it seemed familiar because it began with a 312 area code. Chicago. It was probably just a business associate of Michael's. Or possibly his friend, Tomaso.

But I peered at it. And then I recognized it.

It was Liza's number.

19

When Michael came out of the bathroom, I was sitting on the bed with my legs crossed, his phone in my lap.

"What are you doing?" Michael said. "I thought you were under the covers, waiting for me to serve you."

I pulled the robe tighter around me. "Why is Liza calling you?"

"Liza called?" His eyebrows scrunched together the way they did when he was confused or thinking about something.

"Yes."

Michael walked toward me. I watched him for signs of guilt, but his face betrayed nothing.

He took the phone from my hand. "Let's find out."

He dialed. He lifted the phone to his ear. He punched in his password. He brought the phone to his ear again and listened. "She was calling you."

"What?"

"Here, I'll start it again and put it on speaker."

Michael touched something on the phone and Liza's strong, confident voice filled the room. "Hey, Michael and Kate, how are you lovebirds? Actually, I was calling Kate but she doesn't have a cell phone yet, and no one bothered to tell me where you were staying, so I thought I'd try this number. So Kate, remember those sandals we saw at that shop in St. Marabel? Well, I just saw the same ones on Armitage Avenue for fifty bucks less. Can you believe that?"

Michael clicked off the speaker and handed the phone to me. He turned away, going through the minibar and finding the corkscrew.

I listened to the rest of Liza's message, telling me that she would normally buy me the sandals and send them to me, but did I want the black or the crimson, and could I call her soon, because they only had two pairs left in my size? Her chipper voice told me she was sad. Liza sometimes compensated for the blues by shopping and acting cheerful, as if she could physically and mentally force herself into being happy-go-lucky.

I erased the message when she was done. I looked at Michael, and I felt like an ass. When I moved, I'd canceled my Chicago cell phone. I'd planned to get a Canadian one, but with all the craziness and the wedding, I simply hadn't had time. Liza normally called at the house.

"I'm sorry," I said to Michael's back.

He turned and handed me a glass of wine. "What are you sorry about?"

"What I was thinking."

He sat next to me. "And what were you thinking?"

I shrugged, marveling how fast I'd gone from feeling fantastic to suspicious to absolutely foolish. "I guess I wasn't thinking."

He touched my chin and moved my face to look at his. "You know that it's *you* I'm in love with, right?"

"Right."

"Not Liza."

"Right."

"*You,* Kate. I've never felt like this before. And I want this to last forever."

I said nothing for a moment. The truth was, I no longer believed in forever. And not because I was bitter about the way my first marriage had ended. I'd done a lot of thinking over the last year, and it seemed to me that promising someone forever was a false promise. How could anyone know what forever looked like or what forever held for either of them?

"I love you, too," I said. "But sometimes it seems like you and Liza have some kind of connection."

"Do you think I'm having an affair with Liza?"

I stared at him. "No."

He laughed. "Good, because I am *not* having an affair with Liza. But I'm flattered that you think I could attract the both of you."

"Sorry."

"Quit saying that."

"No, I am sorry. I don't want to ruin our honeymoon."

He pushed the robe from my shoulders. "Let's make sure that doesn't happen."

I let Michael take off the robe. I let him draw me back onto the sheets.

But my mind kept wondering—why hadn't he denied that Liza and he had a connection? He said he wasn't having an affair, but he didn't correct me when I'd said there was a connection between them.

Annoyed at my splitting of hairs, I pushed the thoughts from my head. I let myself surrender to the feel of Michael's hands.

20

Thirty-six years earlier
Khiem Hanh District, Vietnam

Michael awoke after only three hours of sleep. He'd been on a night ambush the evening before, but he was expected to be up and prepared to lead his ICEX team every morning just the same. ICEX—he had finally learned the name of the program he had been indoctrinated into—stood for Intelligence Coordination and Exploitation, and his team was responsible for ferreting out enemy agents in their district, sharing the information with other ICEX teams and helping to prepare U.S. troops for combat. Which didn't mean that the ICEX team sat on the sidelines. Far from it. They usually ended up fighting along with them.

Michael entered the kitchen of the villa where his team was staying. The villa had been occupied by the French many years ago and had concrete walls and sandbags surrounding the perimeter. The interior was spartan but clean and comfortable. When the water tank outside was full, you could even get a hot shower.

Michael murmured good morning to the mama-*san,* a Vietnamese woman who acted as the villa's housekeeper—she cooked and did the laundry and shined shoes and cleaned. She was a tiny woman stooped either by age or disappointment. Michael suspected it was the latter. Although the deep lines of her face spoke of many years, his minimal conversations with her suggested she was only in her forties.

Michael accepted tea, along with a dish of rice sweetened with cinnamon bark. The mama-*san* avoided his gaze, as she did every morning.

While he ate, Michael composed his report of the night ambush in his head. His commanding officer would ask about body count. He always did. The way he made it sound, the only job of the U.S. troops was delivering a high enemy body count. Michael had even heard that evaluations of the commanders were based, in part, on body count, something that made him extremely uncomfortable.

For better or for worse, Michael could report a high number of "dispatches" of Vietcong last night. It was always hard to get an exact count, since the Vietcong often stripped their dead of anything valuable, including clothes, and if possible carted off their bodies. But last night they'd been unable to carry the dead away, and Michael was left to count naked bodies in the sticky silence of the night.

In a way, nude soldiers made it simple for Michael. If the dead weren't stripped by their own team, a U.S. military man was sure to do it. It made Michael sick to see troops pulling off the black pajama-like clothes and

Ho Chi Minh sandals from an enemy-deceased. He knew they would trade these goods for food or send them home as souvenirs. Since many of these men weren't technically under Michael's command, he couldn't say a thing, but it was something else he hated about combat.

Michael didn't know what he thought combat would be like. Maybe exciting or like he was doing something for his country. But really it felt like failure. The ultimate failure of humankind. Yet it was either him or them, so he did his job.

After breakfast, he thanked the mama-*san*, who again averted her eyes, then went to his desk and radioed the commander as usual.

"You're wanted at Go Vap," the commander said. "Transport arrives at 1300 hours."

Michael acknowledged this and asked no questions. He'd gotten good at that.

At one in the afternoon, a helicopter set down in the vacant field behind the villa. Forty minutes later with him on board, it touched down in another field behind a different, larger, much nicer-looking, villa. The Go Vap District was not far from Saigon, but that was all Michael knew about it.

He was led in the back door of the compound to an office decorated with rows of metal file cabinets, all gray. Right below a window that overlooked the yellow-green field were two leather chairs. Michael couldn't imagine where they'd gotten them. The chairs were like something his parents would have at home in Rhode Island. Home, where it would probably be snowing now, not blazing hot.

"Have a seat," he heard from behind him.

Michael turned and saw a man whose blue eyes smiled intently. "Colonel Kingsley," he said, snapping a salute.

"At ease," the colonel said, gesturing toward the chairs.

Michael sat while Colonel Kingsley poured two scotch and waters. He handed one to Michael without comment. Michael accepted it, waited for the colonel to take the first sip, then let the liquor slide into his mouth and his insides.

He sat on the edge of his seat, at attention, pulled again by the colonel's intense eyes, by the man's imposing physical presence. He had steel-gray hair, worn in the standard military cut, and yet the colonel didn't look ridiculous, like Michael thought he and many other army men did. With his square jaw and tanned skin, the colonel seemed made for the buzz cut.

"You're doing a fine job, son," the colonel said.

"Thank you, sir."

"You displayed a high degree of maturity, and we've given you responsibility that goes along with that."

He nodded.

"You've got a knack for languages, and the men you come into contact with respect you."

"Thank you, sir."

"Your reports are consistently D-3 or C-3."

Michael nodded again. D-3 and C-3 were high ratings given to information collected by agents like him. They indicated that his reports tended to be consistently accurate.

"Body counts are also high," Michael said, hating himself for it, but wanting suddenly to impress the colonel.

Yet his statement seemed to have the opposite effect.

Colonel Kingsley frowned. "That's not how I like to quantify success."

Michael's posture lost some of its stiffness. "Me neither, sir."

"Is that right?"

"Well, sir..." He paused, wondering how candid to be.

Colonel Kingsley ran a hand over his chin. He seemed to be waiting, interested, in Michael's answer.

"It's just that it feels random, sir," Michael continued. "Like there isn't always a point." He realized that he sounded now as if he had no point whatsoever. He braced himself, waiting for Colonel Kingsley to give him a gruff dressing-down about how the army didn't care about feelings.

Instead, the colonel nodded. "And how do you like ICEX?"

"Fine, sir."

"Tell me what you're working on."

He told the colonel about how he met with chiefs in his district, ostensibly to visit and to give small amounts of money for village needs, but also to learn the word around the village about the movements of the Vietcong, whether they'd heard any sounds in the night, whether someone had gotten news passed down by a cousin in another village. He told the Colonel about the agents under his command who were spread out around his district, seeking similar information. He told the colonel how he'd employed Montagnards, men from a mountain tribe in Cambodia whose families had been killed by the Vietcong and whose extreme hatred of them led to exceptional loyalty to the job the U.S. was doing.

Colonel Kingsley nodded as Michael talked. He probably knew all this, but Michael again felt the need to impress.

"You realize it's bigger than all that?" the colonel said.

"Sir?"

"You're part of the Phoenix Program, son."

"I'm not familiar with the term, sir."

"You can drop the 'sir,'" the colonel said. "And you better take another sip of that drink. Because we have matters to discuss."

21

Go Vap District, Vietnam

The Phoenix Program, Colonel Kingsley explained, was a covert, highly classified operation designed by the CIA to gather intelligence for the U.S. military and, if necessary, eradicate any threats.

"What you're doing with ICEX," the colonel said, "is part of the Phoenix Program."

"Yes, sir," Michael had said, unable to lose the "sir." He was fascinated by the thought of this Phoenix Program, by the thought that he was part of something larger than he'd known.

The colonel stood, groaning a little as he did so. "Bad knee."

He walked to one of the file cabinets, put a key into its round lock and turned it. The cabinet opened with a screech, and the colonel removed a sheaf of papers, which Michael recognized as his daily reports.

The colonel took his seat again, took a sip of his scotch, then flipped through Michael's reports, thoughtfully studying them. "I think you've left some information out of your reports, son."

Michael swallowed. "Sir?"

"Toilet facilities."

Michael almost blushed. He'd been taking some of his operating payroll and using it to help build outhouses for different villages in his district.

"The way they live is hard, sir," Michael said. "And if the villagers are happier, they provide us with more intel."

"And your photography. How's that, son?"

Again, Michael felt heat from embarrassment on his neck. He had a 35 mm Minolta camera that his father had given him for his sixteenth birthday. In the early-morning hours, he sometimes rose before everyone else in the compound (everyone except mama-*san*) and took pictures of the light as it hit the Boi Loi woods in the distance. He had no idea how the colonel knew about that.

"Fine, sir," he answered.

The colonel nodded. "Here's what I want to tell you about the Phoenix Program." He looked up at Michael. "Gathering intelligence isn't enough."

Michael gave a brisk nod of his head, although he wasn't sure what the colonel meant.

"High body counts aren't enough," the colonel said. "ICEX, as I told you, is a big part of this program, but the Phoenix Program is designed to be more purposeful. It's designed to target specific threats to the U.S. How does that sound?"

"Very good, sir."

The colonel took out one of Michael's dailies and handed it to him. "Let's take this chief, for instance."

Michael glanced at the report. It was a week old, and in it he'd told of his suspicion that a local chief was helping the U.S. while also doing favors for the Vietcong.

"How sure are you of your report?" the colonel asked.

"Quite certain."

"Then he has to be eliminated."

"I believe I can turn him." Michael pointed to the area of the report where he'd said just that.

The colonel dropped his chin and stared intently at Michael. "How long will that take?"

"I'm not sure. A week, possibly two."

"And in that time, the Vietcong can ambush and kill three, maybe four American troops."

"With all due respect, if we make an example of the chief by killing him, his villagers will go wild. We could lose everything we've been working toward with them."

"That's exactly why you won't make an example of him, son. The Phoenix Program isn't about glory. It's about doing the right thing for the United States. Often, it's about doing the quiet thing."

"Yes, sir," Michael said, not entirely understanding, but liking the sound of the colonel's message.

"You know the chief's habits?" the colonel said. "You know when he takes a shit, when he goes to bed, when he sees his villagers, when he's alone?"

"Yes, sir."

"You know when he's alone?"

"Yes, sir," Michael said, starting to comprehend.

"So then that's when you'll dispatch him."

"How?"

The colonel put the reports aside and leaned forward on his knees. "You're an intelligence officer, son. The *how* is for you to figure out. This is intelligent intelligence. Understand?"

"Yes, sir," Michael said, louder and more enthusiastic this time. He was thrilled at the prospect of thinking for himself, of doing the right thing, of having a real purpose over here in this hot, crazy country.

That night, at 1700 hours, Michael pretended to retire for the evening, but ten minutes later, he slipped out of his bedroom and left the villa. He drove fifteen miles or so, then walked the remaining five to the village. Darkness had fallen now. The village was quiet, with only an occasional laugh or murmur heard. Michael cased the chief's home. It was a three-room house with hard walls and, Michael knew from being inside, wood floors. In front was a small porch, and Michael knew the chief would soon come out onto the porch by himself and survey his village.

Michael flattened his back against the side of the house, right next to the porch. He was sweating more than usual, drops of it running down the side of his face. Part of him fought against the thought of being here, without backup, without anyone knowing.

But he thought of the Colonel, and his words about doing the right thing, the quiet thing.

When the floorboards of the porch creaked and the chief stepped out into the night, his small legs spread wide, his arms crossed in front of him, Michael didn't think anymore. In one movement, he was on the porch, directly behind the chief, grabbing him. As the chief struggled, he turned and his eyes met Michael's. He opened his mouth to call out, but in that instant, Michael got a better hold on the man, wrapping one arm around his neck, his hand tight over his lips, grasping his chin. He managed to get his other arm around the top of his head. Michael tightened his grip, then pushed down on the man's head and wrenched it with the other arm, breaking the chief's neck with a loud, grisly snap. The man went still. Michael listened for indications of anyone approaching but heard only the usual sounds of the village—a distant, crackle of a fire, the faraway murmur of discussion. Still, Michael felt a momentary rise of panic. What if the chief survived? He'd seen Michael. What if he identified him?

Just to make sure, Michael sharply rotated the chief's neck again, then once again, pulling the chin up and to the left. Gently, he laid the body on the porch and began his long walk back to the jeep.

22

Chicago, Illinois

Saturday afternoon, Liza tidied her bedroom, then listlessly meandered around her Lake Shore Drive apartment, moving a few things here, there.

Liza traveled so much that she often neglected her apartment. Not that it wasn't clean. A housekeeper, whom Liza had met on only a few occasions, slipped in on Tuesday mornings and scoured the place whether it needed it or not. But the rooms lacked the details of someone who'd really settled. Sure, there were books on her nightstand—a Somerset Maugham novel, a historical book about the building of the Panama Canal, a thin novel with a pink cover she'd picked up in an airport on a whim—yet those books had been there for months. They were just sitting, waiting for her to do more than start them. They were waiting for her to dig in and relish.

The rest of her apartment was the same. She had silver plates for serving appetizers, and thousand-thread-count sheets in both the master and guest bedrooms. She had a telescope that faced the big wall of windows and out to the lake and an area the locals called "The Playpen," which was now bobbing with pleasure craft and was packed with people drinking beer and soaking up the sun.

Liza opened the glass door leading out to her balcony and stood there, staring at those bobbing boats, and it was almost as if she could hear the laughter bouncing into the air, surrounding her and her pristine apartment.

She felt an intense jab of loneliness. And she let herself think of Aleksei. There'd been no information this week; the Russian government was being typically reticent, lest they be accused of some kind of wrongdoing or oversight. No one knew why his plane had gone down. The captain had called in shortly after takeoff, stating he was turning the plane around due to weather, as well as a suspected problem with one of the engines. There were low clouds, Liza had learned, but nothing that a twenty-year veteran pilot shouldn't have been able to handle. Two minutes and thirty-eight seconds after the pilot's request for a runway, the plane crashed.

Liza's jab of loneliness became heartache as she thought of Aleksei, of what he must have suffered.

She and Aleksei had spent three wonderful weeks together in Rio. Over the next two years, they'd managed to meet up once in Moscow, once in Miami, once in Denver and once in Venezuela. Each time they came together with ferocity. The word *love* was never spoken, but both of them felt it. She knew that. She knew it because she'd never felt it with a man before and she hadn't since.

Their affair was discovered by the Trust; of course it was. She'd been reckless, and she had loved her recklessness. Liza was removed from duty for three months while an investigation was made into whether she had told Aleksei about the Trust. Once the Trust was satisfied she hadn't, she was handed a demotion—she literally set her career back five years with her affair with Aleksei—and she was told in no uncertain terms to end their relationship. She did, but she never regretted their affair. Not even for a moment. And as for its ending, the truth was that both Aleksei and Liza had known that it couldn't work in real life, anyway. Aleksei had his family to take care of in Russia, and she would never be allowed to move there. She tried to tell herself that she didn't like Moscow, anyway—while she appreciated its underground trendiness, she found the city cold and unfriendly. Living there would have seeped out what vitality she had and left her carved out and empty. She would have blamed it on Aleksei, and their relationship would have died, slowly and bitterly, and she would never think of it the same. That's what she told herself, and eventually she believed it. She was good at that.

And so they stopped seeing each other. It was a cold ending in some ways, but the memories were nothing but warm. Some very, very hot. The truth was, she had always carried around a small nugget of hope that someday their situations would change and they would be together.

Honking sounds from Lake Shore Drive, many stories below her, cut through her thoughts. Aleksei was gone now. And so the memories couldn't fill her the way they used to, the hope had died with him.

Liza went back inside. She had to do something. *Something.* But what? She wasn't due to leave for Bangkok for a week. She would spend this next week in the office, getting ready and preparing reports of her other missions, just the way she always did.

But now it was Saturday. A shimmery Saturday in Chicago, and the night was coming. Liza could taste the energy from the city—no one loved their summer-time Saturday nights like Chicagoans—and although she usually ignored that energy, Liza gave in to it this time. Because tonight was the start of something new. She could feel that in her body, a nervous stomach mixing with the pain about Aleksei, her body's knowl-edge that for better or for worse, she was on the verge of a new Liza.

She went into her bedroom, an immaculate place with furniture made of light, smooth maple. She found her briefcase in the closet, and inside she located Rich Macklin's business card. She stared at his cell phone number, with its Boston area code, re-membering their meeting in the elevator, remember-ing that cocky, sexy grin of his. She couldn't believe she was even considering this. Although they hadn't been together in years, Aleksei was only barely gone now. Shouldn't she be mourning his memory, mourn-ing what they'd almost had? Well, she was. But she also wanted to obliterate that grief with something spicy and succulent in her personal life, something completely unlike the usual.

She picked up the phone on her nightstand, and she dialed Rich Macklin's cell-phone number.

A few nights later, Liza walked into Landmark, a bar on Halsted Street.

They had chatted easily last Saturday night, and after a few minutes, he'd brought up Landmark. "I'll be in town for the week, so why don't we meet there for a drink?"

"You don't have other plans?" she'd asked.

"Nothing I wouldn't cancel to see you. And besides, when I'm in Chicago, it's usually all work. I could use a friend." He didn't say this last part seductively, but it hit her that way.

"Oh." She sounded like a twelve-year-old. She reminded herself that she could play this game. She'd done it dozens of times—picking up men in Berlin and Buenos Aires and Phuket. But of course she was always on the clock. It was just part of her job, a means to an end she'd been ordered to accomplish. Now here was this Rich Macklin, upfront and offering to be her "friend." She needed that kind of friend.

"I'll be there at seven," she said.

At seven, she was standing inside the front door of Landmark, dressed in jeans and her highest heels and a low-cut black shirt that twisted around her midriff, tied in the back and showed off her breasts. She felt tarted up, and she loved it.

The bar had zebra-skin walls in the foyer, and inside, a towering, two-story ceiling with exposed beams. The burgundy leather bar to her left was packed with people—women her age with their girlfriends, men fawning over them. She stood there for a moment, panicked. She never went out to bars for fun anymore. What was she supposed to do here?

A waving hand caught her eye. Rich sat at the end of the bar. His dark hair was a little longer than she remembered. His grin was the same—too confident, but undeniable. He stood and swept a hand toward his bar stool. As she walked toward him, he looked her over, not bothering to hide his appraisal.

When she reached him, he smiled. "You're as gorgeous as I remember." Just like that. Not *Hello,* not *How are you tonight?*

She laughed. Frankness was something she appreciated more and more every day. "Thanks."

She put her bag on the bar, and then she looked him up and down, just as he had done to her. "You look pretty delicious yourself."

23

Manhattan, New York

Roger Leiland sat as his desk in his Fifteenth Street office. He'd been working for six hours straight, and he hadn't paused once, not even to use the bathroom. He liked to test himself like this. He might not be in the field any longer, but he still had the toughness of a top-notch operative.

His phone rang, and Roger saw that it was a call to his private line, a number to which very few had access. He decoded the scrambled numbers on the display and smiled.

"Roger Leiland," he said, answering it.

"Silvia Falconiere," he heard. A sultry, confident voice, an Italian accent.

"Silvia, it's wonderful to hear from you." He'd been waiting for this call since he'd sent Liza to Anguilla.

"I wanted to personally thank you."

"You're very welcome."

"Your organization is everything you said it was."

"I'm glad you think so."

"And now I believe I owe you payment."

"That's right." He stood and looked down over grimy

Fifteenth Street. *Soon,* he told himself, soon his office would be in a much different place. The Trust would be in a much different place. And all thanks to clients like Silvia Falconiere.

"I can certainly take care of that today," Silvia said, "but I like to conduct such business in person, if I'm able. Is there any chance you'll be in Italia this summer? I am spending most of my time in Tuscany."

Roger thought about the one time he'd met Silvia Falconiere. Like many Italian women, she had a beautiful, lean body and a sense of style most American women could only dream of. Plus, she was cold-blooded in her business dealings, which he liked most of all.

"I think I might be in the neighborhood..." Roger said.

24

St. Marabel, Canada

It's widely known that a person can attend a spectacular party and still feel spectacularly lonely. Sometimes that loneliness stems from not being with the person you treasure most. Other times, it might be caused by the fact that you don't particularly like the people around you, and you sense they don't exactly find you thrilling, either. After our honeymoon, back in St. Marabel, I felt a whole new kind of loneliness.

I was living with Michael, the most beloved person in my life, and I truly liked what I knew of the townspeople. I enjoyed the smiles I received when I walked into town in search of a *USA Today*. The problem was, my French wasn't good enough to capitalize on those smiles. I could only have the shortest of conversations, spanning how hot it was or how fresh the baguettes in the bakery case appeared.

I could not say to someone, "I miss Chicago, you know? I miss the wine bar I used to go to on Webster, and I miss my friends. It's not that I don't adore

Michael—God, I do—it's just that I'm adjusting. My existence is completely different from the way it used to be, and the way I thought it would be when I married my first husband. Oh yes, that's right, I was married before, but I had three miscarriages. It has to do with a high level of protein in the blood. Anyway, I feel like having a glass of wine. You?"

I was not skilled enough yet for such in-depth, discuss-your-feelings type of conversations. So I learned to smile wide, to tolerate the kind of loneliness that comes from a language barrier—which feels like a true physical barrier around yourself—and to save those conversations I wanted to have for Michael.

"You're restless," Michael said one morning.

We sat in the kitchen, where the clean rays of light shone through the window over the sink. There was coffee on the table. One pot of regular for Michael. One pot of decaf for me—something I'd gotten used to during my fertility treatments when everything from caffeine to nail-polish fumes were considered potentially harmful. Michael had cut up a green apple, and he'd placed the slices on a plate surrounding a few croissants. I loved these croissants—I loved how they were dropped off every morning before we were even awake, how they were more buttery than flaky, and heavier than the ones in the U.S.

But today, the croissant tasted filmy and bland. The coffee seemed to have gone lukewarm already.

"I'm fine," I said to Michael, mustering a smile, which really wasn't that hard. I smiled nearly every time I saw him. And of course, I was fine. Nothing to be unfine about.

"Kate," he said simply.

"What?"

"You're blue."

Is it a sign of love when someone knows what you're thinking before you say it out loud? I suppose my mood had something to do with the fact that Michael would soon stand and turn away from me. He'd walk through the arched doorway and out the front door. He would work all day on the restaurant, and I wouldn't see him again until late tonight.

"Nothing I can't handle," I said.

He put his napkin on the table. "Let's go. I'm taking you to the restaurant."

"I thought you wanted me to wait until it was finished. I can hang in there for a few more days."

"No, it's finished enough. I want you to see it."

"You're sure?"

"I'm positive. In fact, I can't wait to show you. It's killing me. Get dressed and let's go."

Soon we were walking hand in hand down the streets of St. Marabel. A couple of sleepy tourists strolled with coffees and newspapers tucked under their arms. The residents of St. Marabel moved faster toward their jobs. Michael nodded to many we passed.

I'd seen the outside of the Twilight Club before. It was in an old mill that stood in front of a river's curve. Michael had told me that in the 1700s and 1800s the mill was used to process lumber for the town. Due to fires, it had been rebuilt three times. Now the lower walls of the place were made of brick and stone, with stucco the rest of the way up to a series of black, steeply angled roofs. Stone columns held a roofed portico. Michael led me to the massive wooden door, pounded with brass nails.

"Ready?" he said.

"Ready."

He opened the door.

I stepped inside and gasped.

The front hall was a long room, two stories high with thick, dark beams supporting the vaulted ceiling. Black-painted French doors made up the wall to our right. The other wall was filled with shelves that held old books and antiques. Michael flipped on a switch and the small sconces on the walls gave the room a rich, warm light.

"So this is the dining room," I said.

"Exactly." Michael took me through it, pointing out where the tables and hostess stand would be placed.

Next, he took me to a cozier, smaller room behind the dining room. The walls were curved and made of rough-hewn fieldstone with a fireplace tucked into one of the bends. The bar was carved wood. Beams overhead ran the length of the flat ceiling. And just to the right, there was a small polished-wood dance floor and beyond that a small stage with a baby grand piano.

"The jazz bar," I said.

"You got it." I could hear the pride in Michael's voice.

He took me downstairs next. "The private rooms," he explained.

The smaller of the private spaces was a wine cellar with a table accommodating twelve people. The larger was decorated with leather and wood detailing and could seat forty.

"Do you think you'll get much business for these rooms since this is a vacation town?"

"Definitely. Corporate getaways and that kind of thing. Plus, people, especially wealthy people, place a premium on privacy and luxury. We'll have security outside the rooms and only select waitstaff will be allowed downstairs."

"Is that necessary?"

Michael shrugged. "I think so."

He led me down another hallway. "Here's my office."

The room was small but beautifully appointed with moldings and floor-to-ceiling bookshelves behind a desk. Michael opened the French doors on the other side of the room.

"A garden," I said. "That's perfect."

"I know. I can get some air. Or just take a walk without having to go through the restaurant."

I perused the items on the bookshelf behind Michael's desk—thick binders full of restaurant info, reference materials, a photo of us from our wedding. I was about to turn away, when I saw another photo on the lowest shelf. It was of Roger and Michael. They stood next to each other, both dressed in khaki shorts and shirts. In the background were large tents and an orange setting sun.

"Where was this taken?" I asked.

"Africa."

"I didn't know you and Roger had traveled together."

"It was a company thing."

"Presario sent you to Africa?"

"Yeah. They made a lot of money there—still do."

I looked at the photo again. You could tell by the clothes that the picture had been taken at least a few years ago. "You left Presario over ten years ago, right?"

"Right. So that trip was probably ten or eleven years ago. I can't remember anymore."

He walked over to me and took the photo from my hand, replacing it on the shelf. I was about to say that I thought Roger hadn't worked at Presario that long ago, and that the clothes in the photo didn't look that dated. I wanted to ask more questions—about Presario, about Africa. I found Michael, and all that he'd done, fascinating. There was so much still that I didn't know about him. But he led me from the office and upstairs again.

When we reached the jazz bar, I imagined it filled with people, a musician pounding the piano keys, dancers gliding across the floor, waiters slipping through the crowds.

I walked behind the bar, and ran my hand over the smooth metal of the draft-beer taps. "Sometimes I miss being a bartender."

I'd told Michael various stories about my part-time bartending gig after college. I had been working during the day for Riser Consulting, the largest accounting firm in the nation, but two nights a week I worked behind the bar at the Red Lion Pub on Lincoln Avenue where my friends hung out and where we knew the manager. I loved having an excuse to chat with everyone who sat down, not just my friends. I liked the simple motions of pouring beer, opening wine bottles, polishing glasses. I liked the easy busyness of it, so different from my number wrangling and tax-code analysis during the day.

"Do you know how to make a dirty martini?" Michael asked.

"Of course." I ticked off the ingredients on my fingers. "Gin, dry vermouth, olive juice. And olives. Preferably two of them."

"What about a Green Demon?"

I touched my fingers with each ingredient— "Vodka, rum, melon liqueur, lemonade."

"Okay, here's a tough one. Have you ever heard of an Adios Motherfucker?"

I laughed. "A what?"

"It's a very legitimate drink."

"Where? In a Mexican border town?"

"We get all types here. You'll have to be prepared, Kate."

"What do you mean, I have to be prepared?"

"Would you consider bartending for me? I didn't want to ask because I wanted you to just enjoy the town and get your bearings, but I think you'd be perfect. And we could spend—"

Before he could talk any further, I tackled him with a hug. I swelled with the thought of Michael and me working together, learning about each other, making something of this restaurant *together.*

"Yes!" I said. "Absolutely, yes!"

Four days later at the grand opening, the Twilight Club was packed. From my vantage point at the bar, I couldn't see past the throng of people to the door. In the corner, a jazz guitarist, pianist and vocalist whipped people into a feel-good frenzy. Waiters circled the place with trays of appetizers—caviar on toast rounds, scallops with watercress, tiny pizzas with goat cheese and porcini mushrooms.

"I had no idea it would be this insane," I said to T.R., the other bartender, a big man in his late forties. T.R. was a Texas transplant who'd lived in St. Marabel for over twenty years now. He'd come here to paint, and he'd never left. Michael was able to woo him away from another local pub where he'd tended bar for years.

"Darlin', I didn't see this coming either," T.R. said.

All night, we poured wine and popped corks and created drinks in a rush. I found the work exhilarating. At the Twilight Club, I was meeting and I was greeting and I was talking and I was *moving*.

I marveled at the crowd. I'd expected largely a local group, but there were couples from Italy and a family from Japan. At the end of the bar were two men from Germany and earlier I'd seen a group from Australia.

"Quite the international bunch, huh?" I said to T.R. as we stood next to each other mixing cocktails.

"Yep," he said, flipping a vodka bottle, catching it by the base and pouring a shot into a glass. "That's St. Marabel. I've never understood it, but this town has always seen its fair share of foreigners. It's one of the reasons I decided to stay here. I could meet so many different folks in just one little place."

"Do you ever miss Texas?"

T.R. put his customer's drink on the bar. He crossed his big arms and paused for a moment. "I visit every so often. But I still miss pickup trucks. And I miss *pico de gallo* and Mexican beer, but other than that, I'm okay with being here. What about you?"

"I miss Chicago." I delivered a gin and tonic and started to open a new bottle of sauvignon blanc. "I miss my friend, Liza, even though I didn't really see her that often. And I miss seeing baseball on TV and visiting my family. But Michael is my family now."

"So you're in the right place."

"I think so."

"Why don't you go find your man and tell him congrats? I can handle it on my own for a minute."

"You're sure?" I looked around. We'd gotten cocktails for nearly everyone who'd come in the door, and now we had a momentary lull.

"I'm fine."

I untied the white apron from around my waist and smoothed down the black cotton shirt that was our uniform. I threaded my way through the crowd, hearing nothing but praise for Michael and the Twilight Club.

When I reached the doorway between the bar and the front room, where Michael had been standing earlier, I didn't see him. I went into the dining room and said hello to Anna, the hostess, a woman in her mid-fifties with short gray hair.

"I think Michael is with some diners in the private rooms," she said.

"Are those booked tonight?"

"Both of them. Tonight and tomorrow."

"Wow, that's great."

I went to the stairs to see if I could catch Michael, but I was stopped by a man in a dark suit. He had terrible skin and a nice smile. "My apologies." He held an arm across the top of the stairway. "These rooms are off access."

"It's all right. I work here," I said.

"Only authorized personnel."

"I'm sure I'm authorized. I'm Michael's wife."

"My apologies, *madame,* but you have not been placed on the authorized list."

"Look, if you can just find Michael for me, I only want to say hello."

"I will tell him when I see him, Madame Waller."

"Can you tell him now?"

He shook his head.

The two men from Germany who had been at the bar came to the top of the stairs. They spoke a few words in German. The bouncer in the dark suit responded, also in what sounded like German, and stepped aside to let the men down the stairs.

When they were gone, he nodded at me. "*Madame,* I will have to ask you to step away."

"What's your name?"

"Jean."

"Thank you, Jean. I'll be sure to tell my husband I met you."

If Jean was put off by my words, he didn't show it. He gave me another nice smile and a dismissive bow of his head.

I walked back to the bar, curious and slightly deflated.

"How's your hubby?" T.R. said when I reached the bar.

"I don't know," I said. "I don't have any idea."

25

In the small private dining room, Michael clasped his hands behind his back and greeted the four men from Australia. "How is everything?"

"Brilliant, mate," one of them said. "Congratulations on your opening night."

"Thank you. Thank you very much."

The group was made up of a father and son and two business partners. Like many of the visitors to the Twilight Club, Michael expected this group would enjoy their time in St. Marabel. They would sail on the lake—*Lac Marabel*—drink at the club and take pleasure in being away from their wives, but they were here on business, too. They were investing members of the Trust.

Michael chatted with them for a short time about the restaurant, the food and the music. Then the son asked, "How's the situation in Rio?"

Michael raised his hands in a surrender sort of gesture. "Gentlemen, I'm not involved in that side of the operations anymore. I'm only here to run the club."

"Just update us on Gustavo."

Michael put on a pleasant look. "I'm really not the right person."

"Well then, who is?" asked the father, a hearty man with a ruddy complexion.

"I'll have someone come in and apprise you."

"I should hope so," said one of the other men. "That's why we came all this way."

Michael heard the irritation in the man's voice, and it made him anxious. The Australians, although notoriously friendly, cared deeply about their politics and their business, and they wouldn't hesitate to pull their funding if they weren't kept happy.

Although he'd never been assigned to Brazil, Michael had spent a good deal of time in Australia, and he'd helped bring these men—and their capital—into the Trust. They had different interests than the Trust. Rather than being concerned with United States, per se, they just wanted to be on the bandwagon to help defeat people like Gustavo in order to further their own business agendas. In particular, they were concerned about Brazil's iron ore industry. The Australians were the owners of a private company that mined such ore in Brazil and owned land there with rich reserves. But Gustavo was talking about nationalizing the ore industry. If he came into power, there was a real chance that would happen, and the country would take over all of the Australians' land and machinery. And that billion-dollar investment would disappear in an instant.

Michael knew that if the Australians weren't getting real assistance from their membership with the Trust, if they weren't kept happy, they would walk in a minute. They were paying too much not to get results. And the Trust needed capital.

Meanwhile, Michael shouldn't care about any of this

anymore. How many times had he told Roger that he was out? That he was only running the Twilight Club? But the fact was he did care. He had spent his life believing in, and working for, the Trust. He would do nothing to tarnish the group's reputation or jeopardize its missions.

"What about the Russians?" the man said. "Have we heard whether they're interested in Gustavo, too?"

Michael took a breath. The intel he'd collected in Moscow had shown that the Russians were, in fact, very interested in Luis Gustavo. They only cared if the Russians intended to do something about Gustavo. If that was the case, the Trust might step out of the way or get involved depending on their own analysis of Gustavo. Still, that was no longer Michael's problem. "I should have someone else update you."

"If you know something, tell us," the son said. "We don't have time to wait around."

On the contrary, these men had more than enough time. They were in St. Marabel for a few days, and yet Michael found himself nodding. He felt the tweak of excitement that had kept him in this game for so long. He pulled up a chair and briefed the men for a quick five minutes on what he knew about the Russians.

When he was done, he stood. "Your entrées are on their way," Michael said. "I'll make sure you're updated on Gustavo after that."

"Before," said the son. "We'd like to get business out of the way before our meal."

"Of course," Michael said. "Can I get you anything else to drink?" He hated the solicitous tone of his voice.

For those five minutes discussing the Russians, he was a crucial player again. He wasn't simply someone who oversaw menus and ordered around waitstaff. As much as he wanted out of the Trust, he hated forcing himself to the periphery. Simply watching others carry on what he'd done for years made him feel like he was on the downswing of his life.

But then he thought of Kate. Gorgeous Kate. He loved the smart, funny Kate, whom he'd seen bantering with the patrons at the bar. He loved the vulnerable way she looked in the morning without mascara on her brown eyes, when her messy, blond hair looked like a halo around her face. He loved the way she studied him when he talked, when she listened like she just got him; she just loved him; she just saw him. Kate was one of the reasons he could embrace the Twilight Club and life on the sidelines. She made the struggle worthwhile, and at the thought of her, his spirits buoyed. He took drink orders from the men and left the room.

As he stepped into the hallway, he was approached by a young operative, Angus Laslow, whose cover was working part-time for the Twilight Club. Angus, Michael knew, was one of Roger's favorites, although he wasn't sure why. The guy had a mean streak a mile wide. In fact, they'd had to reprimand Angus when Michael was a board member. Angus had been ordered to conduct surveillance on an arms dealer in Mexico, and while planting audio equipment he'd startled the guy's mother, who came at him with a knife. Angus disarmed her, which was protocol, but then he turned the knife back on the woman—over and over—and left her, so that she nearly bled to death. Such an incident went against the "no collateral damage" rule the Trust had always held fast to. Upon hearing about the incident, Michael wanted to end Angus's operative status and make him office staff. Roger argued successfully against that. Now Angus was posted here at the Twilight Club, and Michael could tell he still resented him.

"Call from home," Angus said with a smug smile, which made Michael want to punch him.

A *call from home* was not Kate. A *call from home* was meant to convey that a member of the Trust's board wanted to talk to him.

Michael took a few steps down the hallway and stopped at a closed wooden door with no markings. He lifted the flap of a keypad and punched in a series of numbers. A *beep* sounded, followed by a click, and Michael slid the keypad to the right, revealing a glowing, neon-green screen. He put his palm against the screen and waited. Another click sounded—the door unlocking.

Michael stepped inside. It was a secure phone booth, intended only for communications with the board. He took a seat at the small table and looked at the black phone placed there. A flashing red light indicated a waiting call. Michael lifted the phone.

"Hey, buddy," he heard.

"What are you doing, Roger?" Michael said. "I thought you were in Korea."

"I am. How's the opening?"

"Great. When are you going to see it for yourself?"

"Soon, soon. But in the meantime, we need to talk."

Michael went still. Roger was one of his best friends,

but he knew the cold tone to his voice. This wasn't a friendly call.

"Mike," Roger said. "No briefing the guests, okay? You've only got pieces of the puzzle now."

There were cameras and listening devices in the private rooms. Michael knew that well. Someone had been listening, and that someone had reported to Roger, who now wanted him to back off.

"I *know* my role," Michael said. "I asked for it."

"Then stick to it."

Michael felt his jaws grind, an old habit that awoke when he was pissed off. "I'd be happy to stick to it if the Trust was being run with the precision it requires. Those men should have been briefed immediately. They should not have had to ask me for information."

"Jesus, Mike, they can wait."

"Not when they're giving the Trust the kind of money they are. They deserve the utmost respect. They deserve to get what they paid for. I don't like the lackadaisical way the Trust is operating these days."

"Lackadaisical?" He heard icy anger in Roger's tone.

"Hell, yes. Details aren't being given due attention, things are slipping through the cracks. Coleman wouldn't have wanted it like this."

"Coleman is long gone," Roger scoffed.

"Coleman Kingsley deserves reverence." Michael's voice was loud. "Even now."

"He *deserves?*" Roger said, his voice full of scorn. "Kingsley wasn't omnipotent, Mike."

"He was the strongest, most intelligent man we've ever known."

Roger scoffed. "Strong? He caved when Colby died. Absolutely melted."

"Wouldn't you? If your only son passed away?"

"No," Roger said without hesitation. "I had a feeling Coleman wouldn't be able to handle it. And he didn't. He wasn't as tough as you thought."

Michael opened his mouth to say, *You're a son of a bitch.* But the conversation, the reminders of Coleman, had suddenly taken the steam out of him.

"Look," Michael said, letting his voice drop quietly, "all I'm saying is that if things continue this way, other things will slip, too. I can guarantee it."

"Maybe so. But you're in no position to lecture me, or to rectify anything. You can't have it both ways, my friend."

"I'm aware of that."

"We *want* you in…"

"I know, I know."

"…but you opted out."

"I get it."

"Good. I'm glad. You want back in, just say the word."

"Look, I've got a restaurant to run. Is there anything else?"

"Give my love to Kate," Roger said.

It was a kind thing to say. Michael should have been grateful that his old friend had accepted his new wife, but somehow Roger's words felt like a threat.

26

Is intuition really accurate? Or is it just paranoia that occasionally hits the mark?

The next morning, I waited for Michael to open his eyes. I lay in bed next to him, my head propped on a pillow, and watched him sleep, willing him to wake up.

The rest of the previous night had been a success for the Twilight Club. The bar had been packed until 2:00 a.m., the band having been convinced to play an hour later than planned. It seemed that every ten minutes or so, Michael was walking someone to my bar, proudly introducing me as "my wife, Kate." I knew he had friends in town, but I had no idea he knew *that* many people or so many of St. Marabel's visitors. He'd gotten home an hour after me at 4:00 a.m. and had crashed on the bed in his clothes, like a little boy tired from too much play.

He groaned now and rolled over.

I cleared my throat, and instantly he was awake. Michael was like that. The smallest things could bring him straight from slumber to wakefulness. He looked shocked for a second, like he often did when he woke up, then his eyes found me, and his whole face smiled.

"Congratulations," I said.

Michael's smile got bigger.

"The restaurant was great last night," I said. "*You* were great."

"Thanks, my love." His voice was a little foggy, his face still content. He snuck an arm out and put it on my hip. "C'mere."

"No, no. I have to hear about last night. No sex until I hear about last night."

"You were there last night."

"I want to hear what *you* thought of last night."

He sat up and undid the buttons of his shirt and tossed it on the floor. "You're sure?" he said, giving me a lascivious look.

"We're only talking!"

"All right." Michael leaned against the headboard. "What did you really think of the opening?"

"I really thought it was a smash. An absolute success. I'm thrilled for you."

He nodded. "Thank you. I can't believe we pulled it off. Of course, there are kinks to work out."

"Like putting me on the private dining room list."

His head turned. "What do you mean?"

"I tried to come visit you last night, but Jean stopped me."

"That's what he's supposed to do."

"Can't I visit you?" I was struck with a wary feeling about those downstairs rooms, about feeling shut out of certain aspects of Michael's life.

"Well..." Michael shifted around on the bed. "The rooms are really just meant for clients who reserve it."

"I understand the need for privacy, but c'mon, it's not like I plan on being there all the time."

"It doesn't work like that."

"Says who? You're the owner."

He gave a slow dip of his head to the right. "Yes, but I have investors, and we have a business plan, and our plan includes allowing no one into the private dining rooms except the clients who reserve them and the wait-staff who works them."

"Who are these investors?"

"Just people I've met over the years."

"Like who?" I'd asked this question a few times, and I'd never gotten a straight answer. It wasn't necessarily such important information, but I was struck by how vague Michael always was.

"You know," he said, "people I've met through work."

"Okay, different question. How does an average guy like Jean, the doorman, know how to speak German?"

"What do you mean?"

"There were two Germans there last night, and when they came to the top of the stairs, he spoke to them in German."

"We'd hoped we'd have a lot of international customers, so we made sure to get staff with language skills."

"A bouncer who knows different languages?"

"What's your point?"

I shrugged. "Maybe I should be private dining staff." I wanted to leave it alone. I truly did, but something about Michael's reticence made me push.

Michael laughed. "Your French isn't so hot, and I need you at the bar. You don't want to work in the basement."

"I want to work with you. I want to keep getting to know you, Michael."

"You know me." He moved toward me, his arms reaching around my back.

I wiggled away. I felt caught between two emotions—one that said I should just enjoy my amorous husband and another that wanted to know more about him. "I don't know you enough."

Michael looked uncomfortable. "What does that mean?"

"I want to be closer to you. I mean, look what happened last night. I couldn't even walk downstairs and kiss my husband congratulations. You own the place, and yet I wasn't even allowed to say hello to you."

"It's just the way it has to be."

I lay back, confused. I wanted it to be Michael and me against the world—working at the restaurant together, creating a life. And yet I sensed Michael had worlds I knew nothing about. There was little to help build that belief, I reminded myself. It was more of an indistinct suspicion from deep inside me.

Michael looked uncharacteristically helpless. "Let's go out and get some coffee, and we'll talk about this."

"Why do we have to go out when we talk?"

Michael was always tugging me out into the streets of St. Marabel when we discussed things. It usually worked. It brought reality back to our lives and made everything okay. But it was eight in the morning, and I was tired and suddenly cranky.

"I like to walk and talk," Michael said.

"I like to lie in bed and talk."

He laughed. "You win. Talk."

"Tell me about the private dining rooms last night. Who was there?"

He sighed. "Kate, let's talk about something other than the dining rooms."

"Why? Why won't you share that with me? I moved here, to another country and out of my home, to be with you. I need to be a part of your life."

"You are. You *are* my life." Those were pretty words, and yet I felt Michael growing annoyed with me for the first time in our relationship.

For some reason, his annoyance fueled me. "Why won't you tell me?"

"There's nothing to tell!" His voice was slightly raised now.

"Then why is there a list of people who can get down there? Why is it all a secret? Why are your investors a secret?"

"Jesus, Kate, let it go." He stood up. "Can we please take a walk and talk about this later?"

I pulled the sheets around my chest. "We're talking now, Michael. I'd like to just keep talking."

"Well, I wouldn't."

In stony silence, Michael went to the closet, took off his pants, replaced them with jeans and pulled on a blue golf shirt. Then he left the bedroom.

I heard the dull thud of his footsteps across the wood floors of the living room and into the kitchen. I heard the scrape of keys as he lifted them from the brown ceramic bowl on the counter. I heard the front door open. And close.

27

Chicago, Illinois

Liza watched the rise and fall of Rich Macklin's chest. She let her eyes trail from his chest to his abdomen. Unfortunately, everything lower than that was covered by the sheet, but Liza had no problems remembering it all. He had an incredible body, a body crafted in the gym, so different from Aleksei's body, which had been slim and lean. Rich had sculpted muscles over nearly every inch of his body and a faint scar under his right ribs in the shape of a jagged triangle. And Liza couldn't get enough of him.

Years ago, when she'd let the relationship with Aleksei fade into her past, she'd been morose and melancholy. She'd recognized the need for their break, but it didn't make it any easier to live with. She missed Aleksei. She missed interacting with, being with, sharing her life (in some way) with another person. She missed their talks about the intelligence business, about the Russian Mafiya he'd been investigating for years, about random daily things she'd rarely talked with anyone about except

Kate. Even when they'd ended things, the idea of Aleksei made her happy. She thought of him, in some ways, as her other half, and she liked the thought that he was out there walking around somewhere.

Sex with Aleksei had been wonderful. It was meaningful sex—the best kind, of course—but she'd forgotten that there could be another kind of sex—raw and fast and wholly engaged. Sex purely for sex's sake.

Rich was giving her a fast primer on that other kind.

She couldn't believe how quickly she'd left celibacy behind. That night at the Landmark had been heady. They'd sipped wine with eyes locked, their words light and filled with benign information. He was an estate lawyer, he said. He'd gotten lucky after law school and worked for a well-known attorney who represented some of the nation's wealthiest families, many of them in Chicago. And when that lawyer retired, the families had stayed with Rich, and their business had led Rich into a partnership at Toffer and Brodley. Now he split his time between offices in Boston and Chicago. What did she do? he asked. Liza gave her pat answer. She was in international sales for Presario Pharmaceuticals. They focused on immunization drugs. This part was true. She didn't tell him the other part—that Presario was owned by the Trust, that her sales job took up only fifteen percent of her time, that her real profession was that of a covert intelligence officer.

After two hours of this ordinary and yet somehow entirely heated conversation, Rich had leaned in and said, "If I don't kiss you, I'm going to lose my mind."

He pulled back and looked at her again. He lowered his gaze to her lips.

She bit her bottom lip. For the first time in years, she felt not just desirous of sex but one hundred percent sexy. She delayed the moment with silence, loving it.

Then she said, "Well, I wouldn't want to have to visit you in a mental hospital."

He smiled. The crowd around them was loud and large and provided a buffer that seemed to pulsate.

He leaned in again. This time directly toward her. Their mouths met. Softly, then with more insistence. She grabbed his shirtfront and pulled him closer. The people around them faded. After a minute, she sat back and stared at him with awe.

"Want to get out of here?" he said.

"Yeah," she said without hesitation.

"Your place?"

"Yours. Okay?" She'd never brought a guy back to her apartment. Somehow she couldn't even imagine it.

"Whatever."

In the back of the cab, they kissed, harder this time and with a sense of direction. Somehow her leg was thrown over his, and then somehow he was lifting her up and she was astride him. Fully clothed, yes, but in a cab!

Liza had replayed the evening in minute detail to Kate. She'd described Rich's amazing body and told her about the kissing session in the cab. Kate was thrilled. She jokingly said they should make out on an El train next. That was something Liza loved most about her friendship with Kate—the lack of judgment. Kate would chide her about her busyness and tell her honestly that she thought Liza needed to take time off, to sleep more, to get laid even, but Liza always knew Kate would back off when Liza wanted her to and that she would support her unconditionally. It meant a lot, even if Kate didn't always know what she was supporting.

Liza smiled now as she stared at Rich's sleeping form. This whole relationship was so unlike her. The make-out scene in the cab had led to sex in Rich's rented West Loop loft until the early-morning hours. That had led to coffee together the next morning, and more sex that night. He'd gone away for a few days for a Fourth of July trip with friends, while Liza spent the time working, although her mind was preoccupied with thoughts of him, of this chest she was staring at right now. He called her as soon as he was back in town for work, and here they were again, back in his bed. Exactly where Liza wanted to be.

She looked at the clock: 7:00 a.m. She had to go home to shower and get to work. She liked work so much more now that she had a social life. A sex life, anyway.

Her phone beeped. It was a tone really, meant to convey that it was a phone call from someone high up at the Trust, and Liza had taught herself to listen for it, no matter what she was doing.

She was out of bed in one fluid movement.

"Yes," she said, answering the phone. She looked over her shoulder to see if she'd disturbed Rich. But he was a heavy sleeper, and his chest continued its contented rise and fall.

"It's Paul Costa."

Her face fell into a hard cast. "Paul Costa"—Roger—was her superior, but she'd lost respect for him when he'd hit on her at Kate's wedding.

"Yes," she said again, taking the phone out into the passageway.

She closed the bedroom door tightly behind her and went down the hall, into Rich's coat closet. She climbed inside, stepping on a pair of Rich's shoes and ducking under a coat hanging there, and pulled the door closed behind her. There were rarely any listening devices in closets. Not that she expected Rich to have any, but aside from her recklessness with Aleksei, Liza was always cautious.

"We've got a problem with your friend," Roger said.

"What friend is that?"

"The friend who married your other friend, Kate."

"Let's cut the crap. What do you want to say about Michael?"

"He's treading on thin ice."

"How's that?"

"He can't decide if he's in or out."

"I think he's made it clear he's out, except for the Twilight Club."

"That's what he says. But he's doing some rogue things."

"Like what? The Twilight Club only opened a few days ago."

He exhaled. "You know I can't say, but it's…well, it's worrisome, Liza."

He sounded genuine, which formed a little pocket of fear inside her. "What are you trying to say?"

"I'm just saying that your friend should be careful."

"Michael should be careful?"

"Both of them, actually. I'm calling out of concern."

"I bet."

"I am," he said with sincerity. "I'm his friend, too."

That was true. Liza had never had a reason to doubt the friendship between the two men.

"That's what makes this hard," Roger said. "I care about him, and I just want him to be cautious. He's as out of the game as we can get him. But there are a number of things only Michael knows about. He's still going to have to do some work. And yet I'm concerned about him not following orders because he thinks he knows what's best."

Liza said nothing. Michael was used to being on top at the Trust, and she'd learned from her years of working with such guys that no one took easily to stepped-down status, even when they had requested it.

"I'm also worried about his ability to be discreet," Roger said.

"You don't have to worry about Michael's discretion."

"I wouldn't have thought so before. But your friend Kate has caused a chink in his usual armor. She's suspicious. She already senses that there's more to the Twilight Club than she knows. And he's in love with her. I don't want him to make any mistakes and think he can tell her anything."

In that instant, Liza understood. Members of the Trust promised never to discuss their organization with outsiders, and the Trust promised that anyone who learned about the organization risked being eliminated. With Aleksei, Liza had been beyond reckless, but she'd never told him who she worked for, she'd never told him what she was working on. She'd let him assume her employer was a government agency. And when she'd gotten caught, she'd told the board exactly what she'd said to Aleksei. It helped that Michael had been on the board then. It helped that she was Coleman Kingsley's daughter. But her father's name didn't seem to be carrying much weight these days.

"You brought Kate into this life," Roger said now.

"And so I need to keep her safe," she said.

Silence.

"Got it," she said.

Liza turned off the phone. She sat in the dark, feeling cold and scared.

28

From her office later that morning, Liza called Michael's cell phone. "Secure?" she asked when he answered.

"Yeah, I've got the CTAC," he said, referring to a device that provided secure voice communications via cellular phone. "Do we need it?"

"How's Kate?"

"She's…fine," Michael answered.

"I got a call."

"From?"

She said nothing.

"Roger," he said with frustration. "Christ. It's fine, Liza. We're fine."

"You're sure?"

"He shouldn't have called you."

"He says I'm responsible."

"Going around me is unforgivable. He's treating me like a new recruit."

"I guess he wants you back in."

"Hey, he's got me in for a few other missions he says only I can handle. He's got me in for what's in my head, and he's got me in for the Twilight Club. What else does he want?"

"I don't know." She swung her chair around and stared at the picture of her family. "So much has changed about the Trust."

"Indeed it has." He breathed out hard. "Liza, I wanted to tell you that I'm sorry about Aleksei."

Her eyes welled in an instant. How did that happen so fast? She quickly wiped the tears, but she knew they'd be back. Lately, her emotions were always lying in wait.

"Thank you," she said. "Do you know anything more about it?" She had been meaning to ask Michael. He and Aleksei had never dealt with each other, but she'd hoped that with Michael's contacts in Russia he might have learned something.

Michael paused.

"What?" Liza said. "Tell me."

"There's nothing official yet."

Liza sat up straight. "Don't give me that. Cut to it."

"They haven't released their official report, but they're saying it wasn't pilot error. There was a small explosive mounted on the engine."

Liza shot from her chair to her feet. "Why didn't we know about that sooner? It's not something you can hide."

The tears welled right back up and spilled from her eyes. She couldn't stop them this time. Aleksei had been killed. Or someone on that plane had been targeted, taking everyone else with him. Liza felt a crashing wave of grief coat her.

"I just found out yesterday. It seems the Russian authorities didn't want to say anything until they could figure out who planted the device."

"And?"

"They have no leads."

"Can you find out more? Can you ask around?"

"Of course, if that's what you want."

"Yes. Please. God, Michael, I need to know." She pursed her mouth, but she couldn't stop herself from saying it. "I loved him."

"I know."

"Who can you call? Who was the contact who gave you the info about the plane?"

A pause. "I shouldn't say."

"Does this contact swing both ways?" Liza was referring to a Russian government official who'd been successfully recruited by the Mafiya.

"Not exactly."

Liza thought about it for a moment. "Is your contact someone who already made their money and *now* wants to swing both ways?"

Michael was silent again. They both knew who Liza meant—a prominent Russian oil tycoon who was talking big about running for government office, but who was also known to be a member of the Mafiya.

She was just speculating, but Michael stayed silent; that told Liza everything.

"Call him again," she said. "Get everything you can out of him."

"He won't talk on the phone anymore. He's already said too much."

"So visit him. Please."

"Now you're asking too much. I'm trying to get away from his type, remember? I'm doing that for Kate."

"I know, but Michael, please. *Please.*" Those damn tears kept racing to her eyes again, and she let them fall.

"Liza, he's gone. You need to move forward."

Liza thought of Rich Macklin, who wanted to meet her for dinner after work. She could feel herself being drawn closer to him. Relationships were always difficult when you were a member of the Trust. But despite Roger's warnings, weren't Michael and Kate making it work? Couldn't Liza, too? Shouldn't she at least be able to try? And yet she wouldn't be able to make the effort if she couldn't lay Aleksei to rest properly.

"You've got to help me."

He made a sound of slight exasperation. "I want to, but seriously, I'd have to see him in person."

"So go. For me."

"He's in Miami."

Liza thought of the time she'd spent with Aleksei in Miami. "That's closer than Russia."

"Jesus, Liza."

"I'll beg."

"What am I supposed to tell Kate?"

"The truth. Tell Kate you're meeting with an investor for the restaurant. That's true. Morgan Hadings lives there."

Morgan was a Trust board member. She was a reserved woman, which led many to think she was unopinionated, only a worker bee, but Michael and Liza both knew better. Coleman had brought Morgan in because she was exceptionally smart and exceptionally shrewd. And now, because of her position on the board, she was one of the people who controlled Michael's fate.

"You'll go to Miami," Liza continued, "and you'll meet with your contact, but you'll also meet with Morgan to reiterate how you're getting out of the biz. Plus, meeting with Morgan will actually further your point with Roger that you're on your way out. You keep quiet about your meeting with the Russian, and it will all be on the up-and-up."

Silence again. Finally, Michael spoke. "Fine."

"Thank you, thank you," she said. Then, "I'm going with you."

"Not necessary. He won't meet you."

"He might."

"He won't."

"I'm persuasive."

"Liza, trust me on this."

"I just want to be there. I can't stay here." She thought again of Rich in his office twelve floors down. She didn't want to see him, to consider *being* with him, until she closed this thing with Aleksei. Until she knew what really happened. Until she made people pay for hurting him. Then she could close the chapter. She could wash her hands and come to Rich with an open heart.

"Do what you want," Michael said. "I'll be at the Delano Hotel."

"When?"

"It'll take me a few days to get everything straight at the club."

Liza thought about Miami. She had some contacts there she could meet with. It was always good to keep up relationships, especially before you needed something from them.

She pushed her chair back from her desk. "I'll see you in Florida."

29

St. Marabel, Canada

If I'd learned one thing from my first marriage it was the need to adapt. And so, after our fight a few mornings ago, I'd waited for Michael to come home, I'd let him take me out for a stroll, and we made up. Michael had been a bachelor for a long time, and I knew I needed to give him some space to let me grow into his world.

We went on to have another hectic night at the club that evening. Michael was busy, mostly because the large private room was rented again. There were twenty or so guests, and they were an interesting group, including five Japanese men and one woman who'd come early and sat silently at the bar, most of them drinking whiskey, before they went downstairs for dinner. There was also a group of elegantly dressed Brits and a handful of people who, from what I could tell from serving them a predinner cocktail, came from different Central American countries.

The group was a business trip, Michael had said, a retreat of sorts. When I asked what kind of business they were in, Michael mentioned private equity. And then he'd taken the group downstairs, and disappeared.

He didn't come back upstairs until midnight, and by that time, we were both so exhausted we walked home fast and fell asleep even faster. The next few days were the same.

Now here we were again, headed to work on a gorgeously sunny afternoon, but Michael had just announced he was off to Miami.

"You're leaving during opening week?" I said.

"It's bad timing." He nodded hello to an old man sitting in front of his newspaper stand. "Some of the investors are in Miami, and they couldn't come in for the opening. We need to finalize some financial aspects with them."

"How many investors do you have?"

He laughed. "Too many."

I asked him a few more questions about the investors, but he just have me typical responses like, "It's hard to explain."

"I'm an accountant," I said. "I can understand finances."

He didn't meet my eyes. "It's rather complicated."

"Why are you being so evasive?"

He shot me a sideways glance.

"I'm sorry," I said. "I just want to be close with you, and I guess what I want you to know is I can handle the specifics. I *want* the specifics."

He stopped and turned to me. "Kate, the specifics are boring. Look, I don't necessarily want to hear about every detail of your day. I don't want to know about the ingredients of every drink you poured, and by the same token, I don't want to tell you every little thing about my day. That's how I operate, all right? And I don't think it's a bad way to operate. You're my wife. I *do* want to share all the big pieces of my life. I'm trying, okay?" His brown eyes were earnest and worried.

"So, there was this one woman who wanted a sweet martini," I said, "but she told me to hold the vermouth. And I said, well, that's not a sweet martini if you don't want the vermouth, and she gave me this look, and..." I smiled. "No? You sure you don't want all the details?"

Michael gave a relieved laugh and kissed me, and we walked the rest of the way to work.

Two days later, when I arrived home early from the restaurant, the house was bathed in blue moonlight. It was so beautiful I wanted someone to share it, but Michael was in Miami.

I called his cell phone. It made an empty ring and went to voice mail. I looked at my watch. Michael might already be in bed, tucked into the luxurious sheets of the Delano Hotel, someplace I'd always wanted to stay. We'd talked briefly about me joining Michael on his trip, but the Twilight Club staff wasn't established enough yet. There was no one who could take my shift. And I was happy to help look after things for Michael.

I switched on lamps, killing the moon's blue and filling the house with soft amber light. I took off my black pants and my bartending shirt, limp now from the heat of my body. I dumped everything in the wicker hamper in the closet and changed into a pair of gym shorts and a gray

T-shirt that proclaimed the name Evanston Township High School, where Liza and I had attended.

I checked my watch again. It wasn't too late in Chicago. I poured a glass of wine in the kitchen and settled at the table with the phone. I dialed Liza's cell, usually the best bet, but it too went to voice mail. I tried her at home. Another message.

Was she with the new guy, Rich? Or was she home, ignoring the phone, still mourning Aleksei? I felt terrible that Liza had lost him, even though she hadn't seen him in a long time. True to form, she hadn't told me all the details of their relationship, but I knew she'd loved him. And I knew that was very, very rare for Liza. It hadn't worked out, what with Aleksei being Russian and neither of them wanting to move, but God, for her to lose another person she loved was awful. I wished I could do something for her.

I took another sip of wine in the golden, empty quiet of the kitchen. I remembered that Liza had told me she was thinking of visiting her mother, who was now living in South Carolina.

I decided to call Information for Liza's mom's number. It would be nice to say hello to her, even if Liza wasn't there, and I craved anything that reminded me of Chicago.

I got the number for Delia Coleman in Palm Springs. In seconds, the number was ringing, and Delia answered with a dainty "Hello."

"Mrs. Kingsley?"

"Yes."

"Hi, it's Kate Greenwood."

"Oh, my gosh, Kate! How are you?"

"I'm great, thanks."

"Congratulations on your wedding. Liza told me all about it."

We chatted for ten minutes about Michael and the golf community where Delia now lived.

As our conversation wound down I told her the other reason I was calling. "I was trying to track down Liza. She said she might be visiting you."

Delia sighed. "Oh, you know Liza. Always with plans to visit but always too busy. She's actually in Miami."

The wineglass froze on its way to my mouth. "She's in Miami?"

"Yes, some work thing."

Why was Liza in Miami at the same time as Michael? "Where is she staying?"

"The Shore Club, I believe."

At least it wasn't the Delano. Then I thought about the vague reasoning Michael had given me for his trip to Miami. And some inner voice said, *As far as you know, Liza isn't at the Delano.*

I put down the wineglass and pushed it away from me. I said a polite goodbye to Delia Kingsley and began calling Michael.

30

Miami, Florida

Michael entered Crobar, one of Miami's nightclubs, and tried not to grimace. There was nothing worse than being over fifty in a club that pulsed with twenty-somethings. The bass thumped so loud it rattled his molars.

The Russians loved this crap, even wealthy, educated Russians like Viktor Shenko. And so Michael hadn't blinked when Viktor had mentioned Crobar. He arrived early, as he always did, and followed the instructions Viktor always required—he had brought no one and he'd turned his cell phone to silent. Viktor would find him, and he wanted Michael's undivided attention when he did.

His meeting today with Morgan Hadings had gone well. She'd expressed sympathy for his dilemma, and she'd agreed that the Trust needed to be run with the same degree of honor with which Coleman Kingsley had started it. And then she'd reiterated what Michael already knew—there was no getting out of the Trust. She'd thanked him for his work at the Twilight Club and told him to keep up that fine work. Michael had appreciated her candor, and he'd left feeling respected for his new job within the organization.

But here he was at Crobar, acting like it was the old days.

Michael pressed through a crowd of young men, all virile and very pretty. He was glad he'd grown up when he had, before the days when men waxed their eyebrows and went to tanning salons. And as he skirted a pack of women, all wearing tight jeans, skimpy tops and artfully messed hair, he thought how grateful he was for Kate. Lovely, classy, wonderful Kate. He would talk to Viktor tonight for Liza. He felt a certain sense of duty to Liza because of her father. The last conversation he'd had with Coleman, he'd promised to keep an eye on Liza—not that she needed watching. Yet she'd asked him for this favor. So he would do it, then he would get back to his wife.

Michael made his way down the steps to the bar. The jostling for the bartender's attention was incredible, and Michael knew these young people would run him over if he let them. Instead, he drew himself up to his full height, elbowed his way into a pocket of space, took a hundred out of his wallet and laid it on the bar. It wasn't the first time the bartenders had been flashed cash, Michael knew, but the strategy was generally still effective.

A young black guy with biceps the size of pumpkins was in front of him in a second. "What can I get you?"

"Glenlivet on the rocks."

Michael gave the bartender the hundred and then turned to survey the club. With a systematic, practiced eye, he ran his gaze over the dancers, then the other clubgoers to the side, then those patrons on the upper level. His eye caught a woman standing by herself, hand on a railing. She had black hair cut in a severe line at her shoulders, and she wore a kelly green dress. She looked more elegant than the rest of the crowd, but that wasn't why he'd stopped to stare. It was the practiced insouciance of her lean. Michael would have known that stance anywhere.

He swore under his breath and began to push toward the stairs, keeping his eye out for Viktor or any of his crew. He climbed the stairs and kept moving through the crowd until he found the woman.

She turned just as he reached her and smiled. "Hi."

"Liza, what the hell are you doing here?"

"Getting a cocktail."

"And compromising me in the process."

"I'm simply hanging out."

"I'm helping you. You do as I say. I'll meet you later like we planned."

"I just want to talk to him. I might be able to ask him something that you wouldn't. I'm the one who knows Aleksei."

Michael took a step away and put some distance between them. "Don't be stupid. He'll run. You know that. Don't you want me to find out anything? You're risking one of our only contacts on this matter. Now, please, get out. I'll call you when I'm done."

He got no response. When he looked over, he saw emotion on her face.

"This whole thing has me so twisted up," she said. "I'm sorry, Michael. I appreciate what you're doing."

"It's okay. Now go."

Liza turned without another word. The green of her dress blended into the crowd and disappeared.

Michael went back downstairs and made his way to the corner of the dance floor. He stood there until he felt a tap on the shoulder. He turned to see one of Viktor's bodyguards, a young man with old, mean eyes.

"This way," the man said.

Michael followed him. His pulse beat a little faster as he did so. He always got a quickening of the heart whenever he met a contact, especially one of the Russians. They were volatile, and he'd found that even their most refined businessmen could be street thugs at heart.

They spoke for an hour. When they were finished, Michael stood from the couch in the upstairs VIP room. Viktor Shenko, a tall man with dark, wavy hair cut close to his scalp, was already looking over Michael's shoulder at a group of women.

Michael checked each of the women quickly to make sure Liza wasn't among them, and said his goodbyes. He knew that Viktor, who was married with five children, was essentially faithful to his wife while in Russia, but while he was in the States, well, that was a different matter.

Michael had known Viktor for over ten years, having gotten to know the man when he was legit, or as legit as someone like him could be. He was an oil tycoon with friends in high places, and he'd been a valuable source of information. When he'd decided to think about a government office, he'd also accepted the support of the Mafiya in the process. Even after that, Viktor continued to provide Michael with intel. He had even given Michael the early information he needed to infiltrate

Radimir Trotsky's operation, and thereby to take out Trotsky by breaking his neck. Michael still felt conflicted about that job. The fact that he was feeling some guilt over a man who was so dangerous, who had terrorized whole communities in the United States to get what he wanted, meant he truly was ready to get out.

"Thank you for the information," Michael said, shaking Viktor's hand, holding it a bit longer than usual. "I know you'll be careful with it."

"Of course. And you'll be careful too?"

Russian Mafiya members tended to have short lives. And Michael liked Viktor. He liked the tall man's heartiness and the candor that Michael found rare among Viktor's countrymen.

Viktor gave a shake of his head. "You have no need to worry about me, my friend."

He wished that were true.

Michael made his way back through the main area of the club, which was even more packed than earlier. He stepped out into a humid, starry night, glad to have completed his duty.

He took his cell phone out of his pocket and saw that there were four missed calls—all from Kate.

He immediately called her. "Hi, love. What's going on?" he said when she answered on the first ring.

"You tell me."

"What do you mean?"

A group of people, laughing loudly and stumbling slightly, bumped into him on their way into the club.

"Where are you?" Kate said, her voice uncharacteristically soft.

Michael began walking, his eyes habitually checking up and down the street, then left and right for anything that looked out of order. "I was in a nightclub for a meeting," he told Kate. "How are you?"

Kate said nothing for a moment. "Michael, just answer one question."

"Anything."

"Was Liza at that nightclub?"

Michael stopped on the street. He stood absolutely still. He looked up and down the street again. Nothing. He wasn't being tailed. More importantly, there was Kate. And her question.

He'd never lied to Kate. Not once. Yes, he'd evaded and yes, he'd answered with generalities and yes, he'd omitted, but he had never lied.

So there he was, immobilized on a muggy South Beach sidewalk, completely stumped for words, something that rarely happened to him. "What are you talking about?" he said in an indignant tone, hoping for some more time.

"Answer me. Was Liza at that nightclub?"

How had she found out Liza was in Miami?

"I don't have any idea where Liza is," he said finally. It was the immediate truth, and it was a balm.

"Well, I'll tell you where she is, Michael. She's in Miami. Just like you."

"Great. Maybe I can meet her for coffee tomorrow if I have time. Do you know where she's staying?"

"I don't know. Do you?"

"No."

"Michael." His wife's tone was sad again. And now confused. And it stung him.

"What?"

"Have you seen her?"

What was he supposed to do now? Should he tell his wife that yes, her best friend had been with him at the nightclub, but it wasn't like that? He could imagine how well that would go over. No, he couldn't tell her that. And he couldn't confide what he and Liza were involved with. It was not only against every rule of their organization, but it could put Kate in danger.

Michael started walking again, and then he did what he'd never wanted to do. He lied to Kate.

"I haven't seen Liza," he said, making his voice sound as if he was just a little disappointed in his wife and her implied accusations.

He lied. He loved his wife. So he lied.

31

Liza sat at the bar of a tiny Cuban place, watching her cell phone display. Rich's number had flashed once, then Kate's a few times. Liza loved messages from Kate, but it was not Kate whom she wanted a phone call from right now. It was Kate's husband. So she left her messages unchecked, while she sipped on a Pacifico beer and watched the screen for Michael's number.

She looked around once or twice. There was a rather quiet, local crowd eating Cuban food and drinking Hatuey beer. They'd stared at her—the white girl in the green dress—when she'd come in an hour ago, but now the curiosity had worn off, and Liza sat alone. Waiting.

She could be at her hotel bar right now, a bar filled with people closer to her age, people who made a lot of money and were out for a fun, luxurious evening in Miami. But it would only remind her of how alone she was.

Finally, her phone made two beeps, indicating a call from the Trust. Liza grabbed it off the bar and opened the phone. "Ready?" she asked Michael.

"I'll meet you on the veranda of the Delano Hotel."

"Fine."

She'd been to the Delano a number of times, and the

front veranda had couches surrounded by billowing curtains that could obscure if pulled in the right direction. And there was a constant stream of cars circling the front drive, which would help block audio surveillance, not that they expected any. You just never knew.

Michael rattled off a few directions, then hung up abruptly.

Fifteen minutes later, Liza sat on the hotel's veranda with her back to the wall, as Michael had instructed her.

The couch was white and plush, and under different circumstances, she might be able to enjoy such a setting, but now she was jumping out of her skin in agony, waiting for information about Aleksei.

Michael suddenly appeared to the right of her, pushing aside a white curtain. He was good, Liza thought. She was about to make a joke about his catlike skills, but she saw the grim cast of his face. "What's wrong?"

He took a seat on the couch, a full foot and a half away from her. He looked away, saying nothing.

"What?" she said. "What is it? Did you find out something about Aleksei?"

"Yes. It's clear an explosive was on the plane, but no one knows for sure who the intended victim was, or why. However, Aleksei's apartment had been broken into a few times before the crash, and after he died, the apartment was apparently wiped out." Michael still wasn't looking at her. "Maybe it was just an overeager family member."

"Or maybe he knew something about a big story. And someone wanted to make sure that knowledge wouldn't spread."

"Maybe." He looked at her now, his expression angry.

"What's wrong?"

"You're on your own. Aleksei is not my concern anymore."

"What's going on with you?"

He shook his head in a terse fashion. "Kate knows you're in Miami."

"What?"

"Yeah, that's right, Liza."

"How?"

"I don't know. Did you tell her?"

"No!"

"Well, she knows. And she's suspicious and confused."

Liza felt her shoulders slump. "Oh, God. Poor Kate. I don't know how she knows. I only told one person." She thought of her mom. "Is she okay?"

He shook his head. "I gave her the impression it was a coincidence we were both here. I told her I didn't know you were here. I *lied* to my wife, Liza. I had to."

"I know. And it was because of me. Because I made you come here."

He said nothing.

"I'm so sorry. I'll call Kate first thing in the morning. I know she's been feeling left out lately, but I'll make it better. I'll help smooth this over, I promise."

"I think you've done enough." He looked away from her.

Neither of them said anything for a minute.

Michael gave her a grim look. "Like I said, you're on your own with this, okay?"

She nodded. She put her mind into work mode, thinking of the next avenue to run down.

"I could talk to his brother," she said, thinking aloud, thinking of when she'd met Aleksei's brother in Moscow.

"The priest?"

"Yes."

"That probably won't help much."

But then Liza thought of something—a tactic she'd taught Aleksei. And she knew then that the priest might be very helpful. She felt a tingle of anticipation.

She started to tell Michael that, but something halted her. It was the way Michael had mentioned Aleksei's brother, "the priest." Granted, she'd asked Michael to inquire about Aleksei's death, but she was surprised he knew so much about his family.

Some voice in her head was saying, *Stop.* And Liza always listened to that voice.

"Thanks, Michael," she said. "Really, thank you."

"Hold on." He stood and signaled a waiter, who approached with two coffee cups on a tray.

"What's this?" Liza said.

"I told Kate I might meet you for coffee. When I go home, I don't want to lie to her again. So drink the coffee."

"It's okay, I just had a beer, and I really should go."

"Liza, drink your goddamn coffee."

She thanked the waiter and took the white cup from his tray. She took a few sips. Then Liza got up and left.

Back at her hotel, she looked at her schedule. She was due in Finland in two days. A side trip to Moscow would fit in nicely. She logged on to her computer and booked a flight.

32

St. Marabel, Canada

Michael moved in and out of me. Our eyes locked as our bodies met. The only light in the room came from a street lamp through the nearly closed curtains.

"This is where I'm supposed to be," he said, his voice low, his body still moving.

I nodded. I didn't trust my voice. Instead, I simply felt him inside me, and I let the feeling of seduction transform into one of love, and I let the feeling of love transform into one of completeness, and I let completeness turn into safety. And then I closed my eyes, and I let the feeling of being seduced return.

Later, with the streetlight making a white band across our bedroom, Michael and I faced each other. "I missed you," he said.

"Me, too."

I almost said *I'm sorry. I'm sorry I was suspicious when I found out Liza was in Miami.* But I held back. Because the truth was, I wasn't sorry. My reaction had been an honest one, and honesty was something I wanted to cultivate with Michael, something that had been missing in my relationship with Scott.

"So this Liza thing," I said.

Michael's jaw tightened. It was almost imperceptible, but I could see it. It was one of the few physical clues he gave when something was making him unhappy or uncomfortable. "There is no 'Liza thing.'"

"I know that." I shifted closer to him and put a hand on his arm. "I know there's nothing going on with you and Liza."

"Good."

"It was just so odd that you were in Miami at the same time."

Michael nodded. "Stranger things have happened."

"Yeah." I took my hand off his arm. "Yeah, I guess."

"What is it?"

"I don't know. I mean, this might sound crazy, but it seems like there are other strange things with you and Liza, too."

"What do you mean?"

"I was just thinking about our first date. We were talking about Liza, and you knew so much about her and her family. I mean, you even knew how Colby died when we were in high school."

"So?"

"It seems like that's a lot of information to know for two people who only worked together briefly."

Michael closed his eyes, then opened them again. I couldn't tell if he was annoyed or sad or none of the above. My husband was a hard man to read.

"Did you know Mr. Kingsley?"

Michael looked the tiniest bit surprised. "Why do you ask that?"

"Because he worked for Presario. He passed away a while ago, but maybe you met him?"

Michael gave a quick nod. "I did meet him."

"He was a great guy. Tough. But great."

I watched Michael closely. He said nothing.

"Is that how you knew about Colby?" I asked.

He shrugged. "I'm sure I talked to either Coleman or Liza about his death at one time. Is that really so weird?"

"It is for Liza. She doesn't talk about Colby to anybody."

"What can I say? I have that effect on women."

I studied him—his beautiful, sometimes sad brown eyes and the gentle lines that sloped away from them and disappeared into the smooth of his cheeks. I loved this man. I *trusted* him, I reminded myself.

I wrapped an arm around his waist and pulled myself to him. "Well, why don't you try to affect me?"

33

Thirty-five years earlier
Khiem Hanh District, Vietnam

Michael laid his head on his pillow at 0200 hours, but he knew he wouldn't sleep. He was used to working late, only sleeping four to five hours a night, and usually sleep came easily. But all day he'd been jumpy and jittery.

He supposed his restlessness had something to do with the birthday card he'd received from his parents. On the front was a bunny wearing a top hat. It was a card better suited for an eight-year-old, not a young man who felt very, very old. Had he been at home in Providence, Michael would have rolled his eyes at the card, and told his parents that he wasn't a child. He might even have gotten mad at how little they understood their son. And yet that card had made him cry today. He'd shoved it back in the yellow envelope and went outside to the latrine, where he opened it again, read his mother's script—*We love you*—and allowed himself to weep quietly for about fifteen seconds. Then he wiped his eyes and went back to the villa. He left his breakfast uneaten in the kitchen.

An hour later the mama-*san* brought him a fresh bowl of rice with cinnamon bark and, for once, she looked him in the eye when she did so and he saw a hint of something there—sympathy and an aliveness she didn't usually show.

Later that morning, one of his agents visited with a report of Vietcong action in the Boi Loi woods, not far from Khiem Hanh.

The agent was a small man, a few years Michael's senior, with exceptional Vietnamese language skills and a knack for slipping into places unnoticed.

"Is it a staging action?" Michael asked the agent, who was sitting in front of his desk.

The agent nodded.

Both men were quiet. It was well known that the Boi Loi woods had been used as a tactical for the Tet attacks on Saigon. Additional staging by the Vietcong now could only mean one thing—the planning of another major attack.

When the agent left, Michael filed a report and had it sent on an urgent basis to his commanding officer. He wondered when Colonel Kingsley would see it. He wondered why the colonel hadn't responded to his other reports on this topic.

After the meeting with the colonel in the Go Vap District and after Michael's elimination of the chief on his porch, he'd received occasional coded messages from Colonel Kingsley. The first one praised him for a job well done. Other times, in response to his reports, the messages would give Michael clearance to take measures into his own hands. He'd killed eleven men since the chief. They were people known to be helping the Vietcong, or they were ranking members of the North Vietnamese. Always Michael performed the assassination with his bare hands, and for some reason he continued to do so with three breaks to the neck. With the chief, it had been his way to ensure death, now it was just the way he performed the job. Michael did not enjoy this job. Quite the contrary. He was often sick and unable to eat for days afterward. But he preferred these dispatches to the impersonal and unsystematic killings of combat. With each personal dispatch, he was targeting real threats to an American victory, to the United States. And so Michael lived his days at the villa with a small measure of pride and a great deal of purpose.

But lately, things had been changing. There were the growing reports of riots and protests back home, and maybe because of that, Michael's budget had shrunk and many agents had been pulled and assigned other posts. Michael's district was short-staffed now, and everyone was edgy and overworked.

And so usually, Michael slept hard. Yet tonight, he could barely keep his eyes closed, so filled was he with a sense of isolated, agitated dread. He kept thinking of how the colonel hadn't responded to his reports about the Boi Loi woods staging, or Michael's veiled requests to perform targeted eliminations of individuals who might be helping them.

He twisted around on his bunk. He put his flat, military pillow over his head. An hour later, he heard the sound of mortar fire and sat up immediately. Mortar fire at night wasn't uncommon, but the amount of incoming rounds sounded substantial. And very close.

Michael ran from his room, shouting orders to others in the compound who were already in the hallways. He kept running until he reached his office where he radioed for clearance to return fire. This was one of the worst parts of combat—getting shot upon, getting ready for your balls to be blown off, and then having to sit on your hands and wait for someone to tell you that you could go ahead and shoot back.

He yelled orders to have all hands ready at the fence of the perimeter and to check that the ground mines were set. The mortar fire kept coming, the explosive sounds banging and violently shaking the foundation of the compound. Finally, a full fifteen minutes later, Michael received clearance to return fire.

He was about to leave the office, when the radio crackled. "Ground force closing on your perimeter," he heard.

Michael's blood felt as if it had stilled in his veins.

He shouted into the radio for air assistance. If they could get choppers with door gunners above the compound, or maybe a Cobra gunship, they could turn back the enemy.

"Air assistance denied," he heard in return.

He stared at the radio for a second, flabbergasted. He picked it up and yelled into it, again asking for air assistance.

In return, Michael heard the same flat denial, then an explanation. "Air assistance not in range."

Michael wanted to yell "Bullshit!" into the radio. As

far as he could tell, over the last year and a half, there were always choppers or Air America helicopters in range.

Michael ran from the office. He yelled orders for napalm, which they kept in 55-gallon barrels, to be fired as needed. The compound was filled with men running and firing weapons. Gunpowder singed Michael's nose, followed closely by the unmistakable scent of blood. He looked to the perimeter fence and saw enemy troops throwing themselves over it with ease. Diving into a bunker, he grabbed an M-16 and began shooting.

Minutes later, a grenade went off in front of him, blowing a body into the air, showering him with shrapnel, and something much worse.

It seemed like the fighting would never end. The grenade explosions, the screaming, the gunshots, the anguish went on for hours. The vibrations from the mortar fire made his body pulse and twitch.

But then came the sound of aircraft. Two Spooky gunships—U.S. C-47 aircraft—appeared overhead, firing 20 mm high-speed machine guns.

"Thank God."

The Spookys did their job. Efficiently, almost easily, making the hand-to-hand combat they'd been going through seem like a child's game.

At 0600 hours, the sound of gunfire diminished, the Spookys lifted off and the first rays of hot sunlight appeared. Bodies lay everywhere, blanketing the compound. Michael gathered the remaining personnel, and they stood around him, scarred and blackened, their eyes vacant. He barked orders at each of them, knowing he had to keep them busy. Then he turned away and began the task of counting, a job that made him grow more and more angry with each increasing digit. If the Spookys had been here sooner, this wouldn't have happened. Why assistance had been denied at first, Michael couldn't fathom.

Michael's fingers grew black with old blood as he checked pulses. He stepped over one corpse, then another. He stopped when he came to a female civilian corpse facedown. He bent over and took the corpse by the shoulder, the only place on the body that wasn't drenched with blood. He rolled it over. It was mama-*san,* her lifeless eyes not looking anywhere now.

34

Two years after Vietnam War
Washington D.C.

Michael Waller clipped his Minolta on his shoulder strap and checked his bag for film, light meters and flashes.

"Honey, I'm going," he called to his wife of one year.

"Wait for a kiss," he heard her say.

She padded into the apartment's kitchen, wearing a yellow nylon nightgown, her brown hair mussed and puffed up in the back. Michael knew that like the good Southern girl she was, Honey would be showered and dressed within forty minutes, even though she probably had little on her agenda today except for grocery shopping.

Before he was drafted, Honey had been Michael's girlfriend for a brief time. Her family had moved from Atlanta to Rhode Island because of her father's job. They'd dated during their senior year, but he'd broken it off because he found her a little too quiet. He wanted someone with opinions, someone not afraid to be loud, even crazy. But following Vietnam, Michael wanted nothing but quiet simplicity. After living at home with his parents for a few months, he landed a job as staff photographer at a small newsletter in D.C., and two months after being in D.C. he'd called Honey and asked her to visit. They were married seven months later.

"What do you want for dinner?" Honey said, kissing him on the cheek.

She was always like that—planning their meals or arranging a weekend card game with the neighbors. He knew such planning was important for her. She was lonely and bored otherwise, but sometimes Michael didn't want to chart out his days. He wanted to just be.

Michael requested pot roast, which he knew his wife liked to make, and gave her a hug and kiss. He left the apartment and went out into the sticky D.C. morning. Sometimes the humidity in this city felt exactly like Vietnam's, and Michael wondered why he'd ended up here. He supposed it was a perverse decision on his part. He hated the military and the government as much as he loved them. It was like being in a bad relationship. He'd broken up with the United States government, but he couldn't help wanting to be around her just to see what she was up to.

At the office of *Capitol Watchdog,* Michael greeted the newsletter's owner and main correspondent, Larry Chentworth. Larry was an old newspaperman who'd been demoted from a major newspaper and eventually let go for too many caustic questions at White House press conferences. He now considered himself a whistleblower and a straight talker who would analyze the Capitol's bullshit and give it to his readers straight.

The fact that the *Watchdog* had only a couple thousand readers didn't seem to bother Larry.

"Waller, hey," Larry said. "Capitol steps. Fifteen minutes. Press conference. Two senators. Brenda's already there." Larry always talked in newsroom bullets. Brenda was his sole reporter.

Michael nodded and hustled to the Capitol where he took the requisite photos, made a log of the names and said hello to Brenda, who was busy scribbling notes on the senators' comments. Then he left.

Since Vietnam, Michael was no longer the one who had to listen to what was being said. He no longer had to analyze words and actions and decide who was telling the truth. That was the job of Brenda and Larry. It was what he'd wanted, but he had to admit, his self-imposed mental vacation was starting to bore him. His mind had needed the rest, and yet now it was flexing and stretching and asking for more purpose. He glanced back at Brenda, who was biting her lip and scratching something out on her notepad. He felt a twinge of envy.

Michael walked down the Mall toward the White House, taking the long way back to the office. The humidity settled into his skin, the way it used to in Vietnam, but he could handle its weight now. At the White House, he took a right. As he passed the Hay Adams Hotel, a man stepped from the hotel's gold-trimmed glass doors and blocked his path.

Michael took a step to the right, about to go around the person, but then he glanced up and saw the man wasn't moving. And then he saw the eyes. Those teal-blue eyes.

"Colonel Kingsley," Michael said, surprised.

"Good to see you, son."

Michael took in the colonel's outfit—a gray civilian suit and red tie. He raised his eyes in a silent question.

"We're just a couple of regular joes, huh?" the colonel said.

Michael almost laughed, but then his surprise at seeing the colonel turned into something else—anger. "Goodbye, Colonel."

"Can I have a word?" The colonel gestured toward the hotel.

"Not unless that word is an apology. You abandoned me, sir. You abandoned my team."

The colonel's nose twitched in what seemed like an effort at control. "You'll get that apology. You'll get an explanation, too."

Michael paused for a moment, considering the man's words. He looked over his shoulder, then past the colonel. How had he known Michael would be here at this particular moment? Had he been followed? And if so, why? There were too many questions unanswered for Michael to simply pass by.

The colonel led him into the plush, soothing lobby of the Hay Adams. They walked past the wood-paneled walls and the gold-leafed furniture and downstairs to the bar, halfway below ground level. Two women sat at the bar, reading newspapers.

Michael and the colonel took a seat at a round corner table, out of earshot. When the bartender came over, Colonel Kingsley ordered a scotch and soda, Michael an orange juice.

They waited for their drinks in silence. Sunlight

filtered in the window near the colonel's face, and Michael noticed how much older the man looked. But then didn't they all? War changed a person.

The colonel sipped his scotch once it was delivered, then put down his glass, studying Michael in silence. Michael returned his gaze, not allowing his nervousness to show.

Finally, Michael broke the stare by looking at his watch. "I'm waiting for that apology."

"Son, you were left out to dry. And I'm going to apologize on behalf of the Phoenix Program and the United States Army. But I'm going to tell you, I was in there fighting for you."

"With all due respect, you failed to respond to my requests for eliminations in the Boi Loi woods. And that failure led to our team being attacked brutally and almost decimated. We lost twenty-eight that day."

"As I said, you were left out to dry. But it wasn't my doing."

Michael eyed him disparagingly. "You ran the Phoenix Program."

"I commanded it, yes, but don't forget I had a brigadier general above me. And the CIA above that."

Michael stared at the bright orange of his juice and said nothing.

"I thought the Phoenix Program had the right idea," the colonel continued. "At least at the beginning. 'Identify and neutralize.' But I had a few lieutenant colonels who took their orders too far. Neutralized far too many. Didn't always report them. By the time I figured out what was happening, the government got wind of the mess, too, and they were planning for evacuation. By the time you requested clearance for the Boi Loi woods, they were shutting down the operation."

"We should have been advised."

"I agree."

"And when we were attacked, we should have received air assistance sooner."

The colonel's nose twitched again. "Agreed."

"The Spookys saved us, but they came too late."

The colonel nodded. He seemed to be holding back.

"Did you order the Spookys?" Michael asked.

"I did." He gulped his scotch. "And I was court-martialed for it."

Michael sat in stunned silence. "I'm not sure I understand, sir."

"We had orders to prepare for evacuation. The Phoenix Program had been turned over to the Republic of Vietnam. We were pulling personnel and minimizing air strikes." The colonel rattled the ice around in his drink. He looked as if he wanted to smash the glass. "When your air assistance was denied, well, that was the final straw for me. I was sick of leaving our men out there with no backup. I personally found the pilots and the gunners. I guaranteed them that no one would know they were involved in the mission. I stuck to that promise. I've never identified the names of those men. But the army doesn't like when you disobey orders. Or when you keep secrets from them."

The colonel looked down and gestured at his civilian suit.

"I'm sorry, sir."

He shook his head. "Don't be. I thought the Phoenix Program was something to be proud of. But it ran off the rails."

Michael nodded. He glanced around the bar. The two women had left. He looked back at his companion. "Why are you here, sir?"

"Well, here's the thing." The colonel gave a smile that didn't seem to match his gruff jawline. "I've started an organization. And I'd like you to be a part of it. It's called the Trust."

"The Trust," Michael repeated.

"That's right. Do you know what a trust is, from a legal perspective?"

"Not exactly."

"A trust holds on to something for the benefit of another, in order to protect it. Our government can't protect what's theirs, son. They can't protect our country, and so I'm starting the Trust in order to do that. It's a pro-American, counterintelligence operation, privately funded with one goal in common, to secure the United States."

"I'm not sure I understand, sir."

"Look, with our government the way it is, with shifting administrations every four to eight years, it's impossible to keep track of all the groups hostile to us. And when the government does find those people, their hands are tied. You know it as well as I do. They can apprehend, maybe give them some due-goddamn-process, and then they've either got to give them a trial or let them go. And now that the CIA has flubbed the Phoenix Program..." He waved a hand in dismissal. "What we need now is to stop these people sooner rather than later. The goal of the Trust is to protect the United States, no matter what. We'll neutralize anyone who poses a significant threat."

Michael felt a tickle of excitement up his spine, like nothing he'd felt since Vietnam. He made sure not to show it. "With all due respect, it sounds like it could go the way of the Phoenix Program, and—how did you put it?—run off the rails."

The colonel shook his head. "Won't happen. We're tightly controlled. We have strict operations regulations. And we pick the right people. Honest, honorable people. Which is why I'm here."

"What makes you better than your targets?"

"People like you, Waller, who know how to assess and conclude, who know how to neutralize, but won't do it for the glory of it. The Trust *is* different. For one thing, we're not trying to overthrow an existing regime, we're just protecting the country we live in and we love. And we're not trying to draw attention to ourselves by our acts, like many bad guys are. We're just trying to stop others from doing so and harming our citizens." The bartender came over and asked about another round. Both men shook their heads.

"And listen, Waller," the colonel said when the bartender had left, "retribution is *not* sufficient. Our main mission is intel. The objective is to stop the attacks before they happen. If the intel does lead to a neutralization order—" the colonel stopped and rattled his ice again "—our targets won't be innocent citizens. They'll be people we know for certain are planning to carry out attacks on the U.S. or who support people who do so."

Michael sat back and stared at the colonel. His head was swimming. He thought of Honey, probably at the meat market, conferring with the butcher. "Would I be able to talk to my wife about this?" Somehow he knew the answer but felt he had to ask.

The colonel shook his head. "If you're a member of the Trust, the only people who know are other members. We'll give you a cover."

"What's yours?"

The colonel smiled. "Depending on your clearance level, I might tell you when you accept my offer."

"And what exactly is that offer?"

"You'd be an operative. You'll use your smarts to help protect the United States. You'll do it honorably—always honorably—with no waste of life. And you'll be compensated very, very well." The colonel pushed his now-empty glass away. "How do they pay you at that paper?"

Michael laughed. "Something tells me you already know the answer to that question, sir."

The colonel nodded. "You won't regret this, Waller. The Trust isn't a job. It's a life's work."

Michael thought about that. *A life's work.* And what was his life's work now? He had none. He took photos when he was told. He turned in the names of those featured. He went home to Honey.

"What do you say?" The man extended a hand toward Michael. "Join us?"

Michael felt a lifting of his spirits, a spreading of his mind's wings. He grasped the colonel's hand, and he shook it.

35

Peredelkino, Russia

The church of St. Isaacs was an old one. On Sundays, Mass was attended mostly by the few remaining villagers who hadn't been ousted or bought out by the wealthy Muscovites who encircled Peredelkino with posh cottages. Their priest, Father Stefan, although energetic and attractive and probably better off with a younger parish, had remained loyal. They loved him for staying with the old village parish, and he knew it.

On a Tuesday night, he met with Mrs. Rovsky, who visited him every week. She detailed the litany of sins she'd committed that week, including coveting her sister-in-law's new stove and thinking ill of her mother, who everyone knew was not a particularly pleasant woman but whom Mrs. Rovsky cared for and nursed, unlike her siblings. Father Stefan tried hard to tell Mrs. Rovsky that she had too much guilt, that the energy she was wasting on this hand-wringing could be better spent. This wasn't the old-school approach to sins that Mrs. Rovsky expected, but then Father Stefan had never done anything exactly by the book.

After twenty minutes he walked Mrs. Rovsky to the front door of the church, where he wished her a fond farewell. The sky was turning a powdery navy blue, softening the austere ambience of this end of the village. As he was about to close the door, he heard his name called. In English.

He opened the door wider and saw a red-haired woman trotting down the road toward him, a large duffel slung over her shoulder. She didn't move like many women who were embarrassed about their bodies. She was in charge of hers. He could tell even from this distance.

When she reached him, she stopped and smiled. "Stefan."

"Liza," he said. And then he thought of his brother and how much Aleksei had loved this woman, and he thought of Aleksei's bloodied body, and he began to cry.

She didn't flinch at his tears. She stood on her toes and hugged him, and soon he felt her crying, too.

"Why are you here?" he said, getting hold of himself, looking anxiously around the village for any parishioners ready to gossip about their young priest. His English felt rusty, but if Liza noticed it, she didn't say.

"I came about Aleksei."

"You came for condolences? To give them?"

"Yes. But I came for more than that, too."

They stared at each other. He knew Liza was a salesperson in the United States for a pharmaceutical company, but the silent, supremely confident way she carried herself made him think she was more than that. "Do you know what happened to Aleksei?" he said.

She placed her hand on his. "No, but I'm going to find out."

36

"He was working on a big story," Stefan told Liza.

She nodded. She had so many questions, but she'd learned early to shut her mouth when someone wanted to talk.

They were sitting in his tiny living room in the rectory, both on wooden chairs with large arms and red cushions behind their backs. It was dark outside now. Stefan had made them black tea, which they drank from white cups.

Liza felt comfortable in this room, but then maybe it was because of Stefan, because of his special aura of calm, the feeling he was so close to God that some of it might rub off on her.

"What was the story about?" Liza asked.

He shrugged. "I do not know."

"Do you know anything—the topic, the subject matter?"

"We all know what Aleksei liked to write about most."

"The Mafiya."

Stefan's face became grim and stern. "It always brought him trouble."

"It sure did." Liza wondered if Stefan knew that Aleksei's investigative reporting into the Mafiya had eventually pulled him into intelligence work, and that he'd only done that work because of threats against his family.

"We never understood the traveling, the moving from one place to the next," Stefan said.

So Aleksei's family didn't know, Liza thought. Aleksei had suffered his knowledge alone.

"We all wanted him to find a wife," Stefan continued, sipping his tea. "We wanted him to be happy in love." He looked shyly at her. "Maybe with you."

Liza started to laugh at Stefan's earnest yet mischievous expression, but then the laugh stuck in her throat. She remembered that there would be no second chance at love for her and Aleksei.

"We miss him so," Stefan said, tears rising in his own eyes. "He was the center of our family. I do not think he knew that. I do not think any of us knew that until…"

"Until he was gone," Liza finished for him. "I understand. My brother, Colby, was the same way. When he died, my whole family just…crumbled."

"We will never be the same." The priest's eyes began to tear, and he rubbed his face. "I am sorry."

"Don't be sorry. I'll tell you what I've learned from losing family members. You are right that you will never be the same. But you will be okay. You will be okay in a different way."

He smiled at Liza. "I tell my parishioners something very similar when they lose someone dear to them. No one ever believes it."

"But it's true."

"I hope it is true."

They shared a moment of silence, then Liza put her tea on the arm of the chair and leaned forward. "You're certain you know nothing about the story he was working on?"

"Very little. He said it was a big international investigation. He said the story would cause a lot of problems if he understood it right."

"Problems for who?"

Stefan shrugged. "I know he was very close to finishing."

Liza closed her eyes for a moment and imagined herself and Aleksei in Rio, all those nights in the safe house when she felt reckless, but safe enough to tell him about herself, to tutor him on everything from surveillance to storage. And one of the things she'd taught Aleksei was to always back up his work, no matter if that work was a legitimate story for his newspaper or gathering intelligence for the service he worked for. One *always* had to back it up. And then one had to hide it.

She had no idea whether Aleksei continued to take her advice over the years or whether, as they slid out of each other's lives, he'd grown careless again. But she remembered Aleksei confessing to her where he would secrete his intel and his work. She had laughed at him, patiently explaining that he couldn't tell *anyone,* not a soul, not even her, about the hiding place. Aleksei had kissed her, and laughed with her, and said he would always tell her everything. He said she wasn't just *anyone.* He said she understood his soul.

"Are you all right?" Stefan said now.

Liza realized that she'd dropped her forehead into her hands. "I'm fine," she said, raising her head.

And after a breath and a sip of the strong tea, she felt better. Because she was very near Aleksei's hiding place. Very, very near.

37

For robbers and spies, 3:00 a.m. is the magic hour. By three most of the drunks have put their heads to pillows and most of the hardworking haven't picked theirs up yet.

At precisely 3:00 a.m., Liza's internal alarm went off. She had trained herself to be able to sleep anywhere, under the most appalling of conditions, and she could also snap awake whenever she decided. Not that the small twin bed in the rectory's guest room was appalling. Spartan, yes, but Liza had enjoyed five hours of restful sleep on the rough cotton sheets because she knew that Aleksei had slept here, too.

She thought of their last visit. They'd met in Denver, a place where the Russian Mafiya had found an unlikely and yet strong foothold and where Aleksei was covering a story. From the bed, she'd watched him sweep the room for bugs, chuckling at how adept he'd become.

"Finished," he said after a few minutes.

But that was only the beginning of their visit—a weekend in which Liza stayed decadently in bed, waiting for Aleksei to finish interviews and research. Then he came back to bed, and they talked about his work and their families and their friends. Aleksei was the only person in Liza's adult life that she could share nearly all the pieces with.

Aleksei often spoke about his nieces and nephews. He talked about his parents and their failing health. He talked about Stefan and his dwindling but appreciative parish. He described the village of Peredelkino, how it had been a famous writers' colony for many years, and how it was now being overrun by the post-Soviet Moscow sprawl, and that's when he'd told her where he hid his backup files.

This morning, Liza dressed quickly, washed her face and packed the few belongings she'd brought. She wrote Stefan a note thanking him and telling him she had to get an early start back to Moscow. She didn't tell him what she was doing, of course, at least not yet. She couldn't. Because what Stefan didn't know couldn't be used to hurt him.

She carried her small overnight bag out of the rectory and stowed it in a bush near the back of the church. In the light of a distant streetlight, she circled the church and studied its structure—old and yet solid. She considered the high windows before deciding they would take longer to infiltrate than the most obvious of entries—the back door. It was locked of course, but a good rattle told her it wasn't padlocked from inside.

She took a small flashlight out of her pants pocket, clipped it to a strap and positioned it around her head for later. Next, she took out a lock pick and began testing the lock. The first pick stuck. The second one slid in but wouldn't turn. As she selected the third, a howl pierced the night.

Liza dropped on her belly to the ground. She held her breath, listening through the silence for the sound. She heard it again, and her heart stuck in her throat. A dog. Liza hated dogs. She'd rather take on a man twice her size than a dog. The howl came again. And again. Listening closer, she could tell from the strangled yelp the dog was chained. Her breath returned to normal.

Liza stood and went to work again with the key picks. On the fourth one, she felt the pick gain some purchase, and after a few jiggles in either direction, the lock gave.

The church was small and without much adornment, but it still had the revered stillness most churches possess. Liza remembered when her father was still alive, when Colby was still alive, when their family was still intact, how they would go to church, not every Sunday, but every few weeks. Colby hated it. He could never be at rest, a trait which would have made it hard for him to follow their father's footsteps into the Trust, but Liza had always had the ability to just sit. And she loved to simply sit with her family in that church in the suburbs of Chicago, feeling the solidity of the bench behind their backs, the quiet comfort.

She used to go to that church after Colby and her father died, but she could never recapture the feeling. She'd tried other churches around the world—from the opulence of the Vatican to the glass and gold-leaf temples of Bangkok to tiny, steepled churches in Hamburg. But they were never the same.

And yet, Liza always hoped. So before she switched on the light on her head strap, she stood there, waiting for the kind of feeling she used to have with her family—a feeling of calm, of being in the right place at the right time, of needing nothing. Maybe she was looking for God. But she couldn't feel him. Because deep inside, she was thinking of Aleksei.

She turned on her light, and let herself really think of him now. She let herself hear his words, spoken to her in the hotel bed in Denver. He was naked and turned toward her, his glasses off, which gave his eyes an endearing, slightly fuzzy quality.

"I see my brother, Stefan, usually once a week," he'd said. He gave her an impish smile. "I keep my work in his church. Behind the altar."

Liza slapped her hands over her ears. "Don't tell me, you fool!"

He pulled her hands away and held them at her sides. He was still grinning. "There is a cutaway in the wood. It is where they used to hide the religious icons from the Soviets. But the wood is warped now and difficult to remove. No one ever uses it."

"Except for you."

"Except for me. So what do you think, teacher?" He sometimes called her that. He made it sound naughty, which she liked.

She drew her arms away, chuckling. "Too easy. You should probably find something else. Especially since you told me."

"I cannot keep anything from the teacher." He took her by the hands again and pulled her to him.

Now, Liza guided the light of her head strap to the altar. It was raised slightly on a wooden platform and draped in cheap gold fabric. She made her way to the paneled wall against the back of the church. Aleksei had said "behind the altar," so she started in the middle of the wall, running her hands slowly and systematically up and down, feeling for the cutaway. Nothing. She moved two paces to the right and repeated the process. Still nothing. Finding the spot hadn't been as easy as she'd assumed. She checked her watch. She'd been there four minutes. Too long. Even at this hour there was a chance someone might see the movement of her light from outside.

She stepped to the left of the middle and repeated the process. And finally, there it was. She could feel the sliced square in the wood, roughly a foot long and six inches tall. She tried to lift the piece away with her fingers, but as Aleksei had said, years of swelling had sealed it shut. She pulled a penknife from her belt and used it to pry away the sides.

At last she was able to wrest the wood away from the wall. She shined her light inside. There she found a zip drive, a thumb-shaped computer storage device. Just as she'd taught him. She smiled.

Liza reached behind the waistband of her pants and took out a small black satchel. Inside was a handheld computer, designed specifically for the Trust. It could be used to open and read files on an as-needed basis. She knew that she could simply take the zip drive with her and read its contents when she got somewhere safe, but she couldn't wait.

Liza powered up the computer and slipped the zip drive into the USB port on the side. There were two files there, one a document, the other a JPEG, probably a photo.

She opened the document and read it quickly. It was a draft of an article dealing with the murder of Radimir Trotsky eight months ago.

Liza had heard about the killing, of course. But like Aleksei's death, details had been kept to a minimum. No one had been able to figure out who had ordered the hit on Trotsky or who had performed it.

It turned out Aleksei hadn't been able to determine the culprit either, but he had apparently found something even more explosive.

"Oh, my God," Liza whispered into the quiet of the old church.

According to Aleksei's article, besides being a high-ranking member of the Russian Mafiya, Radimir Trotsky was also an undercover CIA agent.

38

Aleksei's discovery made perfect sense. No one had ever been able to determine where Trotsky had come from; but then, no one questioned the lack of background information among Mafiya members.

Aleksei's story detailed how Radimir Trotsky was actually Charles "Charlie" Miller, a thirty-five-year-old from Connecticut. Charlie, who'd received a minor in Russian, had played college hockey and been good enough to be scouted for the pros until a knee injury allegedly halted his career. But the real story, Aleksei had written, was that Charlie's knee was just fine, and that he'd been scouted even more aggressively by the CIA, whose ranks he entered out of college. After two years of intense training, he'd landed in Siberia, played for a Russian pro team and eventually infiltrated the Mafiya, rising steadily in its ranks.

Liza's eyebrows raised as she read the story. "Good for you," she whispered to Aleksei. The story of an undercover CIA agent who'd infiltrated the Mafiya, gotten killed in the process and still not had his identity exposed would have been big, big news. Likely, it would have defined Aleksei's career. She shook her head, saddened and then pissed off that he wouldn't be here to see the story published.

But Liza would. She would make sure this article, or at least its contents, saw the light of day.

She checked her watch. Another ten minutes had passed. She needed to get going, but she wanted to see the JPEG. She opened it. The file was a death photo of the man who was once apparently Charlie Miller, after his neck had been broken. He was slumped over a desk, head turned to the side, eyes open and glassy. Liza grimaced. She'd been in this business for decades, but she still hated the sight of the dead.

She was about to close the file when she noticed something odd about the turn of Miller's neck. It was as if the neck protruded slightly in the middle, and the head had been pulled back. Liza studied the picture closer, her heart rate picking up. She couldn't be sure.

She pulled a loupe from her belt and held it to the photo. Her stomach swirled and sank. The head was slumped forward and slightly rotated. And there was a bony protuberance sticking out of the back of Trotsky's neck, just below the base of the skull. Three breaks to the neck.

This type of killing was rare and practiced, and could only mean one thing… Liza knew exactly who had killed Charlie Miller.

39

St. Marabel, Canada

I hadn't been able to say goodbye to Michael before I left the restaurant. He was taking care of another large group in one of the private dining rooms, and now I was going to bed alone. Again.

I put on an outfit that was becoming familiar—my gray high-school T-shirt, which was worn to a silky sheen, and my old gym shorts. Not glamorous, I knew, but then, who was there to be glamorous for? I couldn't blame Michael for working hard. I'd known he was opening a restaurant when I met him, when I married him, when I accepted a job working for him. I had no excuse for the loneliness I felt. It was simply there.

The shorts and T-shirt felt old and comfortable, tying me to Chicago. I missed the simplicity of the Midwest.

I poured myself a glass of wine and wandered around our lamp-lit house. This was becoming habitual for me—a glass of wine or two to wind down when I came home from work. I spied a potential problem in my future—would one or two glasses turn to three or four, or a bottle and a half? For now it was my vice and I liked it.

I sat down at Michael's desk, an old, nicked-up rolltop he'd told me he'd owned for years. The desk was situated in front of a window, which looked onto the street. Michael's main office was at the Twilight Club, but he liked to work here nights and on weekends. I ran my hands over the desk's closed, grooved top, liking the sensation of touching something that had long been a part of Michael's life. I wanted more of him than I had, but I couldn't seem to figure out if I was asking too much or being ungrateful for the wonderful relationship I already possessed.

Itching for more of Michael, I lifted the rolltop. To the right of a small computer monitor, items were neatly organized. I found reference books on restaurant management and three-by-five cards filled with his notes about waitstaff and stemware and china. I liked his straight, precise penmanship, and I liked his curious little questions to himself—*Buy Wusthof Trident fillet knives or go inexpensive, like Russell Harrington? Would bulge-top pilsner glasses be more European?*

As I was reading, movement outside the window caught my eye. I glanced up and saw a man across the street, his body facing our house. The man was backlit by a street lamp, so I couldn't make out his features, but his form was familiar to me somehow. For a second I wondered if it was Michael, but the man wasn't lean enough. And he was just standing there, absolutely still. A prickling of alarm climbed up my back. This was a tourist town after all, and there were always people out on the streets, but it seemed as if he might be watching me.

I stood up to close the curtains. As I did so, I looked out once more. He was gone. Like he'd never been there at all.

I pulled the curtains closed and sat down at the desk again, holding my breath for reasons I didn't entirely understand. I waited in silence. The door didn't open, bringing the safety of Michael and his embrace. The phone didn't ring with a call from Liza or my mother.

I sat, as still as the man had been outside. I told myself to forget it.

I kept looking through the materials in Michael's desk. In some ways, I felt as if I was spying or being a voyeur, but the overwhelming emotion I had was one of comfort to read Michael's orderly handwriting on mundane topics.

I began to feel calmer. I sipped at my wine and decided it was time for bed. I began returning Michael's things to the place I'd found them—putting his note cards where he kept them—in the brown leather box, laden with stickers from the sixties—and the restaurant management books in a neat stack against the back of the desk.

But as I was adjusting the books I noticed they didn't lie exactly flat. I removed them again to see if the desktop was uneven or there was a piece of errant paper there, but my hand snagged on something.

I put the books on the floor and adjusted the lamp, shining it toward the back of the desk. There I saw a tiny silver stud that the books must have been covering before.

I reached out and tried to pull the stud toward me, but it was stuck at the back of the desktop, as if it had been glued there. I tried again to lift the tiny silver ball with my fingers and just then, something in the desktop shifted. The movement was almost imperceptible, but I felt it.

There was, I realized, a false bottom of some kind. I tugged once more, and this time, the stud lifted, and along with it a six-inch square of desktop. Affixed under that was a metal container that must have been hanging inside the desk.

"What the hell?" I said aloud.

I put the container on the desktop, staring at the rusted metal. On closer inspection, I saw that it was a thin, drawer-like space, with a small latch on the side.

It was probably nothing, I told myself. There must have been many old desks made that way, to conceal their owners' possessions. But did Michael have anything to conceal? I stared at the latch. Should I open it? Or should I respect my husband's privacy and leave it alone?

I got up from the desk and went to the kitchen. I poured myself another glass of wine. I glanced at the clock. I should put the panel back and simply ask him about it. That's what a good wife would do.

Apparently I wasn't a good wife. In three large steps, I was back at the desktop, sliding into the chair. I turned the latch on the panel. It opened easily.

Inside was a sealed, black plastic bag, about the size of a sandwich bag. I took it out and weighed it in my hand. There was something in it.

I opened the bag and reached inside.

I took out the contents—two passports. One had a reddish cover and said it was from France. The other was maroon and proclaimed it was from British Honduras.

I didn't open the passports right away. Something held me back for a moment while my mind shot around, asking questions— Why did Michael have these passports? Why had he hidden them in his desk?

I checked to make sure the curtains were still closed over the window. On impulse, I peeked outside. The street was empty.

I closed the curtains again and stared at the passports. Finally, I lifted the French one and opened the cover. On the left side was Michael's name and photo.

I lifted it closer, feeling my brows knit with confusion. Michael was American. He'd served in the Vietnam War. I knew who he'd voted for in the last four elections. So what was he doing with a French passport?

I put the passport down and lifted the second one. Where was British Honduras, exactly?

I took a breath before I opened it. What was going on here? Finally, I opened the passport. And there was Michael's picture again.

I felt the hair on my arms stand up, a light dusting of apprehension. Because right below the familiar image of my husband was a name I'd never heard before—*Andrew Marson.*

40

Frankfurt, Germany

Liza got off the flight from Moscow and checked her watch. She had two hours until she needed to board the plane to Chicago. She looked around. The Frankfurt Airport was a lot nicer than it used to be, the terminal packed with shops and restaurants.

She walked until she found what she was looking for—a kiosk that rented desks and public computers so travelers could use the Internet and the telephones they provided. Liza had her laptop, and she could simply go to her airline's frequent-flier lounge to use it, but she couldn't risk having any record of what she was about to do.

She changed some money, purchased an international calling card and went back to the computer kiosk, asking the clerk for an hour's worth of time. She also requested the computer at the back of the store, where no one could see over her shoulder.

Once on the Internet, she found the site for Moscow's most prominent newspaper—the paper where Aleksei had worked. She searched until she found the page for the paper's human resources department. She found a name there of the department's assistant—Katrina Katav—along with a phone number.

Liza minimized the newspaper's Web site and ran a few general searches for Katrina Katav. She was single, it appeared. She lived in a less than desirable neighborhood just outside of Moscow. A few more searches and she was able to find the bank where Katav was a customer. Liza couldn't see the woman's bank accounts, but all she really needed was the name of the bank.

She sat for a moment and practiced her Russian in her head. She used the computer to look up the Russian word for "fraudulent."

Liza picked up the phone and used the calling card to dial the newspaper's main number. She asked for Katrina Katav.

"I'm calling from Bank of Moscow," she said in Russian when Katrina answered.

"Yes?" Katrina responded in Russian.

"We've detected some fraudulent activity on your debit card, and we'd like to ensure that some recent purchases were authorized."

"Yes. All right."

"Do you recall the last date you used your debit card?"

A pause. "I do not know," Katrina said. "I don't use it very often. Perhaps Saturday."

"What about last night at Casino Salyut? Did you authorize a charge in the amount of 26,000 rubles?"

"No."

"The specific amount is 26,786."

"Absolutely not."

"Would you like to contest the charge?"

"Yes."

"Are you still currently living at…" Liza rattled off Katrina's street address.

"Yes."

"Apartment 34?"

"Yes."

"For verification purposes, please tell me your mother's maiden name."

Katrina complied.

"And the pin number for your debit card?"

"08970."

"Is this a good number for our investigations department to contact you with further questions?"

"Yes."

"Thank you, Ms. Katav. We will deduct the amount for the Casino Salyut charge until we complete our investigation."

Liza got off the phone and got on the paper's Web site again. She clicked on the link for newspaper employees, and typed in Katrina Katav's name. When it requested a pin number to access the employee page, she typed in 08970. Most people used the same pass number for everything. As the employee page sprang to life, she was grateful that Katrina was no different.

She accessed the newspaper's calendar. Aleksei had told her that the reporters were required to keep a day-to-day calendar, noting the days they would be gone on vacation and, more importantly to Liza, when they had meetings and who they were meeting with. This system had been put into place because a rising number of

Russian journalists had been targets of violence. If something happened to them, the newspaper, as well as the authorities, wanted to find out who a journalist had been meeting with. A reporter's calendar could only be accessed by the individual writers themselves, the top administrators and the human resources department. Which was why Liza had needed Katrina Katav.

Katrina's code gave her access to the company's calendar as well as the archives. She might have been able to figure out Aleksei's own code, but a dead journalist logging on to the system would have probably raised some eyebrows.

In the system now, Liza found Aleksei's calendar, and for a moment, she stopped and looked at his entries, imagining him still here, still alive, still meeting on a Tuesday morning with "H. Krainova" or "B. Yetsinsky." The exercise filled her with overwhelming regret. Why hadn't she and Aleksei ever fought for themselves, for their relationship?

She looked at her watch. She had no time now for such thoughts. Beginning with the date of Aleksei's death, she worked backward, making note of the names of the people Aleksei had met with. The authorities would have already gone over this information, but Liza wanted to see for herself.

She knew now that Michael had killed Radimir Trotsky. What she didn't know was whether it was a hit ordered by the Trust. But that possibility didn't seem right. The Trust should have been able to find out Trotsky's real identity, and once they'd done so, they would never take out someone in the CIA. She kept hearing Roger's words on the phone a few weeks ago, when he was talking about Michael—*He's doing some rogue things,* he'd said. Liza knew Michael had gotten up close and personal with the Russians during his career. He'd been saying he wanted out of the Trust, but was it possible he'd only switched teams? If so, he'd likely begun working for the Mafiya and had taken Trotsky out when he'd learned Trotsky was CIA and had infiltrated the organization. And if Michael had then learned that Aleksei was researching the killing, it was possible he'd loaded the plane with explosives in order to protect himself and those he worked for. *Stop,* she told herself. *Don't jump to conclusions.*

Liza cleared her mind of her racing thoughts and continued scrolling through the notes of Aleksei's meetings, continued noting the names.

Then she came to a name that gripped her heart and filled in the fear she'd been holding at bay. She put the pen down and pushed her pad of paper away. She didn't need to make a note of this name.

Three days before his death, Aleksei had met with *A. Marson.*

41

St. Marabel, Canada

When Michael got home half an hour later, I was still sitting at the desk, wondering. I'd been studying the passports, trying to divine why he had them. Who he was.

"Kate?" he said. His keys hit the ceramic bowl by the door with a *clang*.

I turned around, passports in my hand.

He came to the doorway. He wore a blue suit, an ivory shirt and a yellow tie with small white diagonal stripes. Even after midnight, he looked fresh, composed. His always elegant nature was something that had drawn me to him, but now it seemed contrived.

"You're still up." He sounded pleasantly surprised. But then he must have seen my stern expression. "What's going on?"

"Hello—" I glanced down at the passport "—Andrew?"

Michael's eyes moved to the passports in my hands. "Where did you find those?"

"In the desk."

"Why were you taking the desk apart?" His voice was almost amused, which infuriated me.

I leaped to my feet and flung the passports at his chest. They hit him, then landed on the floor with a soft *flap*.

"Kate," Michael said with a warning tone.

"I'm tired of this secrecy," I said.

"What secrecy?"

"The private rooms downstairs. The investors you won't tell me about. You and Liza in Miami at the same time." My words lost steam. Saying these things out loud, they didn't sound like much. "I just feel so removed from you, Michael, and now the passports." I pointed at the floor. We both stared at them.

Michael bent slowly and scooped them up. He held out the French one. "My mother is French. I was born in Paris. I have dual citizenship."

I opened my mouth and closed it a few times. Finally, I managed to get out, "I didn't know that. I mean, I knew you were French, but I didn't know you were born there."

He shrugged. "It never came up, I guess."

"And the other passport?"

He held out the British Honduras passport. "This is a camouflage ID."

"What does that mean?"

"When I still worked for Presario, they provided this passport for when I was traveling internationally."

"Isn't that illegal?"

"Not if you don't actually use it for travel, which I didn't. I kept it on me for camouflage purposes, so it's entirely legal."

"Why would you need to camouflage who you are?"

"Well, traveling to certain countries can be tricky, even as a businessman. There are terrorist groups in every city in the world. Hostage situations happen. Hijackings happen."

"C'mon." But I thought of all the kidnappings of Americans I'd heard about.

"If something goes down," Michael continued, "and you're an American, you're the first target."

"So you carry that Honduras passport just in case?"

"Exactly." He loosened his tie. "Can we take a walk?"

"I'd like to know more about this passport."

He ran his hand through his hair. Was there more gray in the brown than before? Was the strain of opening the restaurant beginning to show itself? Guilt crept in that I was adding to his stress.

"Kate, the British Honduras is not even a recognized country anymore. It's Belize now. They sell these passports from former countries just so you can use them in case of emergency. They're meant to hide the fact I'm American, if I ever needed to do that. So if I was in another country that had the potential to be violent, I'd hide my American passport and keep this—" he waved the passport "—somewhere more obvious, in case anyone ever looked."

"So you didn't show it at customs?"

"No. I told you." His voice was growing tense. "I kept it in case I found myself in a tricky situation. Lots of business travelers do the same."

"I'm sure Liza doesn't."

"I'm sure she does." He completely untied his tie and pulled it from around his neck. "Why were you searching my desk?"

"Why did you hide those?"

"Jesus, Kate, passports are currency these days. You know that. They're not something you keep lying around."

His annoyed tone threatened to make me retreat, but I knew I wouldn't sleep until I had answers to all my questions. I knew I wouldn't be able to sleep next to him if I didn't trust him. But why *didn't* I trust him? Maybe we'd gotten married too quickly, before we'd had enough time to build up confidence in each other. Maybe I was too scarred from my breakup with Scott, and now I subconsciously fearful that I was going to be dealt another blow.

"Why do you have a desk with a hidden panel in it?" I asked.

"It was my grandfather's. Give me a break."

He looked so tired and sad that I'd questioned him. Again.

"Something isn't right between us," I said.

"We're both exhausted. The restaurant is sapping our energy."

"It's more than that."

"It's not." He crossed the room to me. He placed the passports on top of the desk. "We'll take a day off soon. We'll drive out to the countryside and have a picnic. We'll stay the night somewhere."

I suddenly found myself exhausted from the late hour, the discovery of the passports and the questioning of my husband. I felt more questions lingering, but I couldn't seem to find them on my tongue. Michael's explanation sounded plausible, and I was left feeling off kilter.

I stood and let Michael's arms circle me, and I let my head fill up with the message I wanted to hear—*Everything is fine. Everything is fine*—even though I didn't quite believe it.

42

Michael left early for the restaurant the next day, and I was relieved to have time to myself. My mind swirled with doubts and self-reassurances, questions and then admonitions to believe my husband.

I called Liza a few times. "I know you're traveling," I said on one message. "I know you're crazed. But can you call me, please?"

Ten minutes before I had to leave for the bar, Liza called. "Hey, Kate, are you all right?"

I sighed and took a seat at the kitchen table. "Sorry about the SOS calls. I just wanted to run something by you."

"Anything."

"Well, tell me about you first. Where are you? What's going on?"

"I just got back from L.A. Usual crap." Liza went on to tell me a few vague details about her hectic schedule. She sounded more distracted than usual, her voice almost hard.

"What's going on with that Rich guy?"

She groaned. "He's great. He calls all the time. But

he's in Boston a lot, and that's okay, because I'm trying to get over Aleksei, you know?"

"Do you know any more about the plane crash?"

Liza made a scornful sound, then paused for a moment. "There was an explosive on board."

"What?" I stood from the table, my hand to my chest.

"Yes."

"Why haven't I heard about this in the news?"

"The Russians are keeping it quiet, I guess."

"Do they know who's responsible?"

"They're looking into it—probably just terrorists."

"Just terrorists?" I thought of Michael's words last night—*There are terrorists in every city.* "God, how are you handling this?"

"I'm not." Her voice almost broke. "I'm a bit of a mess."

"Do you want me to visit? I could come for a few days. We could hang out and drink wine. It might make you feel better."

"That sounds great. Maybe soon. But this week I'm in New York."

"Liza, I'll do *anything* for you—you know that, right?"

"I know."

"I want to help. You provided such amazing support to me with the whole Scott thing. Let me return the favor. Talk to me."

"I really can't. It just hurts too much."

"That's why you have to let it out."

"Not yet."

"You're sure?"

"You know me."

"Yeah, I do, but don't push it away too long. You

can wake me up day or night. I can be in Chicago in a few hours."

"Thanks, Kate."

"Love you, sister girl."

"Love you, too." She sighed. "Listen, don't be offended but I just can't talk about Aleksei right now. I get too upset. Tell me what's going on with you."

I sat again at the table, leaning forward on one of my elbows. "I have a question for you. It's about Michael."

No response from Liza.

"I found something of his," I said. "Two things, actually. Two passports. One was French, the other was from British Honduras. He told me that he has dual citizenship because he was born in France. And I guess that makes sense. I didn't know any of this about him, but I suppose there are a lot of things I don't know about Michael."

"What do you mean?"

"Well, we got married so fast."

"Right."

"He told me the other passport was a fake. He had it from when he traveled internationally for work. He says sometimes you have to hide the fact that you're American. Or at least be prepared to do so. He says it's called a camouflage passport and that you probably have one too."

"Okay," Liza said.

"So is that true?"

"Yeah, a lot of business travelers carry camouflage IDs."

"Do you?"

"Yeah."

"Really?"

"Sure. They make them look exactly like a passport, but they're from countries like Burma that no longer technically exist."

I felt somehow deflated. "So he was telling me the truth."

"Sounds like it."

Guilt rushed in now. I was forever questioning Michael when there didn't seem to be any logical reason to do so. "Thanks. Seriously, thanks."

"That's what I'm here for."

"Let me know what I can do, or if I can fly to Chicago and get you good and drunk."

Liza laughed for the first time in our conversation. "Thanks." Her chuckle died away. "Kate, be careful."

43

Porto Ercole, Tuscany, Italy

From the back seat of the town car, Roger watched as the Mediterranean coastline grew more wild and the hillside steeper. Only a few hours outside of Rome, he felt much farther away, thanks to the azure blue of the sea far below him and the quaint villages that sprang up every few miles.

When the car reached Hotel Il Pellicano, Roger stepped out of the car.

"Checking in, sir?" a bellman asked in Italian.

"Grazie," Roger said, "but no."

He walked over earthen tiles into the lobby of the hotel. The glass doors opposite him were open wide, showcasing vine-draped cottages with whitewashed walls and a glittering kidney-shaped pool dotted at the edges with languid, beautiful people all very tan, all very expensively dressed, even in their bathing suits. The pool seemed precariously placed on a cliff's edge, and beyond it, Roger could see the sheer drop to the Mediterranean.

He steeled himself with the thought that although he could certainly afford to stay in such a hotel, he would wait. He would wait until he could stay for months—or until he could buy the whole fucking place. His aspirations would only be met when he'd reached the pinnacle he'd set for himself—he wanted a couple hundred million in the bank, and he wanted the Trust to be running *exactly* as he'd planned it, with no one doubting him or questioning him. Roger feared if he stopped and enjoyed the ride on the way to those goals, he would grow complacent.

He checked his watch. Nearly four in the afternoon. He was perfectly on time, as usual.

A hotel worker passed him, and he stopped her and asked politely in Italian for the piano bar. She pointed to Roger's left. He walked through the lobby. His newly purchased Italian loafers were the softest of leather and made no sound on the tiles.

The piano bar overlooked the pool and was empty, save for the bartender. Roger ordered a glass of local white wine and took it to a table next to the window. Within thirty seconds, he felt someone enter the bar. He waited a moment, then turned.

Silvia Falconiere stood in the doorway. Her lustrous black hair was pulled back, and as she walked to the bar, Roger could see it was held at the nape of her neck and coiled down her back. She was wearing a gauzy, turquoise beach shirt over a white bikini. Her lithe, tanned legs were bare, except for a pair of leather sandals. Silvia looked like what she was—a wealthy heiress, someone who was making the most of the fortune reaped from her father's business. What wasn't readily apparent from her attire today was that Silvia now ran that business. Much more ruthlessly than her father had.

The business was waste management, and Angelo Naponi, whom Roger had ordered Liza to eliminate in Anguilla, had been the Falconieres' main competitor.

Silvia accepted her drink from the bartender and made her way to Roger's table. She slipped easily into the chair opposite him, crossing her bronzed legs. Physically, she reminded him somewhat of Marta, his only love from his days in Rio, and he felt himself become ever so slightly aroused. He knew that arousal would grow when he and Silvia began talking. Cold-blooded ambition turned Roger on more than anything these days.

"What are you drinking?" Roger said without any other greeting. He knew Silvia liked to get down to business, and he appreciated that.

"Prosecco. I enjoy it at all times of the day." She raised her fluted glass. "*Salute.*"

"*Salute,*" Roger echoed, touching her glass with his.

"Thank you again for the work your company did."

Roger nodded modestly. "I hope that it led to the result you wanted."

"Yes." She took another sip of her wine. "With Naponi gone, his company is in…" She searched for the English word. "Shambles? We have been able to take over many of his contracts. And more will follow."

"Wonderful." He said this with a calm voice, but inside he was thrilled to the point of bursting.

His plan to take the Trust in the direction of his vision

was becoming truer every day. He had realized that there was money to be made—an extraordinary amount of money—in the outsourcing of operatives, making people like Liza and Michael assassins-for-hire. Doing so was obviously against the regulations of the Trust. Such a move meant that the operatives could be hired for almost anything, which meant that various jobs wouldn't have, as a goal, the furtherance of U.S. safety. The Trust's rule of *no collateral damage* also went out the window. But Roger didn't care. Such rules were naive anyway.

The Trust had been started by Coleman Kingsley following his court-martial, but it had really flourished after Watergate, after laws were passed that curtailed the NSA, CIA and FBI. The glory days of the Trust were heady, and Roger was glad to be a part of it. But every organization needed to keep its eye on the next big thing. And Roger had found that.

So Roger had been outsourcing the operatives, and because he tolerated no dissenters, he made the missions appear to be in line with Trust politics. Some of the profits of his efforts—the very, very substantial profits—went back to the Trust. Some went in his pocket. In fact, the Naponi killing by Liza in Anguilla had brought in ten million dollars—five for the Trust, five for Roger. It had been simple to design false intel to make it look as if Naponi was supporting Muslim terrorists who would soon target the United States. No one was the wiser, certainly not Liza. And Roger was all the richer.

"I was impressed by the discretion of your work," Silvia said.

"Thank you. Our operatives know how to complete their assignments without detection. You will never have to worry when you work with us."

"Good." She smiled a chilly, stunning smile, so different from Marta's but so sexy. "I have another job for you."

"Then let's toast again." Roger raised his glass once more and matched her smile.

44

Chicago, Illinois

Liza exited the elevator of her apartment and made her way across the lobby. The marble floor was polished to a high sheen, and the flower arrangements were bright and fragrant, but she barely noticed any of this. In her head, she was already at work, making calls, making connections, making plans. And this time it was Michael she was investigating. Michael who had been her father's friend, and *her* friend, and now Kate's husband. Michael, who had killed Radimir Trotsky, otherwise known as CIA operative Charlie Miller, and then killed Aleksei to cover up what he'd done.

Michael had somehow figured out Aleksei was on the story, and met with Aleksei to confirm that suspicion. He feared if it surfaced that Trotsky was actually CIA, they'd really begin the hunt for the killer, and Michael couldn't risk being exposed. So he took out the threat. The fact that Michael had eliminated a CIA man and the fact that he'd killed six innocent people along with Aleksei to hide it, meant Michael was either sloppy or very, very dangerous. And Liza knew Michael was never sloppy.

Liza had ignored her mailbox all weekend. She stopped there now. Inside were a few bills, a home-and-garden magazine she considered a guilty pleasure and a greeting card. She opened the card. It was from her mother, sent from the retirement community where she lived, and where Liza had failed to visit for way too long. On the front of the card was an illustrated bunch of flowers, and inside the card read, *Miss you bunches.* Her mother had written, *Love, Mom.* Then she'd added, *Hope work is going well. Your dad would be proud of you.*

Liza put a hand out and rested it on the cool steel of the mailbox. She let her body fall forward, too, until her forehead pressed against her hand. And then, just for a moment, she let her eyes close, and she let herself remember.

45

Sixteen years ago
Evanston, Illinois

The newly minted college graduate entered the front door of her parents' house and let it fall closed behind her with a slam.

"Liza!" her mom, Delia, yelled from the kitchen in an exasperated voice. "Don't do that."

"Sorry," she called back.

But neither of them was sorry about the door banging. It was something Colby had always done, and it had truly bothered her mother back then. Now Liza had adopted his habit. They both knew that although Delia was a nice Catholic woman who valued manners and quiet, there was nothing that made her happier than a household made noisy by her family. But with Colby dead now five years and her previously larger-than-life husband severely diminished by a stroke, Delia Kingsley didn't often hear the din she used to complain about. Whenever Liza came home from UCLA, she tried to fill up the house with sound—bringing Kate over and blaring music, talking loudly on the phone, chattering to her mother about boys and campus politics. Now, two weeks after graduation, Liza was glad she was under her parents' roof, glad she could create some more noise, breathe some more life into their world, even if she wouldn't be there for long.

Liza had halfheartedly looked for a job with her marketing degree, but she would have to step up the efforts now. It was time to move out, she supposed, time to grab adulthood by the horns and do something with it. Just what, she wasn't sure.

She walked into the kitchen and pecked her mom on the cheek. Delia was peeling carrots at the countertop.

"Everything went okay? You're healthy?" her mother asked. She had Liza's red hair, but she was shorter. And over these past years, Delia's back hunched slightly, giving her a resigned look.

"Everything is just fine, Mom."

Her mother had insisted that she visit a round of doctors today—gynecologist, internist, dentist. Not because Liza had any symptoms of any kind. No, after four years running sprints for the UCLA track team, Liza was in the best shape of her life. But her mother said she should get her health checked, and Liza—wanting to alleviate her mom's fears that she might lose another family member—had gone.

"What's for dinner?" Liza said.

"I'm making a stew."

"Dad must be having a good day." Her father's appetite, normally robust, had diminished since his stroke one year ago. On good days, he asked for stew.

"He is," her mother said simply.

"Where is he?"

"His study."

Liza picked up a halved carrot from her mother's cutting board and bit into it with a loud crunch. Her mother smiled.

In the study, her father was sitting in his desk chair, turned toward the bay-window view of their backyard. Their house was not one of the largest in this neighborhood. In fact, there were some grand homes that tripled theirs in size. But the Kingsley lawn was beautifully manicured with a row of tall hedges that protected it from view. The hedges were cut straight across the top—*Just like I used to wear my hair,* her father always said—and although he no longer pruned and weeded and deadheaded himself, her father still took pride in the lawn.

Liza looked at her father without speaking. From this angle, the slackness of his left side was unnoticeable, but she could still see how the fire in his eyes was muted.

"Hey, Dad." She walked into the study and flopped into one of the black leather chairs that faced his desk.

Slowly, her father used the one foot that still worked to turn the chair. He grinned with the side of his face that would still let him.

"Lizzy," he said.

She didn't kiss him like she had her mother, and he made no move to hug her. He wasn't that kind of man.

"Did you put your mother's worries to rest?"

"Yep. Clean bill of health."

"Good. Good."

They were quiet. This, too, was typical of her father. He never filled silences just for the sake of doing it.

"So your job search..." he said.

"I know, Dad. I know."

Her father hadn't said much officially, but Liza understood that he wouldn't let her hang around the house for long, eating all their food and staying out partying till the wee hours. She'd been getting away with it, claiming graduation celebrations and visits with high-school friends, but she'd known he would have this conversation with her.

Her father put his working arm on the desk and leaned forward. His gaze was unflinching. "What is it you know?"

"I know I've got to find a job. I know I have to work. And I'm going to. I'm just having a little fun. I'm not going to be a slacker, though. Don't worry about it."

Her father made a disapproving expression. "Of course you won't."

There was no room for slacking in the house of Coleman Kingsley. None was tolerated. Liza had always assumed that her dad's unforgiving attitude came from two things—his military background and the fact that he'd been court-martialed. Liza had no idea what had led up to the discharge; it was unlike her father to discuss such things. Only once, in the months following Colby's death, had he mentioned it. And then he'd said he was *heartbroken.* An odd word, Liza had thought. He'd been talking about Colby. He was saying how there was justice in the fact that the drunk driver who ran him off the road and into the ravine had been convicted of reckless homicide, but how, despite this justice, his heart was still in pieces.

She hadn't thought it strange at all that a parent would be heartbroken about the loss of their only son. But then he'd said, "It reminds me of how I felt when I had to leave the army."

Liza had turned her head slowly to look at him, fearful he would stop talking.

Her father just kept staring out the window over the kitchen sink. "It was different, of course. But I was heartbroken then, too."

Now, in her father's study, Liza told her father about the position she'd applied for at a PR firm, another at an ad agency. She was going to rework her résumé, she said. As she talked, she felt a slight sinking of her spirits. None of the jobs she was applying for really appealed to her, but she had to do something. It was time to grow up. And yet, she wanted to be passionate about her job. She knew that sounded clichéd. Every college graduate said the same thing. She thought of Kate, and how Kate had already landed a job at a big accounting firm. She liked the job but hated the routine of it—of having to get up every day and take the train every day and work every day. But it wasn't the routine or the hard work Liza feared. It was the potential for complacency.

"What would you think about working for Presario?" her father said.

"Oh," she said, startled. "Uh…what would I do?"

Liza knew little about her father's job at the pharmaceutical company, except that he was a senior executive, and he traveled a lot.

"Well, you'd start in sales and marketing."

"Wow. Yeah. That sounds cool, I guess."

"You'd have to interview, of course."

"Sure. Should I send a résumé to someone?"

The right corner of his mouth lifted in a smile. "You can give it to your old man."

She laughed. She had an image of taking the downtown train with her father, both of them in suits, reading the paper. She imagined she would say to people, *It's been wonderful getting to work with my dad.*

She thought of how her father had always been vague about his job, but intense. Maybe it was something she could be passionate about, too.

Her father looked over her head for a moment, his expression almost wistful. "I'd always thought Colby might come to work for Presario."

She felt herself flatten a little. "Colby wanted to be a guitarist."

They were both quiet for a few long moments. Liza missed her brother then, and felt juvenile for being jealous of him. The missing felt like a spear that went right through her.

"Liza," her dad said. "There's something you should know about Presario before you apply."

"Sure. What?"

And that's when he told her. That's when her father brought Liza Kingsley into his world, and in one simple conversation, changed hers forever.

46

Chicago, Illinois

As Liza leaned against the bank of mailboxes, her eyes felt misty. Jesus, why was she constantly on the verge of tears these days? There was Aleksei, of course, and her mother's greeting card. And then there was the fact that her mother reminded her of her father, and her father made her think of the Trust, and now all she could think about was how disappointed her father would be at the state of the organization he had started. With protocol being ignored, with men like Michael who switched teams and took matters into their own hands, with men like Roger, who seemed pompous and power hungry—it was so different than the Trust he had intended.

The Trust was supposed to be a watchdog, a silent protector of the United States. Threats to the U.S. would be taken care of, yes, but in quiet ways, always sparing innocent people. When had the organization begun to slip? Maybe that had happened as far back as when her father died fifteen years ago. Maybe it was more recently, when Michael had held a position of leadership. Maybe it was when Roger became a board member.

She shook her head as she straightened away from the mailbox bank. She thought about being in Miami with Michael. After meeting with his contact, he professed to know nothing about what Aleksei was working on. But he must have known the whole time that Aleksei had been working on a story about Radimir Trotsky and the CIA. He'd known and he'd feared for himself and he'd decided to take care of the threat. She suspected the real reason he'd agreed to go to Miami was so he could control the situation. He could pretend to ask his contact for information and tell her there was none.

Liza hated Michael then with a ferocity she hadn't known before. The thought that she'd set up Kate with him, that Kate was now *married* to this man made her sick. God, what had she gotten her friend into?

Liza turned and strode through the lobby. She hadn't been able to save Aleksei, but she would save Kate.

She'd felt terrible when Kate had called her, suspicious and worried about finding the passports. She'd told her friend the truth—camouflage passports from defunct countries were legal but she hadn't been able to resist warning her at the end of the conversation.

She stepped outside her building and looked around for the doorman, who usually hailed cabs. He must have been helping another resident. Liza raised her arm and began looking for a taxi light. Just then, a Yellow Cab pulled up to the building and the back door popped open. Liza bent down. And there inside was a smiling Rich Macklin.

"You don't return my calls," he said, "so I had to stalk your apartment."

"You could have simply stalked my office," she said, but not unkindly. Just seeing him lifted her mood.

"At the office it would have been hard to convince you to take your clothes off."

She slid inside the cab and gave him a look. "I'm not about to take them off here, either."

Rich looked out the window for a moment, as if he was considering this. Then he turned back to her. There was a roguish, impish tilt to his brown-gold eyes, but there was something else there, too. Something more serious. "Look, I've canceled my deposition for this morning and rescheduled the flight back to Boston I was supposed to get this afternoon. I don't know what you've got going on, but here's the thing."

"Yes, tell me the thing," Liza said in a joking tone.

"I miss you."

She said nothing. She wasn't used to scenes like this. What was she supposed to do? "I miss you, too."

"So let me take you to breakfast. We'll go someplace fancy like the Four Seasons, and you can tell me everything that's going on with you, and then maybe you'll let me talk you into coming back to my place…"

"I don't know about that—"

He held up a hand, cutting her off. "We don't have to decide now. You just have to let me buy you some eggs and some toast and a mimosa. You just have to let me take care of you for the next hour and a half, and then we can go from there."

Liza laughed a little. She actually felt giddy at the

phrase *You just have to let me take care of you.* How wonderful that sounded. The part about his apartment didn't sound bad, either. But she had Aleksei to think about. He'd been murdered, ruthlessly, and to cover Michael's goddamn ass. She had wanted to get all those things cleaned up before she called Rich. But why? Life wasn't ever neat and tidy. She ought to know that better than anyone. And when she looked at Rich, she saw potential for her future, for something real and wonderful, for something other than an empty apartment.

She squeezed Rich's hand. She leaned forward toward the cabbie. "The Four Seasons," she said.

47

St. Marabel, Canada

The weekend at the Twilight Club was the way it was supposed to be—all open doorways and summer breezes and chattering crowds and clinking glasses. Michael had booked the private rooms and spent much of his time there, but he made sure to visit me every hour or so, sometimes just coming to the doorway of the bar and mouthing "I love you."

Those things—the little visits, seeing his mouth make those words—made all the difference. I felt light-hearted and in love again. I joked with T.R. and made small talk with customers. Because the bar was busy until late each night, I was able to walk home with Michael, hand in hand in the early-morning hours, savoring the inky darkness and soft quiet.

But Sunday when I woke up, my throat felt thick and pain coursed through my head. I coughed, hearing a little rattle in my lungs.

Michael rolled over and put a hand on my thigh.

"Better not touch me," I said. "I think I'm sick."

"What?" He sat up, his hair in disarray.

I coughed again. And groaned. My face felt warm, my eyelids heavy.

"I'll call a doctor," Michael said.

"It's Sunday."

"This is an old-fashioned town. I know people who make house calls."

"No, no. Just let me sleep. I'm sure I'll be fine."

I let Michael put cold compresses on my head, then sent him off to get the Sunday papers. I turned up the air-conditioning and fell into a fevered sleep. When I woke up, the fever was still there, but worse. My body felt like it was burning up, and the coughing had increased.

"That's it," Michael said. "I'm having Dr. Fenoir come over."

Within a few hours, a tiny man with a trim, white beard had diagnosed me with bronchitis. If I didn't take care of it, he said, he was sure it would turn into full-fledged pneumonia. "You are not to be working," Dr. Fenoir said. "Only rest. Only liquids."

Michael called in sick for both of us, while I watched from the bed.

"Are you sure?" I asked when he'd gotten off the phone.

"Of course I'm sure."

"You've never called in sick before, and you've been telling me you need to be at the restaurant all the time."

He sat on the edge of the bed and felt my forehead. "I do. But you're more important."

Despite my fuzzy head and my aching lungs, I felt a swell of emotion inside me. "Thank you."

Michael spent the day taking my temperature and

making me food—asparagus soup, tourtière (a meat and potato pie) and blueberry cookies.

The next morning when he tried to bring me a buttered scone, I smiled but shook my head. "The doctor said liquids."

"But you have to eat."

I looked at his eyes. There was a line that ran vertically between the skin there, one that was always present, but now it cut deeper.

"Are you worried about me?" I said.

"Yes."

"Michael, don't. It's bronchitis. I've had that before."

"You never know."

"I know. I know my body. I pushed it too hard at the restaurant, and I got too stressed out about…" Our eyes met. "It doesn't matter. I want you to go to work today. Isn't Roger in town?"

"He's coming in tomorrow. Today, I'm staying home to take care of you."

"There's nothing to take care of. I've got more food than I know what to do with, and I'm exhausted. I'll take my medication and go to sleep. I'll sleep better if I know one of us is working."

"Are you sure?"

I pushed myself up to a seated position. Pressure swelled in my head, but I didn't let Michael see. "I'm positive."

I slept that whole day, barely rousing to hear Michael coming back from the restaurant. Tuesday morning, I felt a little better. I was still coughing and slightly feverish, but definitely on the mend. I managed to get up and have lunch with Michael at the kitchen table, and then I sent him back to the restaurant.

I slept most of the afternoon, but by four o'clock, I was getting antsy. In a burst of motivation, I showered, washed the sheets and changed the bed. Finding myself even more energized, I began to clean and organize the house the way I'd been meaning to since I moved in. The house had been Michael's summer place for years, and little had changed since I'd gotten there. If I was going to make the best of my marriage, the way I wanted to, I had to make this *my* place as well.

I pushed furniture across the rooms and shook out rugs. I dusted books and rearranged them on the shelves, making sure to feature those that I'd brought with me, not just Michael's. I cleaned out kitchen drawers and reorganized the dishes the way I liked them.

When Michael called to check on me, I told him I'd have a surprise when he came home. I wasn't tired at all. The movement had made me feel better. I kept working—tidying the closets, sorting through old bills and mail, cleaning every available surface. I even took the screens off the living-room windows, letting in the humid but seductive August air, and began scrubbing the white-painted sills until they were a sparkling alabaster. The work was like a meditation; it allowed my thoughts to drift until all I heard were the soft evening sounds of St. Marabel—distant music, passing laughter, the purr of a scooter.

I was working on the third windowsill, a rag in my hand, when I ran across a raised spot of old paint. I rubbed at it, but it wouldn't budge. I pulled the rag away and saw that it was actually a white plastic disc or chip of sorts affixed to the sill. I used my fingernail to pry it off.

The disc was small and paper-thin with a glass square on top showing red and gray wiring beneath. It wasn't much bigger than my thumbnail. I turned it over, looking at the adhesive backing and the two black slash marks on the lower right corner.

I couldn't imagine what this thing was.

I put it on the desk and stared at it. I thought about calling Michael at the restaurant. Instead, I quickly searched the rest of the windowsills in the living room. I saw no other white chips. Next I went to the small room by the kitchen and removed the screens there. On the sill above Michael's desk, tucked way over to the left, almost invisible, I found another chip. In the kitchen I found another one. In the bedroom, yet another.

At midnight, I stood in the darkened house, four discs in my hand. Most of the windows were still open wide, and the house smelled fresh from all the cleaning, but there was a foreboding in the air now that tainted it all.

48

I had waited for Michael to get home that night, but when he wasn't there by one in the morning, my sickness overtook me again. I felt bleary, hot and weak. And confused. I stacked the four white chips on the counter, where Michael would see them, and crawled into bed, falling deeply asleep.

The next morning, I found Michael already awake, sitting at the kitchen table. He had the papers in front of him, but he seemed not to be reading.

"How do you feel?" he said, looking up at me.

I touched my forehead. I no longer had a fever, and I felt like I could breathe normally again. "Better. Fine."

My eyes shot to the countertop where I'd placed the discs the night before. I saw Michael's gaze follow mine. The discs were gone now.

"So the place looks great," he said, picking up his paper again. "I can't believe you found the energy to clean."

"Yeah, well, I was feeling better."

"Still, you should probably take another day off."

"Michael, where are those things?"

His hands still held the paper but his eyes rose over

it, meeting mine. I couldn't read him. So often I couldn't read him.

"What do you mean?" he said.

I walked to the counter and pointed at the empty spot where I had left them. "Last night, when I was cleaning, I found these white discs…."

"Where?" he said calmly, as if we were discussing what to have for dinner.

"What?" I said, annoyed.

"Where did you find them?"

"They were on the windowsills, but you would never have seen them unless you lifted the screens off."

Michael put the paper down.

"What are they, Michael?"

He was silent.

"A better question—*where* are they? What did you do with them?"

He regarded me for a moment, then pulled the chips out of his pocket and set them on the table.

"So?" I said. "What are they?"

"I don't know. I think they're just computer chips. They're extra memory or something."

"Are you kidding me? Then what are they doing behind the windows?"

He shrugged.

"What kind of reaction is that?" My voice rose. I couldn't help it. He was being so weird about this.

"What reaction am I giving?" Michael asked.

"You're so calm."

"I'm a calm person, Kate. You knew that when you married me. You said you liked that about me."

This was true. I'd dealt with Scott's roller coaster of emotions for so long that when I met Michael, I'd told him I loved his centered, composed nature. But still.

"Don't use that against me," I said. "I'm just commenting on the fact that your wife found something planted all over your house—our house—and you don't even seem particularly curious about it."

"I've rented this place for years. I have no idea what the landlady does, and unless it's affecting us, I really don't care."

I thought of our landlady—a divorced woman in her fifties named Claire, who seemed kind. And benign.

I walked the few steps to the table and picked up one of the discs. "Well, you might not care, but I do. I think these things are weird, and I want to know why they're in our house."

Michael looked at the disc in my hand, and I noticed tenseness around his mouth.

"I'm going to ask Claire what they are," I said, looking for more of a reaction.

"Let me take your temperature."

"I'm fine."

"No protesting. Dr. Fenoir said you're not going to work until your temperature is down."

He took me by the arm and led me to the bathroom. He opened the cabinet and took out the thermometer. He removed the sheath and rinsed the thermometer in water. Then very slowly, my husband slid the cool glass stick into my mouth and laid it to rest on the delicate skin under my tongue.

I watched him, wondering at how fast I'd gotten here,

how fast I'd married someone I really didn't know that well. It was a marriage based on how alive Michael made me feel, how incredible the sex was, how fascinating I thought he was. And yet, what did I really know about him? Had I chased after a romantic notion of marriage, after all the businesslike fertility treatments that had filled my relationship with Scott?

A minute later, Michael removed the thermometer from my mouth. "Still high. You're staying home."

I knew there was no arguing with him. I didn't *want* to argue with him. I got into bed and turned my back to him.

He leaned over the bed ten minutes later and kissed my head. "Feel better. Love you."

I feigned sleep. When he was gone, I got up and went to the kitchen. And I found that the discs were gone, again.

49

Early in the evening, Michael approached Roger in the bar of the Twilight Club. "So he finally visits."

"It's about time I got here," Roger said. "This place lives up to every expectation."

The two greeted each other with handshakes and a loose hug like they'd done many times before. But Michael felt a wariness this time, from them both. For his part, he was worried about Kate. Not just because of her illness, but because of her unease, her questions, and the angst he felt at having to hide things from her. He'd spent his life hiding, and it had never bothered him, but there'd never been someone like Kate.

As to why Roger seemed wary, Michael supposed his old friend was merely preoccupied, being a board member of the Trust, one of only five. Michael could almost laugh, thinking of young Roger, the guy he'd first met when he was recruited by the Trust a few years after Michael. That Roger was intellectual and earnest and eager to learn and please. Now that he was a board member, Roger had a confidence that grew and expanded each time he saw him. As a friend, Michael might have been proud of that confidence. As a colleague, he saw danger there. Roger was an M.D., and he'd been both a field agent and researcher for the Trust for years. But he didn't have the knack for fieldwork the way Michael knew he did or the way Liza did. And yet, Roger had risen through their ranks determinedly.

A group pushed into the bar, making the volume rise. Michael clasped Roger on the arm and steered him to the bar. "A drink before I show you around?"

Roger shook his head. "I want to assess the situation first."

Michael bristled. Roger was doing this a lot lately—tossing out small comments that made it clear he was Michael's superior. Michael hadn't minded at first. Hell, he'd been so relieved to be easing out of the Trust and into a life with Kate that he'd almost relished such comments. They seemed to shift the burden of the Trust squarely onto Roger's shoulders. And that used to be a good thing once when Michael had trusted his former protégé, but now there were too many shortcuts being taken, too many protocols unmet. The capital members of the Trust—many of whom had already appeared in Michael's private rooms—weren't treated with the deference that they used to be, and yet they often knew more than they should.

For example, there were two Philippine manufacturing moguls who'd dined at the club last week. They had been approached about becoming members of the Trust after two other Filipinos had been arrested under suspicion of plotting a terrorist attack on the Philadelphia Stock Exchange. As a result of the arrest, the United

States government, as well as the Trust, was taking a closer look at the Filipino population and any potential terrorist cells. What the Trust liked to do was to approach wealthy locals dependent on American business, like the manufacturing moguls, and use them not only for sources of information, but also as sources of capital. The Trust would investigate possible dangers to the United States and eliminate them if necessary, and meanwhile the moguls could count on their success and wealth continuing via their well-connected American business partners.

The Filipinos had arrived at the Twilight Club and, like the Australians from Michael's first week, they wanted to be briefed upon arrival. Angus eventually showed up to hold the Filipinos' hands. Since he was one of Roger's favorites, Michael expected him to be well-versed in Trust protocol, but when Michael entered the room a few minutes later, he heard Angus giving the men information outside the bounds of the matter they were there to discuss. Whether that was Angus's style or a style new to the Trust, Michael wasn't sure, but either way, he was entirely uncomfortable with it.

The whole point of the Trust was its secrecy and its ability to operate undercover. They informed the capital members only on the precise information they needed to know. Under no circumstances did lines of information get crossed. Michael heard Angus giving the Filipinos more details about other investigative endeavors in their country. He even mentioned once the code name of an operative stationed there. It seemed incredibly sloppy to Michael, and he'd called Roger within minutes to report what he'd heard.

Roger had promptly reminded him that Michael was no longer an inside member of the Trust, and essentially told him to mind his own business.

Now, in his blue slacks and white linen blazer, Roger looked like a vacationing businessman. And yet Roger's shrewd eyes scanned and searched and scrutinized every inch of the club as Michael showed him around.

Michael introduced Roger to the hostess and pointed out the stairs to the private dining rooms, where he would be dining shortly.

"I'll have a drink first before I head downstairs," Roger said.

When they had wound their way back to the bar, Michael introduced Roger to T.R. The beefy bartender, who was not a Trust member and who believed he was simply working for the sleek new club in town, shook Roger's hand good-naturedly.

"Michael, I'm a damn mess without your wife here," T.R. said. "And it's never as fun without Kate around."

"Absolutely true," Michael said. He could feel Roger's eyes on him, silently analyzing.

"Where is Kate this evening?" Roger said when T.R. had moved to the other end of the bar. "Still sick?"

Michael, who prided himself on his calm and his cool, felt himself tighten with anger. He stared at Roger, felt his jaw tensing into hard lines. He had not told Roger that Kate was under the weather. The only way Roger could have known this, arriving in St. Marabel only an hour before, was if he'd heard about it via the bugs planted in their house. The bugs like the ones Kate had found, and which Michael had quickly recognized, based on their markings, as the work of the Trust.

As a member of the Trust, Michael had agreed to intermittent surveillance of his life, even audio surveillance in his home. It was something he hated—something all members hated—but it was always done discreetly, and no one from the board (the only Trust members other than the techs who were entitled to review the audio) ever mentioned anything they'd heard or seen. The surveillance was only done to keep loose tabs on the members, to make sure they weren't, as Coleman would have said, going off the rails.

But now it seemed to Michael that the only one going off the rails was Roger. For him to mention that he knew Kate was sick seemed to be his way of showing Michael that he knew all, saw all. Which made Michael not only angry but humiliated.

He and Kate had made love all over their house. Sex was something that was supposed to be off limits to surveillance. The time when the techs switched off the equipment, or deleted the tape afterward. When Coleman Kingsley was at the helm, Michael had never questioned whether this was the case. When Coleman was around, the Trust was a first-class operation that never compromised its ethics.

But now there was Roger. Roger, with his damn comment.

Michael tried to tamp down his anger.

"Let's get that drink," he said, deciding to ignore Roger's slip.

Because the other problem was the internal sensors on the bugs—they had sent signals to the Trust when Kate had pried them away. Michael had contacted the techs and let them know that the bugs had been inadvertently discovered and removed by a cleaning person. Whether this news had reached Roger and whether he cared, Michael couldn't be sure, but his comment had made it seem as if he did.

They both took seats on bar stools. Roger was here not just to see the club but to meet a group of Russians. They were part of a small organization that was new to the Trust, not part of Michael's old network. And yet previously it would have been Michael meeting with the Russians. He considered for a moment whether he was jealous—an emotion he never indulged in. But subconsciously, was he resenting the stepped-down status that he had requested? Maybe all this wishing for the Trust of old was his way of holding on to something that simply didn't exist anymore.

Michael ordered two glasses of a new Merlot he'd just received.

He decided to be the man he'd always tried to be—a strong man, one who didn't indulge in silly machinations or envies. In doing so, he might be able to lead Roger by example. He would try to have faith that his friend understood enough good from bad to direct the Trust into newer, but even better, times. He wouldn't forget Roger's comment, but for now he would rise above it.

"Good luck with your meeting tonight," Michael said.

Roger nodded in thanks.

Michael glanced at T.R. who was now at the end of

the bar, then quickly over his shoulders. "I want you to know that if there's anything I can do to help, anything that, well…won't compromise my retirement status, I'm happy to do it."

Roger studied him for a moment. He nodded again. "I think that because of your work in this area, we're set up nicely." He turned toward Michael. "Look, Mike, I know I've been hard on you with your retirement and all, but I want you to know I respect everything you've done. Your work with the Russians will be your legacy. And you were a big part of Juliet. She's really coming together now."

"Great." Michael felt a wistfulness for the time when he was all-consumed by the Trust, by its missions, and research projects like Juliet. He didn't want that anymore, but like any retiree, he still felt the company's pull.

Roger patted him on the shoulder, the way a coach would a Little League player. "You did good, Mike," he said with an obvious patronizing edge.

"I did my job."

"And now you've got a different one." He gestured to his glass of Merlot. "I'm not a big fan of this. Have your staff bring me another."

And right then, Michael's wistfulness was replaced with a desire to clock Roger in the face.

50

Roger let Michael show him around the private rooms. He listened intently as Michael pointed out the state-of-the-art surveillance and security equipment in every room.

"Well done." He patted Michael on the arm again in a way he knew was condescending.

Roger could see how Michael hated to be his underling, and so he subtly reminded his old friend of his lowly status every time he could. He'd been trying to get Michael to understand that it was *he* who was the board member now, not him. *He* was calling the shots and taking the Trust in a new direction, the direction that would bring more wealth and less idealism. Because really, what was the point of idealism?

Roger didn't have the pie-in-the-sky, pro-America sentiment that Coleman Kingsley did, that Michael did. When Michael asked to step down, it was exactly the break Roger had been looking for. He'd been weeding out the older board members slowly but very certainly, and trying to keep those that would let him dominate. Michael's desire to get out and then his relationship with Kate had happened at exactly the right times. Roger made the requisite protests, and he liked to give Michael crap about it, but it was precisely what he needed.

Yet Michael persisted in telling him what to do, telling the operatives in St. Marabel how to handle situations, calling Roger with complaints and offering advice. And that was simply not going to work.

"Here's the wine-cellar room," Michael said, leading Roger into a room, where the walls were outfitted from floor to ceiling with bottles of wine. Cut into one wall was a bar. On the wall above it hung an impressionistic oil painting of a golden field.

Roger pointed to the painting. "Isn't that one of yours?" He recognized the artwork. It used to hang in Michael's house in Vermont.

Michael nodded, smiled. "I got that in Theole-sur-Mer. I've always loved it."

Roger furrowed his brow. "So what's it doing here?"

"I'm loaning it to the club."

Roger shook his head. "This isn't your club, my friend."

Michael exhaled. "I didn't say it was."

"It's got to come down."

"Relax, Roger."

"You know the rules."

"We don't have any rules about loaned artwork."

"But we do have rules against letting personal business become part of the job."

Michael scoffed. "I know. That's not what this is."

Roger ignored him. "When do my contacts arrive?"

Michael leaned in. "Don't treat me like a goddamn lackey."

"I'm not."

"You're getting close, and I won't take it."

The two men stared at each other. Roger broke the stare first, only because he knew both of them could keep it up for days, and tactically it seemed smarter to let Michael think he'd won.

He checked his watch. "If you'd show in my contacts when they arrive, I'd appreciate it."

Roger turned his back to Michael. He moved toward the bar and the two open bottles of wine that sat there.

He heard Michael leave.

Roger poured himself a glass of wine and went to the wall panel where the room controls for the audio, video and security systems were located. He punched in a code, put his palm on the pad to gain access, then punched another series of buttons on the panel until the audio and video were disabled.

Out loud, he said, "Code 82," one of the Trust's lexicons indicating an emergency situation.

He waited thirty seconds. When no one came to the room, he knew the system had been properly disabled.

A moment later, Michael showed two Russian men into the room. Roger thanked him, ordered some appetizers and asked Michael to have the waitstaff stay out for the first five minutes. Michael opened his mouth, then closed it. And Roger, who'd had just about enough of Michael's bullshit, closed the door on him.

"Gentlemen," he said, gesturing toward the table.

One of the men had green eyes so light they appeared nearly colorless and a nose that had been clearly broken more than once. His colleague was more elegant looking, with fine features and a slim, tall build. Both wielded power in Russia and both had an incredible amount of money. They were part of a new wave of the Russian Mafiya, which chose to operate on a very quiet basis. Roger had learned of their existence using the initial intel Michael had gained. He thanked God Michael had been unwilling to follow up on the intel and had instead followed his childish desire for a simple marriage to a simple woman. Now Roger was one of the few people who knew precisely what these men were involved with, who they worked with and how much the Trust could benefit from a relationship with them. He'd had to prove himself to the men first. And he'd done it with Michael's unknowing help.

After the men settled themselves with a glass of wine, Roger took his seat across from them. "Gentlemen, I gave you a gift some time ago. I told you Radimir Trotsky was an undercover CIA operative."

Trotsky's CIA status was the piece of information that Roger had been able to find out after Michael requested step-down status. And Jesus, how it had paid off.

The man with the light green eyes nodded. "That was something we thought impossible. Thank you for telling us."

"Of course." Roger bowed his head magnanimously. "You also thought it was impossible that we could take care of the situation for you, making it seem as if Trotsky was hit from the outside so you would never have to admit you'd been infiltrated."

The lean man squinted his eyes. "We appreciate your efforts."

Roger removed a leather wallet from his breast

pocket. "We'll need payment at this time. You'll find all the wiring instructions here. Eighteen million dollars is payable by the week's end."

Both men nodded their assent.

The leaner man took the wallet from Roger and put it in his own breast pocket. "And your operative who performed the service for us?"

Roger thought of Michael, standing right down the hall. "He'll be eliminated."

He waited for some feeling to follow this statement, some remorse, but none came. He felt only elation that the new face of the Trust was starting to show itself. Michael had performed perfectly with the Trotsky elimination. He'd acted on his own prior knowledge of Trotsky, along with some "current" information Roger had contrived. Michael had never known Trotsky was CIA. And when Aleksei Ivanov got wind of the CIA angle, Roger had taken care of him. Just in case anyone checked, he'd made it seem like Michael, under the name of Andrew Marson, had met with Aleksei before his death. The fact that Roger had annihilated Liza Kingsley's ex-lover only made the circumstances sweeter. He'd known Liza was a problem, having inherited her father's sappy, earnest idealism. He'd come to despise her after she'd slapped his hand at Michael's wedding.

Liza and Michael couldn't seem to figure out that Roger was truly on top now, and if his operatives asked too many questions then they would be taken care of, too. No one was indispensable anymore. Except him.

The Russians barely reacted to the news of an operative's soon-to-be demise. Roger felt thrilled that they didn't know that that doomed operative had been the one to show them to this room. He felt a sudden rush of euphoria that he was the one pulling the invisible strings. It was better than sex.

He stood and walked to the wall. He enabled the audiovisual equipment again, then hit the button on the panel marked Manager. "Michael," he said into the intercom, "we'll take those appetizers now."

51

Roger had stayed only the night, thankfully, and the next day, Michael sat in front of his computer at the Twilight Club's office, composing a memo to the board members of the Trust. He knew all of them, of course. He'd been one of them until recently.

The memo, still a draft, was now four pages long, and in it Michael detailed his concerns about Roger. He hadn't worded it exactly like that. His subject line stated only *Noted Violations Against Protocol.* In the text of the memo, he'd been careful to mention Roger's name only when necessary, but all of the violations he detailed came under Roger's jurisdiction one way or another. Roger would not be happy.

Michael felt this was something he needed to do. He had beaten himself up about whether he was holding too tight to the Trust, taking retirement too hard. Yet he couldn't ignore the slide he saw the Trust taking. They wouldn't allow him out of the organization altogether, and so if he was still a member—and still standing—he would fight to keep the organization true to what Coleman Kingsley had started.

He read the memo again. Each grievance, in and of itself, didn't necessarily make a case for a major organizational problem, but Michael was convinced that when taken in its entirety, the other members would see that the tide had turned fast and the rapidly rising waters could drown them all.

Michael saved the memo and closed it. He would send it later, after he'd been over it a few more times. He logged on to the Internet using an obscure e-mail account in Mumbai, India, and sent the memo as an attachment to an equally obscure e-mail account in Adelaide, Australia. He then deleted any indication of the e-mails from the computer's hard drive and server. He did the same for the memo, so that the only copy of the memo now existed as the e-mail attachment, waiting for kirkpatrim36770 @adelaide.net.

The intercom on his phone buzzed.

"Boss?" he heard T.R. say.

Michael pushed the button.

T.R. rattled off a list of things they were running low on at the bar—mixers, vodka, cranberry juice.

Michael told him he'd take care of it and punched the intercom off with a smile. He liked when T.R. called him "boss." It made him think he could be happy with a smaller life, one where he was just a small businessman running a small business.

And then an image snagged his mind: T.R. standing at the end of the bar when he was having a drink with Roger. Michael had told Roger at that moment he would help the Trust in any way he could, and what had Roger said in response? Michael rewound the events in his mind, until he recalled Roger's exact words—*I want you to know I respect everything you've done. Your work with the Russians will be your legacy. And you were a big part of Juliet. She's really coming together now.*

What had Roger meant by *she's really coming together now*? Juliet was the code name for the research project that had been going on for decades in Chicago. Was that research completed? Was it operable? If it was, and Roger controlled it, well… A cold knot formed in his gut. Perhaps Roger's words were just an intended dig, designed to remind Michael that he wasn't involved anymore. Roger thought he was being subtle with his barbs, but Michael could read people well. More important, he'd known Roger too long.

So the comment about Juliet was probably something he should simply ignore. And yet something was behind it. And Juliet was entirely too dangerous in the wrong hands. He wondered if Roger would let him near the Chicago research site. If Roger knew Michael could make trouble for him, maybe he'd do a favor for an old friend and let him view the site and the progress. Maybe this would even satisfy Michael's curiosity and let him put the other grievances to rest.

Michael got on the Internet again and sent Roger an e-mail stating that he was coming to Chicago and he wanted to visit Juliet. Michael also said that he was concerned about Juliet but that his worries would be put to rest if he could simply visit her.

Michael called home to check on Kate, who'd still had a slight temperature that morning. She answered groggily, said she was fine and she would call him later.

He hung up the phone, left with a feeling of dread. He needed to soothe his wife—not just her health but her concerns, her suspicions—and then he needed to truly fade into the background of the Trust. And he could only do that if he was satisfied the Trust was in a proper state.

52

Manhattan, New York

Roger read Michael's e-mail once more with a grim, concerned look on his face. Jesus Christ, Waller was pushing it. He was in, he was out, he was back in. Now he wanted to visit Juliet.

Michael's message had initially alarmed Roger, made him want to respond immediately with a conciliatory tone from old instincts and habits. But he checked that.

He typed one word in response: *Denied.*

He was about to hit the Send button, when he thought better of it. The research was proceeding exactly on the course it had been when Michael had been a board member. In fact, it was nearly complete, and the results were those that the Trust had sought all along. The only thing different about the Chicago research now was what Roger planned to do with it.

He erased the e-mail and typed instead,

Juliet looks forward to your visit. I need to visit her myself. Advise when you'll be arriving.

Roger hit the Send button. Perhaps honoring this ridiculous request of Michael's would get him off Roger's back. And what did it really matter anyway? His self-righteous friend would be gone soon enough.

53

Chicago, Illinois

Liza switched the yoga mat to her other arm and looked at her watch. Almost 8:30 p.m. She was one block away from the yoga studio, so she had plenty of time. She yawned. Whose idea was this? What kind of people went to yoga at almost nine at night?

The city was starting to awaken for a summer Thursday night, and groups of people strolled by her on their way to dinner or bars.

A block later, Liza stepped into the yoga studio on Clark Street. She looked around at the requisite hardwood floors and exposed brick, searching for…whom?

A drop like this one was always interesting. Especially when she didn't know who she would get her drop from.

Liza placed her mat toward the back of the studio, but in the center where she could see everyone. There was already one woman at the front—tall and full-hipped with graying curly hair. Liza doubted it was her, but you never knew. She had been surprised many times before. And besides, the drop wouldn't happen until the end of the class. She'd have to suffer through all the *clear your mind and take time to honor yourself* crap.

In the next five minutes, the class filled in—a minuscule blond girl in purple yoga pants, a thirty-something guy in a basketball jersey, a woman with what looked like baby food on her T-shirt and a stern black man carrying a water bottle. Liza tried to meet the eyes of everyone in the class, but people were already dropping to their mats, legs splayed, eyes closed.

Liza finally did the same. For the next hour and a half she tried not to sigh as she contorted herself and tried to *breathe into it.* It wasn't that she couldn't do these poses. On the contrary, she was probably one of the most skilled in the room. She frequently practiced martial arts and yoga poses on her own. What she hated was trying to quiet her mind. Too many thoughts rushed in, too many memories.

Finally, the class was over. Liza rolled up her mat while she waited.

Suddenly, standing next to her, was the tiny blond girl in the purple pants. "Great class, huh?" she said.

"Yeah, not bad," Liza replied.

"I can never do the plank poses right."

Liza didn't reply. *I can never do the plank poses right.* That was the phrase she was waiting for. She studied the girl. She had cornflower-blue eyes, touched lightly with mascara, and a pink blush on her cheeks. She was so young. How did they get them so young? Liza wondered. She felt suddenly ancient. And sad for this girl, who either had no idea what she'd gotten herself into or didn't know yet how greatly it would affect her.

"Well, have a good one," the girl said brightly.

"You, too."

The girl bent down and adjusted her flip-flop, then left. When Liza looked down, there was the tiniest square of white paper lying on the floor next to her rolled mat. She picked it up and pocketed it.

Out on the street, four blocks away, she stepped into an alley and unfolded it. There was one sentence there, a coded instruction. Liza read it.

"Jesus Christ," she said.

54

St. Marabel, Canada

Michael and I got ready for work together in silence. Technically, *finally,* after days and days at home, I was better—my temperature was down, my breathing clean and clear, my cough gone—but the feeling of unease in our house was palpable.

I'd been feigning sleep the last two nights when he'd gotten home, too confused and tired to make small talk. But now I wanted to smooth things over between us. I wanted us to feel like we had when we first got married. That was only three months ago—technically such a short time—and yet the pace of our marriage, the move to St. Marabel and the stress of opening the restaurant had sped up everything.

"How was it with Roger the other night?" I asked now, applying my makeup in the mirror over the bureau instead of in the bathroom like I normally would.

"Fine."

"I'm sorry I missed him."

He cleared his throat. "He said to give you his best."

"How have the numbers at the club been?"

He moved across the bedroom and opened the closet door. It was old and it made a long creak as he did so. "Not bad. Better than I would have predicted before we opened."

I kept asking questions, about T.R. and the jazz band and what the chef's specials had been. He gave me nothing but short answers. When I told him how I'd asked our landlady about the white chips and how she knew nothing about them, he nodded, seeming disinterested. I'd been about to question him further and ask him what he'd done with the chips, but I was tired of the questions.

"I'll be glad to get back to the club," I said, making a last-ditch effort at a connection.

"We'll be glad to have you. T.R. said last night it's not the same without you. He's right."

"Thanks." It was nice to hear such words from my husband, but having spoken them, he turned away again, fastening cuff links and putting on a peach-colored tie.

After a second, Michael turned back to me. "What do you think about a trip to Chicago?"

"Are you serious?"

"We could visit your mom."

"And Liza."

"Yeah, we could take a few days. See your old friends."

I gave him a hug. "Oh, honey, that would be amazing. I was just thinking I needed to get out of here for a bit."

Michael laughed. "It's great to see you excited."

"I am. But what would we do about the restaurant?"

"I'll handle it."

"You're sure?"

"Absolutely. I've got to see some suppliers on the South Side, so we'll make it a business trip, but we'll have some fun, too."

"What suppliers?"

"Glassware, stemware, that kind of thing."

"But the club has all that."

Michael seemed to hesitate for the slightest of seconds. "Some aren't working out like I thought. The stems on the white are too short."

I thought of the white-wine glasses. The stems seemed fine to me. I opened my mouth to say so but then thought better of it. Why protest when a trip home seemed the perfect antidote for our tension?

"Thank you," I said, hugging him again, this time from behind. Our eyes met in the mirror. "It's a wonderful idea."

My husband smiled at me, but the smile seemed not to reach his eyes. I embraced him more tightly. We needed to get out of here. That was all.

55

Chicago, Illinois

Liza and Rich got into the elevator together. They were both late this morning—it was almost ten o'clock—but they just hadn't been able to get out of bed.

She'd known Rich was in town, and after the yoga class last night, after the directive she'd received, Liza had gone home and called him. She had a compulsion to forget her life. To settle into the simplicity of Rich, the utter lack of bullshit.

"Come over," he'd said. "Now. I seriously miss you. In more ways than one."

"I'll bring some clothes for tomorrow."

"Well, I'm taking mine off."

So she'd gone to Rich's place and spent the night in his bed, drinking red wine and having sex and not thinking about the directive she'd received from the yoga girl.

Now, in the elevator, the doors closed, Rich pulled her to him. "Let's take an hour off this afternoon."

She smacked him on the chest. "I'm not leaving work to have a quickie."

"Why not?"

She pushed him away playfully. "I've got stuff to do."

"Like what? You never talk about work."

Let's see, what did she have to do today? Well, she had to make a call to Roger and talk to him about the order he'd given her. The order to kill her best friend's husband.

But she couldn't exactly tell Rich that, could she? Liza squirmed away from him and was relieved when the elevator opened at his floor.

"Call me," he said, getting out. He waved as the door slid shut again, and Liza could feel all the enjoyment in life seeping away, as if he'd taken it with him.

Once in her office, Liza took a seat at her desk and called Roger. "I got your message."

"Good."

"Just so I'm clear. You want me to eliminate a member of the Trust."

"Yes. Michael."

Liza flinched. "Jesus, Roger, if you're just going to say his name, why make me take a yoga class to get the drop?"

"I like to keep you on your toes. Make sure you still know how to do it."

Liza gritted her teeth and said nothing.

"Any problems with your assignment?" Roger said.

"No."

A pause. "I'm surprised."

"Michael's not the man I thought he was."

"How so?"

Liza could hear a salacious edge to Roger's voice.

"Why do *you* want this done?" she asked.

"I don't want to say too much. You know how it is."

Liza said nothing. In the Trust, walls were intentionally erected around missions. It was better if one arm of the organization didn't necessarily know what the other was doing. But of course, this presupposed that the head of the organization—the board—had eyes that saw all and a collective mind that kept the intentions and ethics of the organization constantly within sight.

But Liza had never had a mission to eliminate her best friend's husband. The walls were going to have to come down.

"What do you know about Radimir Trotsky?" she asked Roger.

"I'm not sure what you mean."

"Bullshit. I know who Trotsky really was. What I want to know is whether you guys knew."

Roger paused. "All I'll say is that Michael knew Trotsky's identity the whole time. I found out too late. I tried to stop the hit, but it was already done."

"And when he found out that Aleksei was looking into Trotsky's story?"

"I'm sorry, Liza," Roger said.

Liza felt her anger boil in her brain. Her anger was then replaced with a despondency that she'd put her friend together with someone like Michael.

"He's running loose," Roger said. "He's taking matters into his own hands. He thought Charlie Miller had become ingrained in the Mafiya. He thought he needed to be taken out, and he didn't care that he was CIA."

"Or was Michael protecting a new master? Had he become ingrained in the Mafiya himself?"

Silence, then "I suppose anything is possible."

Liza clenched her fists and looked around for something to punch.

Roger exhaled loudly. "Liza, Michael is bleeding the Trust of everything your father wanted."

Liza almost laughed. She wanted to say, *You're not much better,* but she restrained herself. "Whatever. I just want to protect my friend."

"Glad to hear it."

"I'll schedule a trip to St. Marabel within the next few weeks," she told Roger. "I've been telling them I have to see the restaurant anyway. It will take a while to figure out how to do it." Liza knew poisons were easy to work with, and, if done right, never detected. She could get something into his food during a time when his guard was down. Then she thought of what Kate's face would look like when she found out her husband had died, and Liza dropped her forehead into her free hand, sick with the image.

"That won't be necessary," Roger said. "We just learned Kate and Michael are coming to Chicago."

Liza got a sick feeling as she realized that the Trust had probably "just learned" that information from surveillance in Kate and Michael's apartment.

"Okay, then," she said. "I'll do it here." Taking care of Michael here would certainly be better than in his own home.

"But no, not in Chicago either."

"Getting cold feet, Paul?" Liza said this sarcastically, more for herself than for Roger. She reminded herself to ignore her own worries, her own cold feet. She would eliminate Michael for what he did to Aleksei and for what he could do to Kate in the future. No matter how much it would hurt Kate now.

"You'll be taking care of this in Rio," Roger said.

"Rio?"

"Yes. We're assigning Michael the Gustavo job."

"Michael's going to take out Gustavo at his political rally?"

"That's right."

"And possibly Gustavo's wife and kids, who he'll have surrounding him as shields."

"Also right."

"Why would you ask him to do the Gustavo job? He doesn't have a history with Brazil."

"But he does have a history as our best shot."

Liza knew that was true. In general, the details of each operative's actions for the Trust were kept completely confidential. But reputations surfaced, and Michael was known for two things—one for his hand-to-hand skills, the way he snapped a neck, and the other for being one of the best sharpshooters in the business.

"Still," Liza said, "you've got other people who could do it."

"Yes." Roger paused. "But think of it strategically, my dear."

"Don't call me that."

"We're using this as a tool," Roger said. "We'll tell Michael that this is his last job. We'll tell him he can get out—even leave the Twilight Club."

Liza started to understand. "He'll do one more job for you, so you get Gustavo taken care of. And then I'll take care of Michael."

"Correct."

"And you'll make sure that it's widely known that Michael killed Gustavo."

"Bingo."

"And I'll get the hell out of Rio, but no one will be looking very hard for me, because I was merely the one who killed the assassin."

"Very good."

"But will Michael buy it? No one has ever been let out of the Trust. It's always been the rule."

"Things change. The Trust has changed. Michael knows that. And I'll tell him I pulled some strings because we're friends."

Liza hated Roger suddenly. Really hated him. She wanted Michael dead more than anybody. She wanted to punish him for what he'd done to Aleksei, and she wanted to save her friend whom she'd gotten into this mess. But Roger was scum.

Liza put her telephone headpiece on and stood up. "How does it feel to order the hit of your friend?"

"How will it feel to kill the husband of your friend?"

She was quiet.

"We do what we have to," Roger said. "Don't forget that."

Liza began to pace. "And what am I supposed to do in the meantime?"

"Your job."

"I mean with Kate."

"Keep her in the dark. Just like usual."

56

We flew out of St. Marabel in the early morning and changed planes in Montreal. The minute our plane touched down at Chicago's O'Hare Airport, I felt better. I looked out the window at the rows of terminals, the vast fields of runways. It was all so different from the tiny commuter airport in St. Marabel, which was just fine with me.

I turned to Michael and squeezed his hand. We would enjoy Chicago; we would enjoy each other. Hopefully, the tension, the questions that I had, would simply lift. If not, we'd have time to talk about them, away from the demands of the club and our daily routine in St. Marabel. And by the time we got back there, we'd have the break we needed. We'd be back to *us.*

We took a cab to the Park Hyatt right off Michigan Avenue. Our room overlooked the old Water Tower, one of my favorite sights in Chicago.

"I'll call my mom and Liza and let them know we're here," I said. I unpacked a few light skirts and dresses from my suitcase and hung them in the closet. August in Chicago could be brutally hot and muggy, and I'd packed appropriately.

"Sounds good," Michael called from the bathroom.

Michael was a meticulous packer—all his clothes and belongings in neatly arranged rows—but he unpacked very little. I liked to make a hotel room my home, if only for a few days; Michael liked to take things out of his suitcase only when required, then return them to their places. Except for a few pieces he hung, Michael was always ready to leave again.

I saw Michael pick up a hotel key and his wallet from the desk and slip them into his linen pants. And I heard him say, "I'll be back in an hour or so. I have some quick business to take care of."

I stood there, holding a pair of high-heeled sandals I'd imagined wearing while we lunched at RL across the street. "What business?"

"Just a quick check on an investment I have here."

"What investment?"

Michael waved a hand. "It's not even worth going into. I'll be back soon."

"And then you have to go to the South Side this afternoon, right? To look at the stemware?"

"That's right." Michael looked at his watch. "But I'll come back here first. I should be able to fit it all in."

"Weren't you going to see my mom? I thought we were going to spend some time together." I hated the resentment that crept into my voice.

"We've got a few days."

I turned back to my suitcase. I tossed the sandals back inside. I was getting tired of not understanding what Michael was doing. Was I overly suspicious? Had I been so hurt by Scott that I was distrustful of all men? I hated the unease I felt with Michael lately. I wanted to take responsibility for it and let that unease fly away into Chicago's blustery winds. But he was making it tough.

Michael turned me around and kissed me full on the lips. I threw my arms around him, and let myself get pulled into him. We embraced and kissed, and then began to tug at each other's clothes.

"First things first," I said, leading him to the bed.

He groaned. "I can't." He straightened himself away from me and tucked his shirt back into his pants. "Let me get this business out of the way, then I'm all yours."

I pushed my hair out of my face.

I watched Michael walk away from me. I watched him open the door of the hotel room, and I watched it fall closed behind him with a sharp, definitive click. He'd said, *I'm all yours,* but it sure as hell didn't feel that way.

57

Michael walked from the Park Hyatt to the Newberry Library. He stood for a moment next to one of its soaring stone arches. Despite the heat, he took a moment and stared across the street at Bughouse Square, a small city park with a circular fountain in the middle. Trees hung over the park, and it was dotted with benches and crisscrossed with a few paths.

He knew well the history of Bughouse Square. He knew of the poets and orators that had held court there in the early 1900s; he knew of the revolutionary soapbox speeches given there in the twenties and thirties. Now it was a place where neighborhood residents walked their dogs and students from nearby schools ate their lunches. But Michael remembered the history because Coleman Kingsley had remembered the history. Coleman loved Bughouse. He'd felt the square was symbolic of the best things about America—a place where everyone got their say, where they got to duke it out if they wanted. And so the Newberry Library, next to the square, had been Coleman's place to keep certain Trust documents.

In the days before the proliferation of computers, the Trust had required actual physical storage. They kept coded records of operatives' missions, reviews, and their whereabouts. The keeping of records at the Newberry program had stopped shortly after Coleman's death, so Michael wasn't sure what he was here to look for. This was about Roger, about Michael's need to ensure that Roger was properly running the organization. It was an itch that needed scratching, and Michael had learned from decades in the business that one had to be patient and scratch around a lot of places before such an itch would go away.

Michael turned and walked up the steps of the library, into the marble-laden foyer. He wished he was here with Kate, prowling through the place together, enjoying each other. He'd been distant with her, overwhelmed by his growing premonitions that something was not right with Roger and the Trust. He wished he wasn't so distracted. After years of acting like someone else, he should have been able to fake the part of a happy, contented husband, but that was the thing with Kate—he was simply unable to fake anything with her.

He went to the front desk where a guard sat. "I'd like to inquire about having an event at the library. Do you have private functions here?"

"We do," answered the guard, a young black woman with a broad smile. "Do you have an appointment?"

"No, I just decided to stop in."

"I'll get you Melinda from events planning." The guard turned and picked up the phone.

As he waited, Michael stepped aside and surveyed

the place. Straight ahead of him were white marble stairs leading up to the actual library and staff offices. To his left was a hallway that led to the bathrooms. To his right was a small exhibit hall and beside that a corridor, which led to the grand ballroom. It was in that ballroom Michael needed to be, and he required a few minutes alone. He tapped his foot a little, remembering the other times he'd done this, usually to drop information, oftentimes breaking in after hours. He might have done the same this time, but most security systems were tougher to get around than they used to be. He wondered if anyone from the Trust remembered the Newberry anymore. With Coleman gone, with so many of the other older members gone, Michael might be one of the few.

He slipped his phone out of his jacket pocket and dialed the number of Sebastian Bagley, his favorite Trust backup and the one person in the organization, after Roger, whom he had considered a friend. He hoped he wasn't wrong about that characterization, because he needed a favor from that friend now.

Sebastian grunted a hello.

"It's Andrew. I need a favor," Michael said in a low voice.

"Sure."

"Don't log this call."

"No problem."

"Thanks. Call the Newberry Library in Chicago—" Michael looked at his watch "—in about five minutes. Tell them you have to talk to an events planner immediately. Make something up. Keep her on the phone for at least six."

Sebastian grunted an assent. "How you doing?" he said.

"Fine," Michael said, talking in a normal tone now. He liked how sure he sounded. "I'm fine. And thanks."

As Michael slipped his phone back in his jacket, a young woman in a suit, black hair pulled away from her face, came trotting down the center staircase. She buttoned her suit coat with one hand as she headed toward him, her free hand extended. "Melinda Waterman. Events," she said breathlessly.

He shook her hand. "Andrew Marson. I'm sorry to stop in unannounced."

"Oh, that's no problem. We're just breaking down from a gathering we had upstairs last night." As she said this, she reached behind the desk and grabbed a key ring. She finally stopped and took a noticeable breath. "Okay. So, what kind of event are you looking to have?"

"It's a ground-breaking party for a new building. Probably two to three hundred people."

She nodded and began walking fast down the hall, motioning for him to follow. "Our grand ballroom is the only space we've got that's large enough. It's fantastic, though. Have you seen it?"

"I have. Once or twice. But it's been a long time."

They arrived at the entrance to the ballroom, which Melinda unlocked. Inside, the floor was marble. The walls, which were paneled with rich wood, rose three stories to an exquisitely molded ceiling. Melinda walked him around the ballroom, her heels clicking efficiently.

Five minutes later, her pager went off. She peered at

it and frowned. "I'm sorry. I've got to take a call," she said. "Some kind of emergency."

"Please," Michael said, "go ahead. I'd like to just stand here and get a feel for the room."

"Great, great," Melinda said, clicking away.

When she was gone, Michael walked to the southwest corner of the room. On the wall hung a large painting of two children, a boy and a girl, dressed in Victorian garb and splashing through a puddle in the rain. The painting was done mostly in moody grays and browns with the exception of the children's luminous skin and their bright smiles. Coleman had chosen this painting because he said the evident joy reminded him of his children, and what they brought to his life.

Below the painting was a brass plaque that bore the title—*Bismarck Children*—and below that three lines that read

Oil on Canvas 1877
Charles Talbot Alderson
Gift of Presario Pharmaceuticals

Michael leaned down until his face was close to the plaque. He pressed the letter C on the word *children,* then C on the word *canvas* and finally the C on the word *Charles.* He prayed the thing still worked.

Nothing happened. He raised his finger again and pressed each letter with more insistence this time. Nothing.

"C'mon, you bastard," he muttered.

He pressed the three letters again, slowly and with a good deal of force.

This time the third C depressed, and he heard a distinctive clicking sound. Michael smiled. He watched as all the letters on the plaque became more raised.

Using the letters, he typed the code word. *Honor.*

Another series of clicking sounds. This time, the plaque unlocked at the side like a small door. Michael opened it entirely and reached into the space behind it. He removed a sheaf of documents on coated, corrosion-intercept archival paper, all covered with the tiniest of coded markings.

He was tempted to simply leave with the documents. After all, who but he would recall their presence? Taking them would be the way the younger members of the Trust would do things—certainly Roger—but Michael remembered Coleman, remembered how the Trust was supposed to be run.

A glance at his watch told him he had less than two minutes.

Michael put on an electronic, magnifying eyepiece and quickly searched the documents. He hadn't read encrypted code in such a long time that his brain initially fought the process. He made himself focus and, faster than he would have thought, the skill returned to him. There was too much information here to photograph it all. He searched for Roger's name. When Michael found it on the operative reviews, as well as the logs of operative whereabouts, he removed a miniature monocular camera from his breast pocket and photographed those pages.

As he was sliding the documents back behind the plaque, Michael heard Melinda Waterman approaching.

Michael pushed the plaque back in its place, but it wouldn't close.

"Mr. Marson?" he heard Melinda Waterman say behind him.

He fought the inclination to straighten, no matter how odd his bent form appeared to her. He pushed at the plaque again with his finger, letting his body's memory take over again. The damn thing would not close. The mechanism seemed not to be working.

"Mr. Marson?" she said again.

He pressed the plaque again, and just then the piece made a soft hum and latched into its original place.

Michael stood. "This is such beautiful artwork."

"Isn't it?" she said in a distracted tone. "So what do you think of the place?"

"I like it," Michael said, slipping his hand in his pocket and patting the monocular camera. "I like it a lot."

58

I took a walk down Michigan Avenue, but I only window-shopped. And even then, nothing I saw registered in my mind.

I felt as if I was waiting—waiting to be with Michael so we could stop at a café and have a glass of wine, waiting to be with Liza so we could dash into a boutique and try on shoes that were way too expensive, waiting to be with my mom so we could look for bras and pajamas and all the other staples that she still liked to shop for.

But Michael was at his meeting, and Liza was working and wouldn't be available for a few hours, and my mother had a luncheon and a book club meeting today, and I'd planned to see her tomorrow.

It was hot in Chicago, the sun bright and bordering on blistering. I went back to the hotel and read a book, a paperback about an Indian woman who'd grown up in the United States but whose parents had arranged her marriage at the time of her birth. She was forced to move back to India to marry the man. The author talked of her loneliness, even though she was in India, a country she loved. She talked about her husband and how although she was growing to love him, she rarely understood him.

The book transported me for an hour. I could understand so much of what the author was talking about. I certainly wasn't in an arranged marriage with Michael—but I often felt lonely in St. Marabel, and often I didn't understand my husband.

When Michael walked in, I stood and threw my arms around him. "How was your meeting?"

He embraced me back, tightly. He buried his face in my neck. "Just fine."

"How much time do you have before you need to leave for the South Side?"

He pulled back and looked at me, almost as if he was drawing strength from the sight of my face. Then he looked at his watch. "Enough time to take care of some other business." He slid a hand into the waistband of my cotton skirt and put it on my hipbone.

"You feel so good," he said.

I murmured "yes" in return and put my hands on the side of his face. I closed my eyes and moved to kiss him, but I felt him go still.

I opened my eyes and saw him staring at me with a gaze full of wonder and longing.

"I love you more than I've ever loved anyone," he said, "*anything*."

"I love you too."

We kissed, softly at first, then with more and more intensity, until I couldn't wait any longer and pushed him on the bed.

A few minutes later, something inside me broke

loose as Michael slid into me. The worries and wonderings that had been separating us dissipated. Afterward, we whispered, again, about how much we loved each other, how happy we were to have found one another.

We eventually rose, and he began to get dressed again. I planned to take a quick shower and leave for Liza's apartment to have a drink on her balcony.

"Why don't you give me fifteen minutes to get ready and we can share a cab," I asked Michael. "You can drop me off and take Lake Shore to the South Side."

There was a seemingly infinitesimal hesitation on Michael's part. "Not sure," he said. "I should probably take the Dan Ryan. I'm actually going southwest." He looked at his watch. "And you made me late."

He turned and gave me a kiss. I returned it, but barely.

It wasn't his words that scared me, but the hesitation. A hesitation that seemed to give him the moment he needed to come up with some kind of excuse. I had no idea what he needed an excuse for, but I was left with the distinct impression he wanted to leave me out of his afternoon plans. I sensed it—I had lost him again.

Michael finished dressing. He kissed me again, this time on the cheek. "I'm going to take off. Call and let me know where we're going for dinner."

"Sure," I said. "Good luck at your meeting."

I watched his retreating back. I listened to that door close again. I desperately wanted a shower, but instead I pulled my skirt on, grabbed my purse and followed him.

59

Roger stood in his office at the Trust's Chicago research center. The center was really just a building in what was otherwise a residential neighborhood. At first glance, the center might be another redbrick McMansion, the kind that had been springing up all over the North Side. But it was bigger than the norm, and there were no windows, only strategically placed glass blocks. There were also the odd architectural details like the stone lions at the top corners of the building, which Roger had found in Katmandu. He'd reprimanded Michael about having a personal painting at the Twilight Club, but that was because Michael was a mere operative now, a lowly one at that. The research center, however, was filled both inside and out with Roger's finds, things he'd seen throughout his years of travel and which he'd brought back, slowly and certainly making the research center *his.* Just like he was doing with the Trust.

Roger's office itself was a replica of an office he'd been to once in Santiago, Chile. The office of a man he'd been asked to eliminate. He accomplished his mission. Later, he'd heard the man's office was stripped and completely redone by the greedy son who took over the business, but Roger never forgot that office with its dark paneling and rich carpets. Instead, he'd tracked down much of its original decor.

He walked over those carpets now, and took a seat behind the desk. He picked up his cell phone and dialed.

"Where are you?" he said when Michael answered.

"In a cab. Should reach you shortly." Michael sounded tense.

"Everything all right?"

"Just fine."

Roger smiled. He knew that things were not fine with Michael and the missus. Which was perfect, because Michael seemed to want to do anything to make it work with Kate, to get out of the Trust. And so he would agree to one last job in Rio. And when the Rio job was done, there would be one less member who had strong attachments to the Trust of old.

The new Trust was already starting to shine. After Liza's elimination of Angelo Naponi in Anguilla and Michael's even more stellar dispatch of Charlie Miller, Roger had been able to get the word out about the Trust's new line of service to just the right people. And now he had more offers than ever. Enough offers to make every one of his dreams come true.

But he hadn't come this far to lunge at his opportunities.

Roger swung around and looked at a photo of him and Michael, taken in a pub in Dublin twenty years ago. They were different people then. When Roger first framed that photo and put it on his credenza, he did so because it gave a homey touch to his work environment. He'd never changed the photo or taken it down, even though he no longer needed homey touches. In fact, staring at the photo, it embarrassed him that he'd ever required such a thing.

But the photo would set Michael at ease. And when Michael was gone, he'd break the glass and shred the photo.

"See you soon, friend," Roger said.

60

Michael sat in the back of the cab with his electronic, magnifying eyepiece attached to his head, the cord inserted into his camera. Through the eyepiece, Michael studied the coded documents he'd photographed at the Newberry Library.

It would take him weeks if he carefully read all the information. Instead, Michael focused on any specific mention of Roger.

The first document he found was an abstract written by Coleman Kingsley of a review he'd conducted with Roger Leiland in late April 1985. The words *Highly Classified* were typed at the top, which was slightly different than most operative reviews, which usually stated only *Classified.*

The first line read,

> Deep concern regarding Operative Leiland. Inflated sense of self, as well as role in organization. Continued criticism by operative of organization's methods and beliefs. Suspect inclination to operate solo or in direct opposition to organization's missions. Psychological evaluation requested.

Michael leaned back against the cab seat. He'd heard nothing before about this poor review Roger had received. It wasn't even poor so much as it was alarming. He looked back at the records and found the listing of operative movements to see if there was a record of a psych evaluation being conducted. He found none.

Michael heard the cabdriver grunt, and he looked up. They'd stopped at a light, and the cabbie, a man in his sixties, was studying Michael in the rearview mirror.

"I've got poor vision," Michael said. He pointed at the eyepiece. "This thing helps me read my damn BlackBerry."

"Ah, yeah," the cabbie said. "I've got the same problem. I should get me one of those."

The light changed and the cabbie drove through it, his attention shifting back to the road.

Michael looked briefly at the street. They were at North Avenue and Halsted, only five minutes or so from the Trust's research center. He didn't have enough time to sift through the rest of the records. He shouldn't even be doing it here. But later, he had to spend time with Kate. He *wanted* to.

He had made so many promises to her, and he hated how he'd been failing at them. If he could simply check out Roger sufficiently, if he could send his memo about his concerns to the other board members, he would then be able to make good on those promises to his wife.

Michael focused once more on the documents, reviewing the reports of Roger's whereabouts. He stopped when he noticed a date in May in the mid-80s, about two weeks after the bad review. That day, Roger had been in Evanston, Illinois, at the home of Coleman Kingsley.

Some memory threatened to raise itself in Michael's mind.

He made himself think back to that time. He was living in New York, working as a photographer for an international wire service, a job which afforded him an extraordinary amount of travel as cover for his work with the Trust. He'd visited Chicago often, as well, checking on the research center.

He looked up and saw the cab turning onto Ashland Avenue and then onto Montana, where the research center was located. And right then Michael recalled another time driving through Chicago. A night in May in the mid-80s when he'd told the cab to keep driving up to Evanston and to Coleman Kingsley's house. That night, Coleman had thrown a huge party to commemorate his son, Colby's, graduation from college, an event a man like Coleman, even as private as he was, couldn't help but celebrate. He'd even invited a few high-ranking Trust members who worked in Chicago. Michael remembered the white lights that lit up Coleman's garden, which he'd been so proud of. He remembered Roger being there, too.

And then Michael remembered what happened later.

61

When I followed Michael to the lobby, I saw him disappear through the glass doors. He slipped into a cab on Chicago Avenue. I waited until his cab pulled away, then pushed through the revolving doors and got in the next taxi. I pointed to Michael's cab and asked the driver to follow him. It was the middle of the day, and traffic was relatively light. Michael's cab headed west and then north—nowhere near the South Side, as he'd said.

I followed him down North Avenue then onto Ashland and eventually onto Montana, a mostly residential street. When Michael got out at the end of the block, I told the cabdriver to keep going. As we passed him, I sunk lower in the seat. I turned around and peered through the back window. I saw Michael standing outside a large building, which was unlike the rest of the modest residential houses on the block. The building was made of large red stone and there were stone lion heads at the four corners, their mouths open in midroar, ferocious and silent.

I got out of the cab at the next stop sign, but now Michael was nowhere to be seen. Had he gone into the building? As I got closer to the strange place, I saw that the only windows were on one side, and they were made of milky-glass blocks. Behind the blocks, I could see the blue flicker of TV or computer screens.

I circled the building, noticing it didn't seem to be a public building—no signage of any kind—and yet it was a little too large to be a residence. It took up half the block. There wasn't a front entrance, just a large steel door in the side of the building with no handle on the outside. I peered up at the building, wondering what in the hell Michael was doing.

Just then the steel door slid open and cool air from inside bled into the muggy afternoon. A man stepped out, wearing a navy sport coat and khaki pants, but he had a bouncer feel to him.

He was solid, well over six feet, with blond hair cut close to his head. "Can I help you?" His tone was monotone and cold.

"I'm looking for my husband."

No reaction from the blond guy.

"Michael Waller?" I said.

"There's no one here by that name."

"I think I just saw him. I believe he's visiting someone."

"There's no one here by that name. You'll have to move on."

It wasn't a suggestion, it was an order. But I wasn't in the mood for orders.

I put my hand on my hip. I thought about the camouflage passport Michael had from British Honduras. "I'm actually looking for Andrew Marson."

Finally, a reaction. His eyes flicked around my face. He stepped away from the open steel door. "Step inside."

62

After idle talk in Roger's office at the center, Michael reminded Roger why he was here—to check on the status of Project Juliet. A minute later, he was following Roger into the OR of the research center. It wasn't really an operating room, at least in the sense that no one was actually operated on here, but it had all the trappings of an OR—sterile surgical table, overhead visionary lights, instrument trays, continuous-flow anesthesia machine, gas cylinders, ventilator—the works.

Of those components, the anesthesia equipment was most important for this particular research. Michael was as intrigued by the progress as he was interested in tracking Roger's actions. Michael's job for years had been to oversee the growth of this project, and like a parent whose child is all grown up, Michael felt pride. He still cared.

"It's pretty much ready to go," Roger said, walking ahead of Michael into the room.

Roger, being an M.D., had been the lead Trust member on-site for the research, but Michael had been assigned to supervise it all. That was the way the Trust worked—checks and balances. Or at least that was how it used to work, and it was how Michael was determined to operate now, even though he no longer had an official role in this process.

"How's the reversibility?" Michael asked.

"Great. We've finally got the component to mimic desflurane in terms of fat solubility but it acts like propofol or ketamine times one hundred," Roger said.

"What's the next step?" Michael said.

"More testing. You know how it goes. But I'd say we'll be ready to roll with it within months."

Michael nodded again. He wished he could be more pleased about the research, but the problem was it could be a disaster in the wrong hands. Could Roger be trusted with the research, with the Trust?

"We've got someone who's under right now," Roger said. "Want to see her?"

"Absolutely."

Roger pushed the surgical table out of the way. He walked to an intercom on a far wall and pushed a button. "Bring her in."

A minute later, the silver swinging doors on the left side of the OR opened and a gurney was wheeled into the room and under the lights.

On the table was a woman in her early twenties, covered by a white sheet, which matched the pale of her skin. An elasticized cap hid the dark hair Michael knew she had. As a recent board member, he knew most of the operatives.

Her name was Yonat, an Israeli name. In fact, Yonat was born in Israel as an only child and moved to the United States with her parents who died within years of their emigration. She was raised by different foster families. She'd fought to get her United States citizenship and ended up at Harvard where she got a degree in microbiology. The degree was a key part of why the Trust considered approaching her, but it was her surprising antiwar, pro-American campus activities that sealed the deal. Yonat was now a Trust operative, and she'd signed up to be a research subject for Project Juliet.

Project Juliet, named after *Romeo and Juliet,* was what the Trust had been working on all along—a long-acting, time-released drug that killed someone, or at least made it look as if they'd died. The drug forced the system to zero, but then started it back up and kept the person in an incredibly deep coma.

The drug was actually a combination of drugs—potassium chloride, scopolamine, atropine and a high-dose barbiturate, among others. The drugs were delivered in sequence. First, the subject was knocked out and their heart stopped for a short period of time. Their unconsciousness was then maintained, while their reticular-activating system was controlled and a cerebral protective effect achieved.

For the initial period after the drugs were administrated, the person had a flatline EKG, fixed and dilated pupils and no heartbeat, but they would suffer no compromise of brain function. Following that period, the time-released drugs awakened the person's system, but kept them in a deep coma while the drug was in their system. Or, in other words, until the Trust wanted them to wake up.

The research had been started by the Trust because it met the organization's vow of minimal collateral damage and the goal of harming only those who needed to be harmed. Sometimes the Trust determined that a person needed simple protection from others who wanted to kill them. The Juliet drug could make it look as if they'd died. The person could then be brought back to life when it was safe and given a new identity with no one the wiser.

"How many half lives of the drug does it take until the patient emerges?" Michael asked Roger.

"We've been working with three."

"And which part of the sequence releases the monoclonal antibody to target the RAS-inducing coma?"

He watched Roger closely as he answered. Michael recalled every detail of the research, and he wanted even more specifics now. He wanted to see if Roger tripped up on anything, if it appeared that he had taken the research in a different direction or was using it to his own advantage.

The danger of the drug in the wrong hands was great. It could be used, for example, to make a terrorist on a most wanted list appear as if he'd died. Such a terrorist would have the drug administered, and everyone would think him dead. They would breathe a sigh of relief and cross another bad guy off the list. His colleagues would cremate a different body or bury the body in a pressurized coffin to keep him alive. And then they'd dig him up and reverse the drug. They would give him an assumed identity and he'd be back in business, without anyone having a clue.

As Michael continued his questions, Roger gave only detailed, thoughtful responses without a trace of the condescension he'd been recently doling out. Which made Michael suspicious.

He kept seeing the coded documents he'd taken from the Newberry, and kept thinking about that night at Coleman Kingsley's house.

It was also the night Coleman's son, Colby, died.

The fact that Roger was at the party wasn't what was bothering Michael. After all, he'd been there that night, too. What made him pensive was Coleman's concerned review of Roger, combined with a memory of a recent conversation he'd had with Roger.

It had been opening night at the Twilight Club when Roger phoned from Korea to put Michael in his place. Michael had mentioned Coleman Kingsley, and Roger had said that Coleman wasn't all-powerful. He said that Coleman had "caved" after Colby died. That was true, Michael knew. Coleman had lost his spark, his drive. He'd slowly let others take over the organization, and then a few years later, he'd had a stroke, which doctors said had been brought on by stress as much as carotid-artery blockage.

Michael had asked Roger during that conversation if he wouldn't respond the same way Coleman had if his only son died.

Roger said no without hesitation.

And then he said the words Michael now kept hearing in his head—*I had a feeling Coleman wouldn't be able to handle it. And he didn't. He wasn't as tough as you thought.*

63

I followed the blond guy into a room behind the steel door—a black-painted foyer with a grated metal floor.

"So where is…Andrew?" I said, glancing around, wondering what I'd just walked into.

"Wait here," the guy said.

He turned and slid open an internal steel door, its appearance the same as the one behind me, and walked through it.

I watched the door slide shut, and I felt like an animal about to be caught in a trap. When the door was nearly closed, I leaped forward, putting my sandaled toe right at the end, stopping it. My heart was racing. On the other side, I could hear nothing. The blond guy seemed to have disappeared. Frozen, with my foot in the door's groove, I looked around the foyer. There was nowhere to sit and nothing to look at except a lone oil painting on one wall—a vivid surrealist image of a woman's face, her eyes bulging and stacked one on top of another, her nose and lips in profile.

Soon, I thought, Michael will appear and have some story for me about how this is a restaurant-supply business. I stared at the disjointed painting of the woman's face, feeling utterly disjointed myself. I felt cut off from the person I'd been in my youth, the person I'd been during my marriage to Scott, the person I'd been during my divorce, the person I'd been when I first met Michael. Who was I now? And why did it have so much to do with the damn men in my life? How was it that *they* had defined my adulthood?

Instead of waiting, I turned and pushed at the internal door, stepping through it.

Inside was a dark, plush hallway with zebra-skin carpet runners. Silence. No sign of anyone. I had no idea where to go, or even what I wanted, except answers.

I headed left, toward the back of the building, and tried the first door I came to. Locked. Same with the next one. I kept on down the hallway, my shoes not making a sound. At the next door, the knob turned easily. The door swung open, revealing a tastefully appointed office with dark paneling and decorated with a desk, wood chairs, a lamp made of elephant tusk, thick carpets and tribal-like paintings on the wall. I looked down the hallway. No one. No sounds.

I stepped inside and closed the door behind me. I padded over the carpet to the desk. There were no papers there, no materials that gave away the kind of business conducted.

I spied a photo on the top shelf of the credenza behind the desk, and breathed deeply with relief. It was a photo of Roger and Michael, their faces more youthful than now, their arms slung around each other, mugs of beer in their hands. I realized that this was Roger's house. Or maybe his office. I knew little about Roger's work. Michael had only said that he dealt with vitamin supplements for Presario. This was probably where he ran his operation, and Michael had simply stopped in to see him.

But then again, Michael had mentioned that Roger spent most of his time in New York. And why hadn't the man outside, who appeared to be a guard, recognized Michael's name? Why had he only responded to the name Andrew Marson?

I looked around the study some more. Finally, I left and continued down the hallway. At the end, I stopped before a swinging door. Unlike the steel doors in the foyer, these were made of metal, split in the middle and surrounded with white rubber.

"Where are you, Andrew Marson?" I whispered. I took a breath for bravery and pushed through the doors.

But they only led to another hallway, this one with gray tile floors and white walls. The look had shifted from one of pampered, exotic elegance to a hospital-like environment.

At the end of the hallway, I reached another set of swinging, hospital-like doors. I pushed through them into what seemed to be an operating room, filled with medical equipment. But the lights were only dimly lit, giving the place a creepy feel.

In the center of the room, on a gurney, was a woman, clearly unconscious. A white sheet covered her. Standing next to the woman were Roger and the blond guy.

On the other side of the bed was Michael.

They all looked at me. Michael's face registered

shock, then slid into an expression I'd never seen before—horror.

"Get her out of here," Roger said without any other greeting.

I didn't have to be asked. That look of Michael's had terrified me, as much as his looming presence over an unconscious woman. I bolted from the room and down the hallway. I hit the swinging doors open and ran back down the carpeted hall, through the metal door and finally into the foyer. But the door to the outside was locked.

I pushed at it frantically, trying to force it open.

"C'mon! C'mon!" I said, scared at the desperation of my own voice.

An alarm sounded—long, piercing, threatening tones—and a jolt went through my body. I kept pushing at the door, trying to get out. What was going on here? What was Michael involved with? I heard the thumping of footsteps in the hallway. Finally, I looked up and saw an automatic lock, high on the door, a foot above my head. I jumped up to grab it and missed.

I heard yelling from the hallway and footfalls just outside.

I jumped again and—thank God—I managed to move the lock to the right.

I pulled the door open and ran outside into the hot August afternoon.

64

"Kate!" I heard behind me. Michael's voice. I ran from it. I had no idea what Michael was doing, or even who he was, I only knew with a deep certainty that I had to get away from him.

When I reached Fullerton, I turned and sprinted east toward the lake. My sandals cut into the top of my foot and made my ankles wobble, but I kept going. I waved a frenzied hand at one cab, then another. They both breezed by.

"Oh, God, please," I whispered.

"Kate, just stop," I heard from behind me. I turned to see Michael trotting toward me in a jog, slowing now that he'd seen me. His face looked contorted—with confusion, with alarm?

I froze a moment. *Who are you?*

I turned back toward the street and saw a taxi with its light on. I waved at it, and the cab screeched to a halt.

I dived into the back seat. "Go!" I yelled to the driver. "Please go!"

Through the open window, I heard Michael yell, "Kate!"

But the cab sped away, and I didn't look back.

In the taxi, I tried to control my racing heart, my racing thoughts. What were Michael and Roger doing back there? Why hadn't I simply stayed and asked them? But there was something terrifying about the cold way Roger had said, *Get her out of here,* and then there were all the unexplained pieces with Michael. He was involved with something beyond the restaurant business, clearly, but I didn't trust him to tell me what it was.

"Where to?" the cabdriver said.

"Can you drive east, please? I need a minute."

I took my cell phone out of my purse and dialed the number of the person I always called when my world fell to pieces. Liza. "Can you leave work?"

"I'm done for the day," she said. "I was just about to call you."

"Can we meet at your house?"

"Sure, or we can get a glass of wine somewhere, maybe sit outside on Rush Street or—"

"Liza, I can't deal with a restaurant right now. Can we go to your place?" I didn't think Michael knew where Liza lived, but even if he did, she had a team of doormen to stop unwanted visitors.

"Of course. What's up?"

"It's Michael."

There was a long pause.

"Liza?" I said.

"Where to?" the cabdriver called to me through the divider. I heard annoyance in his voice.

"Liza," I said again.

"Yeah, yeah. Meet me at my place."

I closed my cell phone and gave the driver Liza's address on Lake Shore Drive.

65

Liza paced her apartment, waiting for Kate, wishing for something to do. The cleaning lady had been there earlier, so her hardwood floors gleamed and her windows sparkled and there wasn't even an old water glass to put away.

She went into her kitchen and took an Asian pear from the fridge. She cut with precision through its brown skin and into its ivory center, but once sliced, the pear had no appeal for her. She couldn't stomach anything.

She told herself that Kate and Michael probably just had a simple fight, a basic marital squabble. But the thought of them, of Michael, of what he'd done to Aleksei and of what Liza had gotten her friend into, made her anxious beyond measure.

The phone rang. It was the doorman announcing Kate. A minute later, Kate was knocking on her door. She was wearing a white skirt and a pair of sandals that wrapped around her ankles—breezy summer clothes—but her blond hair was limp and pushed haphazardly behind her ears. Her brown eyes were strained.

"Are you okay?" Liza asked.

Kate stepped inside and hugged her.

Liza thought of all the times they'd hugged like this—after breakups and family tragedies and just because they hadn't seen each other in a while. Kate was the kind of friend Liza had never had before, the kind she would probably never get again.

"Are you all right?" Liza led Kate into the apartment. "Let me get you something to drink."

"I'm fine." Kate sat on one of the stools near Liza's black granite countertop. "I need to know what you know about Michael."

Liza had just opened the fridge. She froze, staring at two other pears, sitting on a white plate, the rest of the shelf bare. "What do you mean?"

"Who is he? I mean, what is he involved with? He's not just a restaurateur."

Liza closed the refrigerator, and her eyes shot around the kitchen, looking for bugs. Of course, she wouldn't see them—the Trust was better than that—and she'd agreed to intermittent surveillance in her own house, like every member of the Trust. She usually didn't even sweep, since she never had visitors and rarely talked on the phone, or did anything else of note in her apartment.

If there were bugs right now, and if Kate seemed to be catching on to Trust business, Kate could be in even more danger than Liza had thought. She could be eliminated.

"Kate," Liza said, interrupting her, "we should enjoy the weather. Let's go outside." She knew from past sweeps of her apartment that they never planted bugs on the balcony, and even if they did, the noise from Lake Shore Drive would mask most sounds.

Kate shook her head. "It's hot as hell out there, and I don't care about the weather."

But Liza touched her arm and steered her through the kitchen and living room and out onto the balcony. She had no table or chairs. She closed the sliding doors. Her eyes shot around the doorjamb. She turned and ran her hand discreetly under the railing. Nothing.

Finally, Liza leaned back on the railing. "Tell me about Michael."

Kate sighed, her eyes filled with tears. "I don't know what's going on with him, but something is off. He's into something. *Something.* It's so vague and bizarre I don't know how to describe it."

"Just try."

Liza listened for the next five minutes as Kate told her again about the two passports she'd found. She listened to her talk about how Michael protected the private rooms at the club with such ferocity, how she'd found the white chips on the windowsills at their place in St. Marabel and how she'd followed him today to a place on Montana Avenue, where she'd found Michael and Roger standing over an unconscious woman on a hospital bed.

When she'd finished her tale, Kate took a breath. She fixed Liza with a gaze that was unflinching. "Liza, what do you know about Michael?"

"I told you. We used to work together and—"

"What did your father say about him?"

"What?" Liza said, surprised.

"Michael knew your father."

"That's right." Liza stopped her words, unwilling to fill in any blanks for Kate. It was for her own good.

"They worked at Presario together."

"Yes."

"So what do you know about him? And Roger! I mean, what in the hell are they doing in that place, with this woman out cold?" Kate ran a hand through her hair, her face anguished.

"I don't know." Liza was relieved to be able to say this honestly. She knew there was a research center somewhere in Chicago, but since it wasn't part of her work for the Trust, she had no idea what went on there.

"Goddamnit!" Kate's voice was a loud scrape that cut through the gusty winds and the sounds of traffic. "I want some answers! I'm married to someone I don't know. I'm not an idiot!"

Liza's mind scrambled. She was used to calmly coming up with plausible bullshit that sounded like absolute fact, but not when it came to Kate.

The sliding door opened, and Kate jumped. Liza's hand instinctively shot to her hip, but she wasn't armed.

"Ladies," Michael said, stepping onto the balcony.

66

Liza stared at Michael with undisguised hatred. She gave him a warning look, then reached forward and put a protective hand on Kate's arm. Surprisingly, Kate squared herself toward her husband, as if now that she'd spoken to Liza she was ready to confront him.

"What in the hell is with you, Michael?" Kate yelled. "Who in the hell are you?"

Michael glanced at Liza. She shot him a look that said, *You're on your own.*

"Baby, I've got to tell you something," Michael said.

He took a step toward Kate, who didn't move. Instead, she put her hands on her hips.

"I'm part of an organization..." Michael said.

Liza felt her eyes narrow. What was he doing?

"It's called the Trust," he said.

"Michael, stop!" It was Liza who was yelling now.

Kate's head swung back and forth between the two of them. Liza felt the stillness of her friend, afraid to ask, afraid to even remind them she was present. Liza knew that stillness. She'd used it often in the field.

Michael took a step toward Kate. "I'm not sure how to explain it."

"It's a pharmaceutical group," Liza said.

"No, it's not." Michael said. His eyes still didn't move from his wife's face. "It's a private organization designed to protect the interests of the U.S. I'm an operative."

"I don't understand," Kate said.

"I'll explain. I'll explain everything." Michael's voice was tender, his gaze not wavering from his wife.

"The hell you will," Liza said.

She took a step toward him, but right then her cell phone, which was attached by a clip to her jeans, beeped, the tone telling her there was a phone call from a board member of the Trust.

Michael heard it, too.

Both of their eyes darted around. Had she been wrong about no bugs on the balcony? Jesus, if the Trust was listening they were all dead.

She grabbed the phone off her clip. "Yes."

"Hello, Liza." It was Roger Leiland.

67

Liza gave Michael a look, this time pleading with her eyes for him to stop. She opened the sliding door, stepped inside her apartment and closed it behind her.

"I'm here," she said.

"We've got problems," Roger said.

Liza stared through the glass at Michael and Kate. Michael had begun to speak again, the idiot. She frantically waved a hand at him to stop, but he was focused on Kate.

"Go ahead," she said to Roger.

"Michael was at the research center today."

"Okay."

"And Kate stopped by."

Liza stayed silent.

"Somehow she got let inside the lobby by a security member who is no longer with us. And she went snooping around. She walked in on Michael and me."

For the first time, Liza sensed that Roger had no idea Michael and Kate were with her right now. If he knew, he wouldn't be telling her all this.

"I hope you had the sense to zip your pants up," she

said. It was crude but Roger liked that. And right now she very much wanted Roger to like her.

Outside, Michael had his hand on Kate's arm and was talking to her. Kate was motionless. Liza had to get off the damn phone and stop whatever was happening.

Roger didn't respond to her sarcastic humor. "Do you know where Kate is?"

Liza's eyes looked to the heavens, and she said a silent prayer of thanks to every god who might be out there. "No."

"Well, she took off before we could stop her. Michael ran after her. We didn't get a tail on either of them."

"So what can I do for you?"

"We can handle this quite well on our own."

Liza felt a chill run through her body.

"I just wanted to give you a courtesy call," Roger said. "To let you know that it appears Kate is a problem that might need resolving."

"No."

"She walked into the research center."

"But did she really see anything?"

"She saw enough. Nothing that will make sense to that sweet little brain of hers, but still."

Liza felt the situation slipping through her grasp. Outside, Michael was still talking to Kate, who was now rubbing her forehead and shaking her head back and forth. "Look, we're taking care of Michael, right?" she said.

"Yes. Gustavo's rally in Rio is imminent."

"And as soon as Michael is gone, Kate's life will crash around her." Liza closed her eyes tightly, and despite the nonchalance of her words, she felt a stab of pain to her heart on Kate's behalf. She would take pleasure in getting rid of Michael, in paying him back for what he did to Aleksei. She'd be relieved to get him out of Kate's life. She knew Kate would be ruined, but she also knew she could recover. Her friend was tougher than anyone suspected, even Kate herself.

"Your point?" Roger said.

"When Michael is gone, Kate will go back to her old life. Michael will give her a plausible explanation now about the research center, and when he's gone, she won't give it another thought."

Roger said nothing.

"Kate is not a problem," Liza said.

"As long as Michael doesn't tell her anything."

"He never would." As Liza said the words, she looked through the sliding glass doors and saw Michael's lips moving faster than ever.

68

One week later
St. Marabel, Canada

"Morning, Kate," Michael said as I walked into the kitchen at 8:00 a.m.

He had always been an earlier riser than I. Before all this. Before I knew about the Trust. Before I knew that my husband and best friend were often required to kill people for a living. But now I felt Michael was getting up even earlier, talking to me for the benefit of bugs that were probably in our house, trying to make us seem as if we were an everyday couple.

"Good morning."

I stopped and looked at him, but his face made me so incredibly sad. God, how I'd loved that face. I'd loved the lines at the corners of his eyes. I'd loved his tanned brown skin that always smelled like the sun. I'd loved the dark freckle by the left corner of his mouth, that mouth I had planned on kissing for the remaining decades of my life. And now? Now, what would happen to us? What would happen to me?

I had known before, but never truly realized, that the person you marry defines you. You become, for better or worse, a part of your spouse's life, and whether you like it or not, that world they live in becomes partly your world. After college, I'd carved out my own life—living in a loft apartment in the West Loop, working at an accounting consulting firm during the day and tending bar at the Red Lion Pub on Lincoln Avenue, in the evenings.

Then I ran into Scott at our high-school reunion, and I fell in love. We got married, and soon I was living in the suburbs, going to barbecues with Scott's friends, whom I didn't particularly like, working for the medical-supply firm that was located in a strip mall. My life had become Scott's.

And similarly, when I married Michael, I'd adopted his world. I threw it around me like a cloak.

Had Scott's life changed so much when he'd married me? Had Michael's? It didn't seem so. Was it just because I was a woman? Or was it me—was I somehow weak and easy to draw in, eager to toss off one life and try on the next? I had to admit, I liked that process. I liked the thought that a new life might be waiting for me right around the corner.

Except now, I was terrified I'd run through all my lives. If I'd known that busting into that operating room could put Michael and Liza and me at risk, I'd happily return to the way we'd been, even if that meant wondering about my husband, always feeling unsure.

That afternoon on the balcony, I could barely understand what Michael was saying—his explanation about the Trust and his job within it. And then Liza came back outside. She threw Michael a murderous look. Michael ignored her, and in a flat tone informed her exactly what he'd told me about. I watched Liza listen and process his words. I thought of how she'd told me she'd known Michael through work, and in that instant it clicked.

"*You,*" I said to her.

She stared at me, her eyes scared.

"You're a part of this, too?"

Her silence was answer enough. I was stunned beyond words, beyond feeling.

It all came out then—how Liza's father started the Trust, how he'd pulled her in after college. Michael filled me in on his own background with the Trust. The story came out in bits and pieces, some of it told that afternoon on Liza's balcony, some as we walked back to the hotel. And then the pretending had started. I had to pretend not to know—I had to pretend in the hotel room, and on the plane on the way back to St. Marabel, and at our apartment and the Twilight Club.

Now, every day, I ran through a cauldron of emotions—incredibly pissed off, deeply heartbroken and scared. Very, very scared.

I went to the cupboard and pulled out a coffee mug. I was aware of every sound—the click of the cupboard opening, the scrape of the mug being pulled off the shelf, the tinier click when I closed the door. I imagined how all these noises sounded to the Trust. Michael had said the bugging was intermittent, as were the times the audio surveillance was actually reviewed. It was simply a random way to control the operatives, to remind them that the Trust was always there. Well, it was working, because I couldn't forget.

"Croissant?" Michael gestured to the table where he'd placed a plate of croissants. I'd loved those too when I first moved to St. Marabel.

"No, but thank you." I tried to keep my tone neutral, light even.

"Green apple?" He gestured to another plate.

I was angry that we had to perform like this. And yet what choice did I have? I had to act like I didn't know I could be killed. Liza and Michael and I could *all* be killed. They'd explained this on the balcony that day—explained that Michael and I had to return to our life in St. Marabel and act as if it was just like we'd left it.

I walked to the table and picked up a slice of apple. I bit into it, making sure to make a distinct snapping sound, my eyes squarely on Michael's. He had meticulously searched our place for cameras, which were not supposed to be used, but he had to check. Luckily there were none, and so I felt free now to stare down my husband.

Michael was not a man who winced, but he closed his eyes briefly, then opened them again. I wondered if he was losing patience with me. I'd been a good actor this week, at least with my words. I let Michael engage me in conversation, and I made it sound like I knew nothing. I talked like a dumb, happy wife who'd been sufficiently soothed. And yet there was no way Michael could mistake my withering looks, my turned back in our bed.

Our bed. The thought made me shudder. All the

times, the *wonderful,* delightful, sensual times we'd had sex in that bed, not to mention the other places in the house—the couch in the living room, against the door frame, on this very kitchen table—and all the while someone might have been listening to us.

That he hadn't told me was unbelievable, I'd said to Michael yesterday, quite possibly unforgivable.

Would you have married me if I'd told you? Michael had asked.

Of course not.

We were on one of our walks through St. Marabel. I now understood why Michael always wanted to walk when we had personal discussions—so that no one could listen. Sex, on the other hand, was something that was hard to take outside on a regular basis.

Michael had stopped me. We were at the top of a windy bluff, the town below us, tiny and quaint, no one else around. He gave me that look—that calm yet intense look that let me know he knew me, saw me—and he said that when he met me he'd adored me. He *had* to be with me. For the first time in decades, he'd loved someone more than his work, more than himself.

I shook my head, not knowing how to respond. Because those were the very reasons I'd fallen in love with him. His feelings for me were nice to hear, I had to admit, after everything.

"I'm leaving for the office soon," Michael said in the kitchen now. "Come with me?"

"I need a shower first. I'll meet you there. You don't mind, do you?"

Our eyes locked.

"Of course not," Michael said. He stood and kissed me on the cheek. "I'll see you at the club."

"Great, I'll see you there."

At work, I'd been putting up a good front, too. I had to. I now knew the club was a meeting place for the Trust, and I couldn't help but wonder which of my patrons were members. Which were watching.

As he turned to leave, the phone rang. We both looked at it.

I answered.

"Kate, it's Liza," I heard.

"Hey, Liza."

She'd called a few times since Michael and I had returned to St. Marabel. Of course, she couldn't say anything on the phone about the Trust, but she'd been trying to have normal conversations like we used to. I hadn't been able to keep up that part of the front. It was exhausting enough—terrifying enough—to do so with Michael, always wondering if I was somehow letting on that I knew. But strangely, I wasn't pissed off at Liza the way I was at Michael. Not really. I was more hurt than anything that I'd been left out of something so big in her life.

But why had she introduced me to Michael? I hadn't been able to ask her this question for fear our conversation was being taped, but Michael had said he thought she'd imagined we'd just go on a date or two. I remembered Liza saying this at our wedding, and truth was, Michael and I had thought as much ourselves.

The other truth was that I had no idea how to relate to Liza anymore. It was hard to relate to either my best friend or my husband, knowing each had killed more than a few people, even though they believed these killings were required and deserved.

"How are things?" Liza asked.

"Fine. Good. Same. I'll call you later, all right?"

"Sure. Talk to you later."

When I hung up, Michael squeezed me hard around the middle. I hugged him back, missing him, missing Liza. And very much afraid that I wouldn't be around to see how this all worked out.

69

Michael sat in his office, spinning his chair from left to right and back again. He wasn't usually a restless person. He was usually focused, usually intent on whatever he was doing. The problem was he had no idea what he was doing anymore.

He made himself stop the swinging motion and rubbed his eyes. He was exhausted. More exhausted than he could ever remember. It was the worry over Kate that kept him awake nights, the worry of whether he'd done the right thing by telling her. On one hand, his confession was born of a desire to share all—to *share everything*—with his wife. He wanted to be whole with her. He wanted no secrets. Wasn't that kind of honesty—that full-blown, it-ain't-pretty truth-telling—what supposedly made a relationship great? And was it so awful that he wanted it for him and for Kate? He didn't think so, and he knew he would lose her if they didn't have that, and so he'd rushed forward at Liza's place and told her everything. The words had felt so good as they'd spilled from his mouth.

But the disappointment on Kate's face had been a

deep, deep blow. And he was plagued now with how selfish his act had been. He'd put Kate's life on the line for the sake of the intimacy he'd always craved.

His phone buzzed. Michael could see it was a call from the upstairs bar. Probably T.R. opening up for the day and needing beverage naps or red wine.

"Yes," he said, picking it up.

"You've got a visitor, boss," T.R. said.

Michael felt a cold fear in his gut. "Who is it?"

"Sebastian Bagley."

Michael smiled. "Send him down."

A moment later, Sebastian's balding, bespectacled face poked into his office. "A man of leisure," he said, glancing around the place.

"Bagley, you didn't let me know you were coming," Michael said as he stood and shook his friend's hand. Michael waved him toward a chair and took a seat behind his desk again.

"They just told me yesterday."

Sebastian sat down. He wore a green blazer over a white shirt that had distinct fold marks. Michael knew Sebastian liked to stay "home" at the Trust's Seattle office, providing intel and tech support around the world, although with his level of knowledge and rank in the Trust, that wasn't always possible. "They want me to present to some Kiwis," he said.

Michael nodded. He knew a few New Zealand members of the Trust were in town; they'd be having dinner tonight in the wine cellar. "What's the topic?"

Sebastian squirmed in his seat. "Not supposed to say anything to you."

Michael swallowed.

"I mean, you're pretty much out, right?" Sebastian said.

Michael relaxed his throat. But he knew Sebastian remembered well when he was a vital member. When he was a board member. He hoped Sebastian kept remembering that, and the friendship they'd shared because it had just dawned on him how Sebastian might be able to help him.

Michael stood. "Let me show you around."

He led Sebastian around the club; he gave him the usual tour. Then he led him out back to where the river gurgled and ran its twisting course around the old mill, where he was sure no external bugs could pick up anything.

He stopped for a second and looked at his old friend. "You wired?"

Sebastian shook his head.

Still. He took a tiny sweeping device from his jacket pocket. "Do you mind?"

Sebastian, like Michael, had lived most of his life in the Trust. "Have at it."

Michael ran the small wand over Sebastian, then for good measure, in case someone had planted something on him, over himself. He tucked it back in his pocket.

"Do you remember Coleman's son, Colby?" Michael asked without preamble.

He had been studying the documents he'd found at the Newberry Library, particularly Coleman's review of Roger. He'd been making himself analyze everything about Roger, about the Trust, about the history of the Trust. And that always led him back to Coleman Kingsley and the words Roger had spoken about his decline—*I had a feeling Coleman wouldn't be able to handle it. And he didn't. He wasn't as tough as you thought.*

"I never met Colby," Sebastian said. "I came on after he died. I only met the old man once."

Michael nodded. "Well, the guy who ran him off the road—his name was Howard Neville—he was drunk as hell. They convicted him of with reckless homicide and sent him away for twenty years. He got out after thirteen."

Sebastian nodded. If he thought this conversation was an odd one, he didn't let on.

"I've been trying to find the guy," Michael said, "but since they turned him loose, there's been no trace of him. I would look some more, but I'm having some… personal problems."

Again, Sebastian showed no surprise, no emotion. He adjusted his copper-wire glasses. "You want me to find him?"

Michael nodded. "I would appreciate it."

"You got it," Sebastian said.

70

As soon as Sebastian left, the phone rang.

"It's me," he heard when he answered it. Roger.

Michael cleared his throat. "How's it going?"

"I think I'd better ask you that question. Have you been able to give your wife a sufficient explanation for what she saw?"

"Of course. I told her it was a research project for Presario."

"She buy it?"

"Yes, as I'm sure you know." Michael left it unsaid that the Trust had been listening in his home.

"Things sound fine," Roger said. "I hope it stays that way. I'd hate to have to do something about it."

Michael filled his lungs with air, right down to the lower lobes, then exhaled that air, without making a sound. He was glad Roger wasn't in front of him. He would kill the son of a bitch himself. He was sick of these threats.

"Look, buddy," Roger said when Michael still hadn't responded. "I feel for you."

"I'm sure you do." Michael made his tone even.

"And I want to help you out. Seriously. So I've got a job for you."

A *job* was Trust jargon for an elimination.

"I don't do that anymore," Michael said. "As you've pointed out numerous times."

"We need the sharpest shot. We need you. You do this and you're done. Really done."

"Don't fuck with me."

"I'm not. I've talked about it to the board, and everyone is in agreement. You will be out."

"That's not how we do things."

"It is now."

Michael paused. Was there a chance this was true? He hated how the Trust was being run, but possibly this new way of doing things could work to his advantage.

"Where's the job?"

"Rio."

"Gustavo de Jardim?"

"Yep. He's appearing at a political rally. Thinks he might make a run for president."

"And?"

"*And,*" Roger continued, "Gustavo is a cancer. If elected, Gustavo will control Brazil's oil and their production of jets. We have intel that shows he's been in negotiations with two terrorist cells to peddle those jets. You know as well as I do what they'll do with those planes."

"Stuff them full of explosives and run them at a U.S. target."

"Precisely."

"Which cells?"

Roger filled him in on the details. Michael felt the

wheels of his mind moving like it used to, and he asked question after question. And despite himself, Michael felt an excitement. It was a big job, the type he used to get all the time. Gustavo's corruption was well known. During his prior political gigs, he'd taken money from the hands of the poor and sick and put it in his own pocket. And now this new intel. Gustavo needed to be taken out for the good of the United States. This was the type of mission that the Trust used to be all about.

Then he remembered something. "Doesn't Gustavo always keep his family around him in public?"

"Yes."

Silence. Michael processed what this meant. The potential sacrifice of Gustavo's family in order to take him out. This was *not* how the Trust had always worked.

"I don't like it," Michael said.

"I'm not asking if you like it. I'm asking if you want it. And I'm telling you you're out after this. Isn't *that* what you want?"

Of course it was. But there was Kate. He'd told her he was already out. And yet this might be the way to ensure that. To solidify that. To be gone for good.

"How do you want it done?"

"Remember the San Francisco job?"

"The sniper cam?" Michael leaned back in his chair and thought about it.

Eight years ago, the Trust had determined that a member of the Russian Mafiya, operating in San Francisco, had to be eliminated. It was impossible to get close to the guy, but they knew he'd been asked to attend a San Francisco 49ers football game and sit on the fifty-yard line. Michael was outfitted with what they called a "sniper camera," which was essentially a camera with a long telephoto lens that had a sniper rifle built into it. The inspiration for the gun was, ironically, what the Russians called FotoSnaiper. FotoSnaiper was a high-range camera mounted on a base that looked like a gun. The camera was used by the Red Army during World War II to spot the Germans' weapons placements. It was Michael's idea to turn the concept around and make a rifle that looked like a camera. Its gun-stock base could be pulled down from the camera and twisted into place when necessary.

He'd gone to the football game, and used the telephoto lens to find his target, a tiny man named Mikhail Kurchenko, who was flanked by bodyguards. Michael spent most of the second quarter seemingly snapping photos of the game, hitting the button that made photographic clicking sounds. When a San Francisco wide receiver caught a pass in the end zone, the crowd leaped to their feet. Michael stood with them, training the camera back on Kurchenko and positioning the gun base into place. The man never showed emotion, and this was no exception. He watched the touchdown with a look of bored calm. Michael trained the sniper cam on his forehead and pulled the trigger. Between the silence and the roar of the crowd, no one heard or noticed a thing. Across the stadium, Kurchenko went down. Michael twisted the rifle base back inside the camera, let the camera hang on the strap around his neck and left the stadium.

"It might work again," Michael said now.

"You'll make it work."

"How do I know this will be the last one?" he asked. "That I'll be done?"

"I'll personally ensure it. You'll leave from Rio. You decide where you'll go and who you'll be. We won't follow, and we won't look. Ever."

Michael didn't trust Roger. Not anymore. Certainly not with his new suspicions about Colby Kingsley. He would still look into that, regardless of whether he was in or out. He had to for Coleman. But the fact was, he'd been considering a disappearance for years. He didn't know if his plans were foolproof but it was time to find out.

"When's the job?"

"Gustavo's got the rally in one week."

"Kate goes to Rio, too."

"You'll both be in the clear." Then they could both disappear. "Like I said, we won't follow you."

Silence.

"Will you do it?" Roger asked.

"I'm in," Michael said.

71

Ten minutes after Kate was scheduled to work, Michael left his office and walked to the bar. He had the sense of tiptoeing around his wife, as if she was a trip wire that could set off a chain of explosives.

Kate was tying her bar apron around her waist when he came in. She looked up and stopped when she saw him. She smiled a sad smile, then she looked down and kept tying.

He walked around the bar and came up behind her. T.R. was blessedly gone for the moment. Michael wrapped his arms around his wife from behind. She froze, as if he might harm her, and that hesitation made him feel as if the explosives had just gone off.

"It's okay," he whispered in her ear, and he felt himself stir as he did so. She smelled so goddamn good.

"It's going to be okay," he whispered again.

She relaxed, letting herself fall back into him.

She covered her eyes with her hand, and he knew she was close to tears. He couldn't let her fall apart, but he had to touch her, and right now. He had to let her know they'd get through this.

He had told her about the four hidden cameras installed in the bar area. He turned her away from them now. “I *love* you,” he said. “So. Much.”

She made the smallest of sounds.

“I won’t give you up,” he whispered. “I can’t. I’m going to fight for us, and I want you to fight for us too.”

She spun to face him. Her expression was a gorgeous muddle of fear and love and something new—a look of determination.

She embraced him tightly. At first, he felt only relief, but then he noticed her embrace was determined too.

And now she was whispering, intensely, in his ear. “I love *you,* Michael. And what I’m doing right now *is* fighting. I am fighting with everything I have. Don’t forget that. And don’t make me fight too long.”

He moved his head back and looked at her, both surprised and relieved by her ferocity.

He heard someone’s throat clear.

“Excuse me,” Sebastian said.

Michael reluctantly pulled away. “You haven’t met my wife. Kate, this is Sebastian Bagley, an old friend who’s in town.”

She hesitated, and he could see her registering the term “old friend.”

“Nice to meet you,” she said, shaking Sebastian’s hand over the bar.

“You, too. Can I talk to you for a second, Michael?”

Michael squeezed Kate’s hip, and made his way around the bar.

"Someplace quiet?" Sebastian said.

He led Sebastian out to the river's edge again. It was muggy now in the late afternoon, and Michael felt impatient.

"What's going on?" he asked.

"I checked into that Howard Neville guy."

"Already?"

"Yeah, I had a few hours."

"Did you find anything?"

"Depends on what you're looking for. The guy has had an interesting life since prison."

"How so?"

"Lives the high life. Spends a lot of time in Maine."

"Maine?"

"Yeah, some town near Bar Harbor. And I mean a wealthy town. *Lots* of money there—filled with Rockefellers and that type."

"And he's got money? He's not just working as a handyman or something?" Michael remembered hearing little about Howard Neville at the time of the accident except that he was a local carpenter. Definitely not a money man. In fact, he remembered Coleman saying that the guy couldn't even afford a lawyer. He'd gotten a public defender to plea-bargain for him.

"He's not working at all," Sebastian said, adjusting his copper glasses. "He's got a huge house on the Atlantic, and he's playing a hell of a lot of golf."

Michael felt a plummeting of his insides. "So where did Neville get the money?"

"That I couldn't find out."

"Shit," Michael said. "Somebody paid him off."

Sebastian's brows knit together. "To do what?"

Michael said nothing. He thought he knew the answer but he would have to do some digging to make sure.

72

I greeted the two women sitting at the bar. Both appeared to be in their early sixties, both dressed expensively but stylishly. One wore white slacks and a blue-and-white striped shirt. The other wore a Pucci-printed sundress. I put cocktail napkins in front of them and inquired about their drink orders. They asked for sauvignon blanc. While I opened the bottle, I listened to their conversation, something about how happy they were to be off the boat for the evening.

I wouldn't normally have eavesdropped. I was usually friendly and interested in my patrons, but I made sure to give them privacy. Now I wondered if these women were members of the Trust. I wondered that about everyone.

"Oops, sorry, Kate," T.R. said as he accidentally sloshed water from the glasses he was carrying to the bar.

I moved aside and gave him a polite smile. Michael had said that T.R. wasn't part of the Trust, that he didn't know anything about it, but I was still cautious around him now. The knowledge of the Trust had made me hyperaware of everything I said, everything I saw.

Michael came inside the bar and gestured for me to come toward him.

I gave him a questioning look.

He gestured again. Worry tweaked at my brain and grasped at my insides. What now?

I set glasses in front of the women and poured their wine. I crossed the room to Michael.

"Can you come outside?" he asked.

I followed him across the back lawn. The air was still and hot around us. In the distance I heard laughter from vacationers strolling by the front of the inn. When we got to the river, he stopped and put a hand on my shoulder.

"I'm getting tired of having all my conversations outside," I said, giving a weak grin. "What is it?"

"I have to go out of town."

"Why?"

Michael swallowed hard. "I don't want to say."

I opened my mouth. I wanted to scream at him. I reined it in, just in case someone was watching. I glanced around, paranoid.

Then I leaned in and said, "No more secrets. No more."

"It's not a secret. I'm just checking out a hunch I've got."

"Does this have to do with the Trust?"

He paused. "In a way."

"Where are you going?"

"Maine. Then I'm coming back, and we're going to Rio."

"Okay, let's take these one at a time."

He shook his head. He seemed unable to speak.

"What? God, just tell me."

"I don't want to, Kate. I don't want you to get upset, and I know I've brought you into all this, but I'm afraid the more I tell you, the more danger you could be in."

"I'm *already* upset, and I'm losing my damn patience. Remember ten minutes ago when you told me to fight for us?"

He nodded.

"I'm asking you to do the same. And the only way to do that is for you to be honest with me. And by the way, it's already dangerous."

He nodded again. "Maine is some surveillance. Like I said, following up on a hunch. I'll explain more if it materializes into anything." He caught my look. "I swear. Now, Rio? Rio is a job."

"A job," I repeated. I knew what that meant. I'd asked for it, but now I could barely believe I was having this conversation.

Michael closed his eyes tightly for a moment. Then he began to speak. He told me about Rio, about Luiz Gustavo de Jardim. I thought I could handle it at first, but then he came to the part about how Gustavo often kept his family around him, making them act, essentially, as shields.

I was so shocked I couldn't respond at first.

"You'll come with me," he said. "This is going to be my last job, and we'll leave from there. If you'll do it, I mean. We'll disappear."

"Wait a minute. You want me to come to Rio with you, and you want me to watch while you kill someone and maybe his wife and kids, too?"

"Of course not, you won't be there."

"I'll be where? Sitting at the hotel while this goes on?"

"You'll be somewhere safe."

"This is crazy. Am I supposed to see my mom ever again, or my friends?"

"Not at first. Not for a while. I'm still working out the details."

"This is fucked up."

"Call it what you will, but it's my ticket out of the Trust, Kate, and I can't exist without you."

I looked at that face and thought about how he made me feel—cherished, adored, worth something, worth everything. Michael was willing to put his life behind him for me, for us. Strangely, I thought I could do it too. I loved him that much. But I couldn't handle the way the job in Rio was supposed to be carried out, and I told him that.

"I'm doing this," he said. "I'm getting us out."

"Michael, I don't want to be a lifelong fugitive. I can live with the Trust. We can stay at the Twilight Club. What I can't live with is you hurting those people."

"Look, there's a chance I can get a shot off without hurting them. And if I don't, someone else will. Seriously, this *will* happen. The only difference is if *I* do it, we're gone. Together. I'll be free of the Trust."

I watched my husband's determined expression. He was working hard to do what he thought was best.

It was time I did the same.

"Fine," I said. "I'll go."

73

Northeast Harbor, Maine

Michael entered the Docksider restaurant, which, with its wood planking, resembled a boat. He slid into one of the booths and ordered a lobster roll while he waited for his phone call.

When his food was delivered, he bit into the bun and into the fresh lobster salad inside. A meal like this reminded him of his parents—both gone now—and the summers they used to spend in Bar Harbor. His father used to dare him to eat lobster ice cream from the shop in town, and he would do it, even though it tasted awful, because he did just about anything his father dared him to. There were more pleasant memories, though, of strolling the main street with his mother and whiling away an afternoon on a hammock overlooking the Atlantic.

His phone rang, and he put aside the memories as he answered it.

"Found him," Sebastian said. "He's on the golf course. Just teed off, so you should have some time."

Michael thanked him, paid his lunch bill and got

back in his rented SUV. He drove along Sargeant Drive, wishing he could bring Kate here to enjoy the twists and turns of the road, the way the Sound looked cobalt blue.

Following the directions he'd received from Sebastian earlier, he pulled in to a driveway and drove its long tree-lined curves. When he reached the house—a log and stone cabin that was rented out weekly and that he'd learned was vacated yesterday—he stopped. A new family would arrive tomorrow, but for now this cabin was empty.

To double-check, Michael knocked on the front door, waited a few minutes and knocked again. When there was no answer, he went to the SUV and opened the back. He changed into shorts, a T-shirt and water shoes. He clipped his equipment belt on his waist and checked that everything was in place. Then he extracted his rented kayak and oar, lifted both over his head and headed around the cabin to Somes Sound, where he put the kayak in the water and began to paddle.

The water was cool and blue and deceptively still. Michael checked his watch. He had a few hours before high tide.

A fast, whistling wind whipped into the sound, and Michael's body tensed. He knew that winds like this could envelop the area and dash the kayak on the granite embankments if he wasn't careful. He paddled farther toward the middle of the sound, no longer hearing his breath over the gusts.

He paddled steadily for five minutes, glancing toward the shoreline, decorated with ferns and shaded with tall pines. He counted the houses until he reached the one owned by Howard Neville.

If Michael was a man prone to showing surprise, his eyes would have grown big. Neville's house was even larger than Sebastian had led him to believe, rising high above the sound. The shingles on the house were weathered to an elegant gray and a wraparound porch clung to the length of the place.

Michael kept paddling past the house. He beached the kayak and stowed it behind a rocky outcropping, then made his way through the thicket of pines toward Neville's house. When he arrived there, he set himself up behind six feet of overgrown shrubs where he had a good view of Neville's porch. And he waited.

Five hours later, at six o'clock, Michael had scarcely moved from his crouched position behind the shrubs. His knees and hips ached, and yet he loved the stillness of his body, the focus of his mind.

When a door to the back porch opened, Michael didn't move even though he knew he couldn't be seen. He watched as a short man dressed in yellow slacks and a white golf shirt came outside. The man walked to the railing, a highball in his hand. He set it on the railing and looked out over the water.

Straight off the golf course, Michael thought. He envied the man his leisurely posture. But Michael was about to change that.

Careful not to make a sound, Michael reached into one of the pockets on his belt and pulled out a retractable telescope. He raised it to his face and trained it on the face of the man he assumed was Howard Neville. He wanted to see what he was dealing with before he approached.

Through the scope, Michael could see that the man was about ten years his senior and had dark gray hair, deeply parted and combed to the side. He was clean shaven and tan. He looked, Michael assumed, like most of the men also on the local golf course today—patrician and made of money. But how many of those men had spent thirteen years at Stateville prison in Joliet, Ilinois?

He thought about how to approach Neville. His preliminary plan was to pretend he was a neighbor, out for a stroll; but since arriving, Michael could see that the homes were far apart for a reason and the undergrowth thick. No one would simply come ambling through.

The hell with it, he thought. He'd show himself and talk to Neville and find out what he could about Colby's accident.

But first, Michael watched as Neville raised the glass to his mouth and took another sip of his drink. He dragged the scope up and down Neville's body, checking for weapons. It didn't appear there were any. He brought the scope back up to Neville's face one last time. At that moment, Neville turned in Michael's direction, although he was still looking at the water. And it was then Michael felt a twinge of familiarity.

He refocused the scope, going in for an even closer look. The guy's chin was off center, as if someone had socked him in the jaw and physically moved it. As he stared at that feature, Michael felt the familiarity increase. Why did he have the strong feeling he'd met this man?

He probed his brain, frustrated with how it didn't sort

as fast as it used to. Or maybe it was simply that he'd done too much, met too many people.

He let his mind travel back through decades, through missions, through cities and countries and aliases. There was something about Neville that made him think of the earlier days of the Trust, when Michael was starting to call the shots, but before he was a board member. Finally he recalled something—he had worked with this guy. But in what capacity?

A recollection of an operation in Chicago came to him—a very lengthy operation, dealing with a local politician. He and Roger were working together on that one, Michael remembered as a zing of warning sent itself through his body. They'd needed to hire a free-lance guy to handle surveillance. Howard Neville had been that guy. Only Roger and Michael had met him. They tried to keep face time as minimal as possible, especially with freelancers. Which meant that Coleman Kingsley had never met Neville.

Michael thought about calling Sebastian and setting him on the case again and asking him to find out what what had happened to the freelancer. But his usual patience had thinned over the last few weeks. He wanted answers. Now.

Michael stood then, in full view, and Neville's gaze turned his way. Neville took his hand away from his drink and shielded his eyes from the setting sun, then he stiffened.

Michael walked through the yard, neither of them saying a word. Michael readied himself to hit the deck if Neville produced a weapon.

But Neville did nothing of the sort. He stood stock-still, watching Michael approach.

When Michael reached him, Neville said, "I've been wondering when someone was going to visit."

74

"You ran the car off the road. You killed a twenty-one-year-old kid. And you went to prison for *thirteen* years," Michael said. "All for a paycheck?"

He was standing on the porch now, a few feet away from the man.

Neville gestured toward his house. "It was a big paycheck."

Michael remembered more about Neville now. The guy went by Bradley Pello back in those days, and he was callous and cruel, but he was also efficient and closemouthed and very skilled, three things the Trust prized in freelancers. Michael and Roger had used aliases, so Bradley Pello hadn't even known who had hired him to watch and report on the politician in Chicago, and he hadn't cared. He was purely out for the top dollar.

"And after the job in Chicago was closed, Paul Costa retained your services with regard to Colby Kingsley," Michael said, using Roger's most oft-used alias.

Neville didn't say anything. They both knew the silence was an acknowledgment.

This was exactly what Michael had feared.

Roger, whom he'd once thought of as his best friend, had hired someone to run Colby Kingsley's car off the road and into a ravine near Lake Forest, Illinois, where Colby was heading to a party after his own. To survive such an accident would have been nearly impossible, and that was exactly what Roger had counted on. To cause an accident like that, and to get the car to plunge down the ravine in exactly the right deep spot, would have taken skill. So Roger had hired Neville for the job, hoping Colby's death would weaken Coleman, and would lessen Coleman's hold on the Trust so Roger could step in. Roger had gotten exactly what he wanted.

Michael felt like telling Neville he was a fucking son of a bitch for taking the life of someone's son, but hadn't Michael done the same? Maybe he'd had better reasons—reasons he believed in—and he wasn't just out for cash, but knowing they had this similarity, Michael found it hard to throw stones.

"I've never had an interrogation go this easily," Michael said with a wry voice.

"Sometimes you want to confess your sins," Neville said. He shrugged. "I'll deny it later."

"What if I'm wired?"

"Ever heard of double jeopardy? I already went down for that kid. You can't get me again."

Michael recognized the truth of the man's words. He felt a weight he hadn't known before and a despondency that was hard to grasp around the edges.

He thought of how Roger had lost Marta in Rio so many years ago. He'd known exactly how horrible and gut-wrenching such a loss was, and that was precisely why he'd killed Colby. And if he'd done such a thing so many years before, what was he capable of doing now? The potential was devastating.

Michael turned without a word and went down the steps. He retrieved the kayak, put it in the water and he left, using fierce oar strokes that cut through the water like a blade.

75

Lyons, Illinois

Liza stared at the rounded head of the target and pressed her cheek on the stock of her shotgun.

In her imagination, she painted the target with Michael's brown hair and elegant jawline. She widened her stance, stared at what was, in her mind, Michael Waller. She pulled the trigger. A single black circle appeared at what would have been his shoulder. Not exactly what she was aiming at. More practice was needed.

She hit the button to reset the automated target and waited. This wasn't the kind of weapon she'd be using in Rio, but it was still morning and she'd rented the public range for the day. She would practice with .22 rifles, 300 Win Mags, 9 mm handguns and single-action revolvers. But she always started with her Caesar Guerini Magnus Jaspe. She loved the glossy chrome barrels and the wood side plates that were marbled with light and dark woods. Her father had also had a Caesar Guerini, and after he'd brought her into the Trust, he'd given her this one.

A new target appeared. Liza tucked the butt of the shotgun in the crook of her shoulder and pressed her cheek against it, firing at the target. In only a few days, she would leave for Rio. Michael would be posing as a photographer covering Gustavo's rally. Fake press credentials had already been issued for him under the name of a freelance photographer specializing in political figures. Michael would use the sniper cam to take out Gustavo, and quite possibly a few of his family members. An escape route had been planned. Only, Michael wouldn't get a chance to use it.

Liza's own sniper rifle would be focused on Michael, and the minute his job was done, he would go down. Her escape route involved spending two days in a safe house in Rio. Then she would be back to the States, where her main job would be comforting her bereaved best friend.

At the thought of Kate's pain, Liza felt a wave of despair. What was she doing? She couldn't let herself think about the grief Kate would suffer. Taking Michael was revenge for Aleksei, but more importantly it was for Kate's benefit.

She inserted new shells into her Caesar and pressed the cool wood to her cheek. She fired, then again. Both shots hit the target precisely where she wanted—at the heart.

Her heart was taking a beating, too. She pressed her hand to her chest, made herself breathe. How had her life come to this?

She unloaded the shotgun and laid it aside with the breach open. She took her cell phone out of her bag and dialed Rich's number.

"Just who I was hoping would call," he said, picking up immediately.

She smiled. "When are you back in town?"

"I have a deposition tomorrow afternoon."

"Can I see you tomorrow night?"

She hoped she didn't sound needy. But she *was* needy, and she was tired of hiding that. Rich was someone to whom she could finally, once again, show her softer side.

He barely paused. "Absolutely."

"Meet you at your place at eight?"

"Done. And Liza?"

"Yeah?"

"I'm really glad you called."

Liza hung up the phone, the smile still on her face, a giddiness inside that made her feel sixteen again.

Then a grim frown replaced her smile as she looked at the target. Using her mind's eye, she filled it again with the details of Michael's face. She reloaded the shells, snapped the breach into place and lifted the shotgun once more.

76

Manhattan, New York

Roger Leiland sat in a boardroom at the Trust's midtown office. At exactly 10:30 a.m., a knock came from outside and the door opened.

"Hello, Angus, you're on time."

Angus Laslow nodded and smirked. "Of course."

Roger waved a hand at the table. Angus sat to his right and leaned back, crossing his legs. He said nothing and seemed entirely content to wait for Roger to speak, even though Roger knew Angus was probably thrilled. It wasn't often that young operatives met on a one-on-one basis with a Trust board member. But then they'd had a few of these meetings since Roger had asked Angus to work on a private matter for him.

"I've got another job for you," Roger said.

Angus nodded again, but there was no smirk this time. Roger could almost feel the man's pulse quickening. Angus was extensively trained and had handled more than a few eliminations, but Roger had asked him to spend some time at the Twilight Club. He wanted an inside man there to keep tabs on Michael, but he knew Angus was growing bored there.

"You're going to Rio for a job," Roger said.

Angus's head kept bobbing. He was champing at the bit. Unlike people like Michael and Liza, Angus enjoyed killing. He didn't need a patriotic reason or a grand motivation. Exactly the kind of operative Roger needed to take the Trust forward.

"My mark?" Angus asked.

Roger folded his hands on the table. "Liza Kingsley."

"Got it."

If Angus had a guilty conscience about being ordered to take out a member of the Trust, a very well-known one, Angus didn't show it. In fact, Roger suspected the guy probably had a hard-on under the conference table. He was a killing machine. The first time he'd realized this was when Angus had mercilessly turned a knife on the mother of a Mexican he was surveying. Michael had wanted to take Angus out of the field, but Roger saw Angus's potential. He'd had to watch the guy, of course. If Angus was supposed to take out a mark, there was a good chance the guy's wife or girlfriend would go with him. Angus seemed to have a thing for hurting women. But Roger felt this trait was worth the risk. He wanted either cool assassins or guys who loved the sport of it, not tortured spies.

The fact that Coleman Kingsley's own daughter would have one job before she died—killing Michael—was beautiful. She'd agreed because she was driven by her own grand motivations—her belief that Michael had killed a CIA agent and then killed Aleksei to cover it up.

Roger had been having Liza closely watched, and while he had no indication that she did anything outside the bounds of her orders, Roger knew that Liza, like Michael, was anxious about the direction of the Trust. And because her father had started the whole thing, she'd never sit back and let it happen. His only regret was that he'd never get to enjoy that delicious body of hers. But then that's what ten-thousand-dollar call girls were for.

"How do you want it to go down?" Angus asked.

"Luiz Gustavo de Jardim is having a rally. Michael will take him out. Liza will take out Michael."

"And I'll take out Liza," Angus said. "And get the hell out of there."

"Precisely."

"My cover?"

"Rio police uniform. There's going to be hundreds of them on duty. Ostensibly, you'll be going after the assassins who took out Gustavo. You'll be able to get out of there easily. Just brush up on your Portuguese."

"Not a problem." Angus stood up. "Anything else?"

Roger thought about the one loose thread—Kate. She wanted so desperately to be a good little wife that she did whatever Michael told her, believed whatever idiocies came from his mouth. And when he died? She'd melt like an ice cube in the sun. She'd go crawling back to her mama in suburbia.

But just in case, he briefed Angus on Kate. "If she's a problem—" he snapped his fingers "—get rid of her."

Then Roger stood. "I think we've taken care of everything."

77

St. Marabel, Canada

Michael and I stood under an awning at a busy café. The early lunch crowd clanged their silverware and talked loudly. The energy of the coming weekend was in the air.

Michael had flown back from Maine that morning and had arrived with a haunted, drawn look. I knew better than to ask while we were in the house, and with the busyness of the restaurant, I hadn't got the chance after that. Now, a day later, he led me outside and to a spot near this café. I felt an impending doom, a stark contrast to the café's vigor, and yet I couldn't imagine how things would get worse.

"What happened in Maine?" I asked.

He blinked a few times. "Remember when Liza's brother, Colby, died?"

"Colby?" I said when I finally found my voice. "What does he have to do with anything?"

Michael started talking, and suddenly the noise from the café receded and all I could hear were his words.

Horrible words. Someone pushed past me on the way out of the café. I jumped at the physical contact and spun around.

An elderly man smiled benignly and apologized in French.

Michael stopped, and we both watched the man amble down the street leaning on a cane.

"Come with me," Michael said. He led me into the cobblestone alley and took a keychain bugscanner from his pocket. He swept it over me, then himself. Both of our eyes trailed it, watching the tiny light, wondering if it would turn from green to red.

Finally, Michael lowered it. "It's okay," he said.

Then he began talking again. But nothing was okay.

I told Michael I needed to be alone, and I walked aimlessly around St. Marabel. I had hours before I needed to be at the club for work, but it would take me much longer than that to get my head around what Michael had told me in the cobblestone alley.

Colby had been killed. Roger had ordered someone to drive his car off the road. And all on the off chance Mr. Kingsley would react badly and slacken his hold on the reins of the Trust. Who *were* these people who could be so careless with others' lives? Who was I to be even peripherally involved with them?

I'd wanted to tell Liza about Colby immediately. She deserved to know. But Michael made me promise I wouldn't until after Rio. We'd get word to Liza somehow that we were gone, we'd tell her about Colby, and we'd let her decide for herself how to handle it.

I promised Michael I'd go along with his plan, but I was making my own plans, too.

I was part of Michael's world now. Liza's world, as well. I knew about the Trust. I knew about what Michael had agreed to do in Rio, and I couldn't live with the fact that there was a good possibility he would have to kill Gustavo's family.

I turned a corner onto an avenue populated with charming old apartment buildings, many hidden by willows and other drooping, vibrantly green trees. I let my mind spin around my problem—how was I, someone with no skills at espionage—supposed to stop an assassination attempt by one of the best—my husband? It was almost ludicrous to think I would even try, and yet I had to figure something out, because I'd seen the determination in Michael's eyes. I heard the steeliness in his voice. He was going to do this in order to help us disappear, and if he didn't, someone else would perform the hit. But I wouldn't be able to live with him if he did it. Or if I just stood by.

I kept walking. I let my mind spill and tumble, letting my shock of the situation mix with possible solutions and worries. As I got to the end of the block, I saw a guy I recognized coming toward me. It was Angus, who worked part-time at the Twilight Club. I'd never quite been able to figure out what Angus did. Now I knew he was probably a member of the Trust, and being alone with him on the quiet street gave me a blast of apprehension.

Angus hadn't seen me yet. He was lifting up the bottom of his shirt to wipe sweat from his brow. He'd clearly been jogging and was slowing to a walk. It was hard not to notice, even in this anxious moment, that he had a great body—pecs that were perfectly muscled, abs that looked like they were cut from clay, and a scar on the lower right side of his ribs that looked like a triangle.

I stared at that scar, and my brain began firing off connections, warnings.

Angus lowered his shirt and saw me. “Hello, Kate,” he called.

I raised my hand and waved.

He kept walking, right down the sidewalk, right toward me.

He was tall, taller than I’d ever noticed at the restaurant, and as he came closer that height made me feel shrunken. And very defenseless.

I stepped aside to move around him, but he moved the same way. I tried to move back the other way and in my haste, I stumbled. Angus grabbed me.

“Don’t!” I said, my heart pounding.

“Whoa,” he said, taking his hands away and holding them up as if he was surrendering. “It looked like you were going to fall there.”

“I’m fine.” But I could feel my body trembling.

Talk like you normally would. “How’s it going, Angus?” I said. “Working today?”

“Heading out of town, actually.”

“Okay, well, enjoy.” I started walking again. I had to get away.

“Thanks. Good to see you,” he said. “And say hi to Michael.”

I walked slowly until I hit the corner a block from the apartment. I turned and glanced back. Angus was gone.

When I reached our place, Michael was sitting at the kitchen table, looking at nothing, doing nothing.

Our eyes met as I came inside.

"What?" Michael mouthed to me.

I shook my head. I picked up the phone and dialed Liza's work number. "Hey, Liza, how are you?" I said when she answered.

"No," mouthed Michael. *"No."* He must have thought I was going to tell her about Colby.

"Okay," she said.

"Hey, I just realized I have something to do. Can I call you back in ten minutes?" We both knew I was referring to the safe phone in St. Marabel—a pay phone at the back of the meat market. Michael had bought me a generic, international calling card so I could phone Liza there. Unfortunately, I hadn't been carrying the card around with me and needed to come home to retrieve it. I wanted to make sure Liza would be available by the time I got there.

"Definitely," Liza said.

Michael stood and held me by the shoulders when I hung up. "Don't, Kate," he whispered in my ear. "Do not tell her about Colby. Not yet."

I pulled back and gazed at him, then stood on my toes and whispered, "Trust me."

I went to our room and found the calling card.

I walked the three blocks to the meat market and said a polite hello to the men in aprons behind the old-fashioned display case made of red metal and glass.

I went to the pay phone at the left side of the store and dialed Liza's number. "Are we okay to talk?" I said when she answered.

"Hold on." A pause, then, "We're good."

"Do you have a picture of Rich you can send me?"

"What?" This was probably the last topic Liza expected me to raise.

"You know, a photo, like one you take from your phone or something?"

"Yeah. It's pathetic, but I took one of him when he was asleep. I just like to look at it when he's not around, you know?"

"Sure, sure. Can you send it to me?"

A pause. "Why?"

"Can you just e-mail it to me? Right now?"

Michael had told me that the Trust might be reviewing my e-mail, at least the address that I'd always used. He told me that in case I needed to e-mail anything private, I should go to the library, use a public computer and take out another e-mail address. When he said "private" he was really just referring to talks with my mom. He knew how uncomfortable I was with the surveillance, even if the e-mail surveyed was one discussing my mother's new landscaping. I'd gone to the library that same day and gotten a new e-mail address, which I rattled off now to Liza.

I walked to the library and gave my card, showing that I was a resident of St. Marabel. I'd never felt more like a foreigner.

The computer section was in the back, and occupied only by a kid who looked about thirteen. I sat at the farthest monitor away from him.

I clicked on the Internet and logged on to my e-mail.

78

Four days later
Rio de Janeiro, Brazil

I walked through the Parque da Cidade barely able to breathe through the huge ball of anxiety in my chest. After the bustle of arriving in Rio, the confusion of not knowing the language, and the stress of what was about to happen, this park in the middle of the city could have been a respite. There were acres and acres of green grass. The lawn was striped with trails, sprinkled with exotic trees and dotted with small lakes. But nothing could pacify me now. Nothing could hide me.

In fact, the Parque da Cidade was a hard place for anyone to hide, which was exactly why Luiz Gustavo de Jardim had chosen this place, Michael had explained. Normally, a politician might hold a rally in a famous *largo* or square, but such places were surrounded with buildings where someone could conceal themselves on a high floor, take a shot at Gustavo and get out fast.

Here, the only building was an old two-story home, now the Museu Histórico da Cidade, at the end of a garden. As I walked across the lawn, the museum came into view. It reminded me of an old New Orleans house with its yellow-painted stucco walls and a high balcony surrounded by black wrought iron. Banners of purple and gold, bearing Gustavo's name, hung from the balcony and rooftop. Similar banners were carried by Gustavo's supporters, starting to stream across the lawn. On the right side of the *museu,* a band was assembling. Next to that, a small bleacher for VPs. On the opposite side of the *museu,* the press corps was gathering—journalists, TV reporters, photographers. Michael was in that bunch, I knew.

I looked up at the sky and said a silent prayer, something I hadn't done since I was ten.

The rally would start soon.

Within forty-five minutes, the park was crowded. The eight-piece band, its members wearing casual, white clothes, played upbeat tunes heavy on the percussion. The bleachers were filled with men and women dressed in suits. Loyal followers of Gustavo's knotted in front of the museum, occasionally glancing up at the balcony, waiting for him to appear. Behind them, where I stood, other Brazilians filed in. Some stood with their arms crossed, ready to listen, while others chatted in Portuguese with friends and appeared to be there simply for the show. The press faced the museum now, poised with notepads, recorders and cameras.

I moved through the casual observers and wedged my way into a group of Gustavo supporters, right in front of the museum. My heart banged louder than the band's drums. It was a beautiful eighty-degree day, the sun bright overhead, but I was sweating as if it were a hundred degrees. I'd worn a dress I'd bought when we arrived last night—one that was a bright pink and that couldn't be missed in the crowd.

I let my eyes roam over the press corps, and I easily found Michael at the edge of the group. He was dressed in a white T-shirt with a khaki photographer's vest over it. The vest's pockets bulged with lenses and extra film. He blended in perfectly, yet he stood absolutely still. He held a camera with a long telephoto lens in his right hand, his eyes trained up at the balcony.

I turned and glanced around the park. Rio's police, dressed in short-sleeved black uniforms, were prowling the perimeter, mixing in with the crowd. A line of officers also stood in front of the museum, barring any entrance. Gustavo's security detail held posts at the corners of the balcony.

The band ended its number and suddenly began drumming with insistence. The drumming became louder and louder, and immediately Gustavo's followers sprang to life—shouting, clapping, hoisting their signs.

A large, smiling man dressed in a blue suit stepped up to the microphone set up on the balcony and began what I assumed to be an introduction for Gustavo in Portuguese. Some people behind me booed, but mostly the crowded clapped and cheered.

The man spoke for another minute, then, waving an arm behind him, he announced, "Luis Gustavo de Jardim!"

More applause and cheers. A group—the Gustavo family—took their places in front of the mic. Luis

Gustavo de Jardim was a short man, as Michael had said, but even from this distance, I could see he was fit. He raised his hand in a pumping motion and the crowd roared again, swept up in the man's magnetism.

Gustavo's family literally surrounded him as he stood at the microphone. His wife, a regal woman with black hair in a chignon, her face a smooth palette of calm beauty, stood to his right. His daughter, a younger, sexier version of her mother, was on his left. In front of Gustavo was a son, maybe ten or eleven years old, and behind him an older son. The wife, daughter and eldest son were all taller than Gustavo, blocking him from the sides and the back. The closeness of the bunch almost ensured that nearly any bullet sent his way would hit one of the family members first or, depending on the type of bullet, on exiting Gustavo's body.

The group remained close together as Gustavo started to speak. I couldn't understand a word, but I felt the excitement of the crowd. The press was in action now, scribbling notes, shooting video, snapping photos. Except Michael. He remained still, his face a mask of concentration.

I gazed at him, hoping he might feel my eyes and look my way. Did it have to happen like this?

I moved toward Michael, past the group of supporters at the front and to an area about thirty feet from my husband. My chest was so constricted with nervousness that it seemed as if my ribs were knitted together with steel cord. All the muscles in my body twitched and tensed.

Gustavo spoke again with emphasis, almost shouting. Once more, he pumped a hand in the air, and the crowd erupted into yells. Some in the audience jumped up and down. The sound was so loud it seemed to fill my brain.

Gustavo watched as the crowd went crazy. He waited for the cheers to subside. When they did, he smiled and took a slight step forward, his hands on the shoulders of his young son.

My eyes bolted to Michael. He shifted the camera to his left hand, and with his free hand, withdrew the rifle's handle from the camera's false base. The crowd went quiet again, waiting for Gustavo to resume, but I could barely register the silence through the blood pounding in my head.

Slowly, Michael raised the camera to his face. If you didn't look closely, you'd see just another photographer, taking yet another picture. But if you focused and looked close, you could see his finger on the trigger.

And now, it was my turn.

I opened my mouth wide, and I yelled the one word of Portuguese I'd learned. *"Fuzil!" Gun!* Then again, *"Fuzil!"*

79

The minute I screamed, Gustavo's eyes, and those of the crowd, shot to me. At that same moment, the sharp, ferocious crack of a rifle pierced the air. The crowd erupted again, but this time in shouts of alarm.

The security guards threw themselves at Gustavo and his family, tackling them. I looked at Michael, the camera now at his side. This time, he looked back at me.

At that moment, another explosive *crack* was heard. Michael dropped the camera and clutched his chest, staring down at himself. Redness seeped through his vest. He returned his eyes to mine for one moment. And then he crumpled to the ground.

I looked around wildly. Some people were running, others cowered on the grass. But kneeling on the lawn was a small figure with a sniper rifle. The person lowered the rifle away from her face.

"Liza!" I yelled.

She returned the scope to her face and pointed the rifle at me. Another crack blasted the air. A powerful force hammered into my chest. I felt the skin rip, tearing through my ribs. I felt something lodge there. Like Michael, I clutched at myself. I sank to my knees.

"Liza," I said again, although it was hard to talk.

She lowered the rifle away from her face. In that instant, I saw Liza in all of her stages; as a freckled, fresh-faced teenager; as a brash college grad; as a bridesmaid in both of my weddings; as my savior during those austere days after Scott left.

All those images cleared, and I saw Liza still holding that rifle. Just then a policeman ran behind her, his handgun pointed.

I blinked, trying to stay conscious.

She glanced behind her, then stood as if to run, but the cop fired his gun.

Liza, too, fell to her knees.

She looked at me again, then Liza Kingsley fell face-first into the grass. And the world went away.

80

St. Marabel, Canada

Roger strode to the podium at the front of the church. The place was adorned with funereal decor. He nodded at the priest, then looked out at the forty or so people assembled in the pews. He recognized a number of faces, since many were Twilight Club employees or members of the Trust.

He exhaled loudly into the microphone, as if he was having a hard time speaking. Although that impression wasn't exactly true, this was harder than he'd thought. When he and Michael had first met during his early years at the Trust, he wouldn't have thought it would end like this. There was something bizarre about it, though bizarre didn't necessarily equate with bad.

"The last time I was in this church, it was for Michael and Kate's wedding." He paused and shook his head. "I can't believe I'm now here to say goodbye to Michael Waller."

He continued, talking about how Michael was a great friend and an amazing man, how he would be sorely missed. But in Roger's mind, he was scrolling through his calendar and his schedule for the next few days. He'd conduct business here tomorrow at the club, then he'd fly to Chicago the next day to attend two more funerals—Kate's and Liza's.

All in all, it wasn't a bad schedule.

81

That day in St. Marabel before we left for Rio, when I saw that scar on Angus Laslow's stomach in St. Marabel, I got the same feeling of raw suspicion I'd been having since living with Michael. But by then I knew I'd been *right* about Michael—he was someone other than just a restaurateur, he was hiding something from me, he did know Liza more than he'd let on. I knew then to trust my instincts.

So I'd called Liza, and she e-mailed me a photo of "Rich." That photo confirmed that Angus Laslow, who worked for the Twilight Club and the Trust, was Liza's boyfriend.

I sat at the library's computer that afternoon, staring at the photo, and I debated what to do. Alarm coursed through me, but I needed to think things through. Was it possible Liza knew about Angus and hadn't told me? Or maybe she simply hadn't been able to, since we really hadn't spoken since that day on her balcony. Was I overreacting?

I would let Liza decide. I went back to the meat market and phoned her with my calling card.

"Are we good to talk?" I asked.

"We're fine," she said. "And I'm so glad to hear from you. I've been worried since you left. Are you okay?"

"I'm fine. But about Rich…"

"What about Rich?" Her voice was wary. Then she chuckled. "He's cute, right?"

I glanced around the market. One butcher was helping an older woman. The other stood with his arms crossed, his eyes on me. He smiled at me. I felt a stab of paranoia. He couldn't be a member of the Trust, I told myself.

Still, I turned my back. "He is cute, Liza, but…" I paused. "Look, he's a member, right? Of the…"

"Why would you say that?"

"Because he works at the Twilight Club."

Complete silence. Then, "Oh, my God."

"His name, at least around here, is Angus Laslow."

"Oh, my God."

"You didn't know."

"He told me he was a lawyer. From Boston." She laughed a short, scornful laugh. "Jesus, I can't believe I fell for it."

We were quiet a second. "What does this mean?" I asked.

"I don't know, but I'll figure it out. I should go." Her voice was brusque.

"No, don't."

"Seriously, Kate, I've got to figure this out."

"Well, figure it out with me!" My voice rose a little, and I turned around to see if anyone had noticed. Both men behind the counter were busy with customers now. I turned back again. "Look, I know everything about you guys now. *I'm* the one that found out about Angus. Let me do something here. Hash this out with me. Let me help."

"I'm not used to that."

"There are a lot of things you're not used to, but maybe it's time to change."

I could almost hear her brain turning the situation around and around, analyzing it.

"What are you thinking?" I said.

"I'm thinking what an ass I am. God, I *really* liked him. I mean…" She made a small sound, a tiny moan of anguish. "I was starting to wonder if I could be in love with him."

"I know. And I'm sorry."

We were quiet. We both knew how rare a statement Liza had made.

"Do you think it was all an act?" I asked. "At least on his part?"

"Yes," she said bitterly.

"Why did he get involved with you?"

"That's what I can't get straight. I mean, obviously the Trust sent him. They clearly wanted to watch me closely. I just don't know why."

"Is there anything you've been hiding from them?"

"Nothing. I'm as clean as they come."

"Well, someone thought you weren't. Or maybe they were hoping you weren't. Who would have sent Angus?"

She scoffed. "Angus. Great name. Much better than Rich, actually."

"Focus, Liza."

"I know, I know." She groaned. "He had to be sent by somebody high up."

"Why do you say that?"

"Because the cover was elaborate. He had an apartment here. He had business cards with the name of a law firm in my building. Damn, I never did see him at the office. He'd just get off the elevator, and I'd *assume* he was working there."

"So who's high up enough to send him?"

We were both quiet for a second. "Roger."

"Okay, but now we're back to why."

"Shit," Liza said.

"What?"

"Roger wanted me for a job in Rio."

I didn't know what to say. I thought about it. I had told Liza she could hash this out, and maybe I was going to take a leap and trust her to let me do the same.

"Michael has a job in Rio," I said.

"I know."

"Does he know you'll be there, too?"

A pause. "No. Oh, God, Kate. This is such a mess."

"What do you mean?"

She exhaled loudly. "Okay. Here it is."

82

Liza made a risky decision to tell me about the hit ordered on Michael. And the fact that *she* was going to be the one to kill him.

I was shocked. I hated her. But she asked me to listen while she explained. After she did, I went to the club and found Michael and asked him to take a walk.

"Kate, what's going on?" he said. His expression was weary, worried.

I pulled him into a café that was crowded and noisy. I held his arm and took him to the back. "Can we talk here?"

He glanced around and nodded.

"Radimir Trotsky," I said.

Michael's weary face shifted into one of alert attention.

"He was CIA."

"What are you talking about?" His eyes narrowed, then blinked, and I could tell his reaction was one of genuine surprise. He hadn't known.

I told Michael about discovering that Angus was masquerading as Rich, and how he'd apparently been conducting surveillance on Liza. I told him everything that she'd told me—how she believed that Michael had killed Aleksei to cover up the Trotsky story, how Roger had said that Michael was running loose and taking matters into his own hands, how she'd been ordered to kill Michael but was having second thoughts, now that she'd found out Rich's real identity. I told him Liza was willing to talk.

The muscles in my husband's jaw worked as he listened to me. "Let's call her," he said. "Now."

We drove to a large hotel on the outskirts of town and rented a conference room. Michael and I took seats at a table opposite each other and, using the speakerphone, we called Liza. She and Michael hashed out everything they knew, and it was then they started piecing together what Roger was doing.

It was an awful moment when Liza heard Colby had been murdered. "Roger Leiland killed my brother," she said, her voice full of astonishment. She strangled a cry. "He killed all of us in a way when he did that. He killed my father."

Michael and I looked at each other across the faux-wood table, and we sat in silence while Liza cried.

When she quieted, I leaned forward to talk in the phone. "Liza, it's okay."

"How is it okay?"

I moved the phone toward me. "Because we're going to make it okay. We are not taking this lying down, all right?"

After a minute, she exhaled loudly. "Right. Let's get that fucker."

Later that day, Michael went back to the club and reviewed his employee logs. Angus had often been gone from the club on "Trust business." When Michael compared those dates to days when Liza had seen Rich in Chicago, they matched up precisely. And then Michael saw Angus was scheduled to be gone from the club again, exactly the time when the Rio mission was scheduled. It was then Michael started to suspect Liza might be in danger, too.

We went to Rio as planned.

We tailed Angus, who believed he was the cat and not the mouse. We found out where he was staying. In the early-morning hours on the day of Gustavo's rally, Liza and Michael broke into Angus's room and sedated him while he slept. They found the police uniform in the closet.

We'd had a plan, but now it needed to be altered.

Instead of Angus wearing the uniform that day, Liza paid Faustino—a man she'd worked with in Rio and whom she knew would do absolutely anything for the right price—to wear the uniform. And to shoot Liza, after she shot us.

The bullets in the guns that day were special, thanks to Michael's knowledge of the Chicago research and the help of Sebastian, whom Michael trusted enough with the whole story.

Essentially, the bullets contained liquid that became a gas when the gun was fired, due to thermal energy. After we'd been shot with these bullets, the liquid, a protein-based enzyme, was inhaled through our lungs and entered our bloodstream. That enzyme in turn metabolized the endothelial coating of the microchips that Sebastian had implanted in the folds under our arms. And when that happened we became the first field tests of Project Juliet.

Because the Juliet drug was really just a series of drugs already available, Sebastian was able to secure those drugs and combine them. Once the coating of the microchip dissolved, it released, in sequence, the Juliet drugs and made us appear clinically dead.

Our bodies were declared DOA by paramedics. We knew what local hospital we'd be taken to, and we'd made sure beforehand that all caskets in the morgue were oxygenated. Later that night, in the quiet of the morgue, Sebastian woke us, and replaced our bodies with weighted corpse replicas, which were then flown back to the U.S.

Sebastian accompanied the caskets and when he arrived he told Liza's mom and my parents that we were okay. We couldn't let our parents go through the anguish of a real funeral. But he asked them to stage funerals with closed caskets. Somehow our parents held up.

And Michael, Liza and I slipped away.

83

Rio de Janeiro, Brazil

Two weeks after her supposed death, Liza walked into the old prison on the outskirts of the city. It was a dinosaur of a facility—all crumbling stone and filthy walls smeared with graffiti and God knows what else. The smell of urine permeated the place, and there was no air-conditioning, making the heat thick and oppressive.

The prison housed mostly petty criminals held for carjackings and thefts. There was a bounty of such crime in Rio, so it took months to process the prisoners and often years to resolve their cases through hearings or trials. It was a place where a person could easily get lost or overlooked.

Liza gave the name of the prisoner she was there to see—Henrique de Tonas.

"You would like to see him in the cell?" the guard said in Portuguese. Faustino had submitted this request for Liza, and she'd paid him well to make sure it was granted.

Soon, she was being escorted down a hallway lined

on one side with grimy cells that were protected by rusting steel bars. Some prisoners rushed to their cell door, calling obscenities to her, telling her what they would do to her if they could. This only made Liza grin. This was precisely the kind of place she'd hoped for.

When they reached the last cell, the guard stopped and nodded at it.

Liza asked if she could have a moment alone. The guard walked down the hallway about a hundred feet and leaned against the wall, waiting for her.

She stepped up to the cell bars. Inside were two prisoners. One, an obese man whose soiled T-shirt barely covered his swollen belly, slept on the top cot, an arm thrown over his face. The mattress sagged under his weight, hardly leaving room for the inhabitant of the lower cot, Henrique de Tonas, to climb in if he wanted.

The man now known as Henrique was sitting on the floor, cross-legged, against the far wall, next to a toilet with no lid that was clearly clogged and ready to overflow. His face was cut in two places and the remnants of an old black eye were still visible.

"Hello, Rich," Liza said. "Or should I call you Angus? Or do you like Henrique now?"

His eyes narrowed. The man on the top bunk groaned and rolled over to face the wall.

"I heard you got picked up for impersonating a police officer and stealing his gun."

Liza had made sure that Rich's drugged body was dropped off in front of a police station. His pocket contained identification, doctored with Rich's picture, and bearing the name Henrique de Tonas, a man who was wanted for everything from drug trafficking to counterfeiting and who'd been eluding the police for years. The real de Tonas had been found, paid off handsomely and told to spend a few years with his family in the countryside. She hadn't told anyone—not Kate or Michael or the Trust—what she'd done. It was her own personal slice of revenge.

Rich stood and crossed the cell floor. He had a pronounced limp, and Liza noticed his right ankle was swollen.

When he reached the bars, one of his arms suddenly darted out to grab her.

She jumped back, just missing his hand. "You don't get to touch me anymore."

The guard yelled from down the hallway for Henrique to behave. Or else.

"You fucking bitch," he snarled at her.

Liza gave him a grim smile. "Why do you have to be like that?"

She knew it was irresponsible to be here—letting Angus see she was alive—but for once she'd let her emotions get the best of her. She was doing a lot of that lately, and she intended to continue it. She was no longer the Liza who was frozen emotionally, who could take care of her depressed friend but who kept herself unaffected. These days, she had all sorts of emotions—grief over Colby and her father; sadness and fear that she was out of the Trust (the only job she'd known); optimism and the occasional glimmer of elation that she could craft an entirely new life now.

"You know why I didn't kill you?" she said to Angus.

She spoke the words softly, because she was starting to feel bad for him now that she was here. Such conditions were cruel. There was no telling when, or if, he'd get out. She'd heard rumors of prisoners getting lost in here for years.

Angus said nothing.

"I didn't kill you because you made me *feel* something for the first time in a long, long time. And even though I despise you now, I want to keep that feeling alive. For me."

"You want to know how I felt when I was with you?" he said in a near growl. "Like I was fucking a cold slab of meat."

"Well, I'm sure *he'll* keep you satisfied." She gestured at his cellmate.

Angus lunged again, his arm shooting through the bars. She easily dodged him.

"Bye-bye, Angus." She blew him a kiss. Then she turned away and sauntered down the hall.

84

St. Marabel, Canada

Roger Leiland greeted the four other board members in the wine cellar room of the Twilight Club, shaking the hand of each one, patting arms and speaking to them warmly. He was on top of the world now in so many ways. He was the head of the Trust, and with Michael and Liza gone, every member would toe the line. It was entirely his show, and he was going to have a blast running it. It was also going to make him very, very wealthy.

He took a seat at the head of the table and gestured for the others to sit. Three of the other board members were men and the last a quiet woman named Morgan Hadings. These members had all been brought in by Coleman. They had enjoyed a long history duking it out in the trenches of the Trust, and now they simply wanted to sit back, out of the line of fire.

They took their seats, and Roger ordered wine. When it was brought and poured, he asked the waiter to stay out of the room.

He deactivated the surveillance system—they always

did when the board met—and he addressed the group. "We have some unfortunate business to discuss today. The loss of two of our members, Michael Waller and Liza Kingsley."

He went on to talk about how both had made significant contributions to the Trust and would be missed. He also addressed the serious concern about the AWOL status of Angus Laslow, chalking up Angus's disappearance to an undetected mental instability. Roger had doctored up some records to make it look as if Angus had been seeing a psychiatrist for post-traumatic stress disorder following a mission in Beijing last year. One of his real theories was that Angus had been more attached to Liza than he'd let on and that the task of killing her had pushed him to true instability. Roger would find the shithead eventually. And he would deal with Angus appropriately.

Roger kept talking, addressing the fact that the Rio mission had gone awry, the shot from Michael failing to hit Gustavo, and Michael and Liza both being killed.

Vincent Lunosi, one of the board members, raised a pointed finger. "If both Liza Kingsley and Michael Waller were in Rio to ensure Gustavo's death, and Gustavo is still very much alive, what in the hell happened? Why did Kingsley shoot Waller?"

Roger had anticipated such a question. He explained that Liza had taken matters into her own hands. Essentially, she'd blown her cool after the loss of her ex-lover, Aleksei Ivanov, and after learning information that Michael had killed Aleksei, she'd eliminated him.

"Why would Waller have taken out a reporter like Ivanov?" one of the other men asked.

"Ivanov was investigating the death of Radimir Trotsky." He paused dramatically. "We ordered the hit on Trotsky based on Michael's intel. Unfortunately, he hadn't told us everything. We've learned now that Radimir Trotsky was actually a C.I.A."

No response from the group. Although they'd all been trained never to look surprised, he'd expected something here.

"But you knew Trotsky was C.I.A.," Morgan said.

Roger turned to her. "Not until after the elimination when we learned that Michael had apparently been working for the Mafiya."

Morgan Hadings shook her head dismissively. She took out a leather folder from her bag and opened it. "You knew Trotsky was CIA well before the job, isn't that right? And you sold that information to the Mafiya, and you had Trotsky killed to prove to them the Trust could do the job, correct?"

He felt a tickle of unease travel from the base of his skull to the bottom of his spine. "You're mistaken about that, Morgan. I…"

"Isn't it also true," one of the men said, interrupting him, glancing at a sheaf of paper he'd taken from his inside jacket pocket, "that you manufactured grievous deeds committed by an Italian named Angelo Naponi so that the Trust would approve a hit, when in fact the only crime he'd committed was acting as competition for Silvia Falconiere?"

Roger's unease turned to distress. He suddenly

realized the precariousness of his situation—no backup, no audio or video operating, none of his handpicked staff. "That's not accurate. And I take great offense to the slander. May I ask what document you're reviewing?"

"This is a memo from Michael Waller and Liza Kingsley," said Morgan. Roger's distress turned into alarm. "A memo?"

"Dated three days ago. Michael is alive, as is his wife and Liza Kingsley." Morgan looked down at the contents of her folder. "The memo also says you ordered the killing of Coleman Kingsley, Jr., in the hopes that Coleman Senior would be devastated and the loss would weaken his hold on the organization he founded."

She wasn't asking questions now, just stating sentences in the affirmative.

"I categorically deny that allegation."

"We don't need your response." She closed the folder and placed it on the table, dropping her hands into her lap. "We have researched and confirmed every assertion in this memo. We've also come to a decision about your status."

Roger glanced at the other board members. Their faces were all placid, unreadable.

"You are no longer a member of the Trust," Morgan continued. "Effective immediately."

Bolts of anger shot through his body. "I don't accept that!" He shoved his chair back and charged to his feet. This was not how this was going to go down.

"You're attempting to make the Trust an organization of assassins for hire," Morgan said. "We won't have it."

"Look, you sniveling idealists," Roger shouted at them, his hands clenching into fists, "we've always killed for profit. Always!"

"That's not accurate."

"How do you think we've funded this all along? What's the difference? Think about it. We might believe, in our esteemed opinion as Americans, that a person like Gustavo is a tyrant, and we'll take him out while accepting a capital contribution by other groups. Right? What's the difference between that and taking Silvia Falconiere's money to eliminate Naponi?"

"The difference," one of the men said quietly, "is that in the first scenario, we have our beliefs. Our work is hard. It is rarely clear-cut. But we know that what we are doing is protecting our country and upholding the beliefs of the Trust, rather than selling our sevices."

"Bullshit!" Roger yelled.

The members of the board stared at him with disquieting calm. Fuck these rubes. He would start over. He would train his own operatives and track down all his contacts and let them know he'd opened his own shop. And he would track down Michael, too, and his pathetic simpering wife, and then Liza, and he would personally kill each of them with his own two hands.

In the meantime, he needed to get out of this room. Out of the Twilight Club. He rolled his shoulders back and began to address the board again. "I categorically deny any wrongdoing and—"

"For God's sake, Roger," Morgan said, "shut up for once."

Her hands lifted from her lap and, too late, Roger saw

the 9 mm in her grasp. He hesitated, his mind scrambling for a solution.

But she didn't hesitate. In an instant, she raised the handgun. And Roger Leiland felt his mind explode as the bullet tore into his brain.

85

French countryside.
The Charente/Dordogne border

I had thought my life was quiet after my divorce, and yet, comparatively, it was a riotous, rocking party compared to the way Michael and I live now. It has to be that way until everything is truly final with the Trust. We have to keep to ourselves and avoid the friendly smiles of the villagers when we occasionally go to town for Bergerac Rouge wine and walnuts and cepes, the local mushrooms.

We have to spend our time all by ourselves. And I love it.

I am no one I knew when I lived in Chicago. I am a woman who knows how to detect poisonous berries from edible ones. I can deseed those berries and make a pie, with my own crust. Baking is a newly acquired skill that I've come to love. But most of all, I am no longer an innocent. I have plotted my own death.

While I am stronger and tougher and more myself than I have ever been, Michael is my world and I am his.

In a way it's familiar—it's the way I thought Scott and I would be. I believed that the children we would have would be like planets that orbited us. We would be a unified sun. Yet Scott had different ideas. About me, about marriage and kids. For that I am glad, because in a way he brought me to this place with the white eyelet bedspread and the massive tub with the brass-clawed feet and the orchard that skims our property, protecting us. Because of Scott's rejection, he sent me down this path, which ended in a place where the sun sparkles over our garden in the early morning hours and the moon always seems like a benevolent golden eye in the navy sky.

Yes, Scott got me here. He and Liza, of course.

When I get up this morning, and put my blue tea kettle on the stove, I'm thinking of her. Where she is now, I don't know. We've got a plan to meet in Paris after the Trust tells us it's okay to come out of hiding. But we don't know when that will be. And I miss my friend.

Roger has been "taken care of", a fact that makes Michael sad and sometimes moody, despite everything. To me, the thought of Roger being killed is surreal. I guess I haven't adjusted yet to my husband's profession. *Previous* profession, I should say.

They don't know where Angus is, and they don't know if there are others like Angus with whom Roger was working closely. Until all Trust members have been screened and cleared, we've been asked to stay away, as has Liza, and we've been asked not to interact at all, for everyone's safety.

Michael is still in bed—he sleeps late these days, something he says he's always wanted to do—and I enjoy my morning moments alone. I open a tin of black tea and scoop the leaves into a strainer. I pour the hot water over it, watching the steam rise and curl from my cup. It's details like this that I notice about life now.

I think of Liza as I lift and lower the strainer from the cup. I watch the tea spreading, mixing with the water. I wonder if Liza is making tea or drinking coffee somewhere this morning.

I imagine her living in Budapest or maybe Barcelona. Her auburn hair might be cut short, possibly dyed dark, although she could never hide those freckles. I imagine she has some job that no one would ever suspect her of doing—possibly she's a receptionist or a store clerk—and yet that job brings her joy in its simplicity. I imagine she is doing the exact same thing that Michael and I are—living small but wonderful lives.

I sometimes wonder if Liza knows where we are, if maybe she checks on us from time to time, just to ensure we're all right. It's something Liza would do, and certainly I feel her around me. Sometimes, when I walk the yard at sunset, checking that the gates around the orchard are latched, I feel her eyes. It usually starts as a warmth that seeps in under the creeping cool of the evening. I glance around, trying to tell if a breeze has pushed some of the heat of the day through from the yard, but nothing moves, the trees don't stir. Then I usually hear a murmur, a whisper more tangible than breeze. But everything is still. It's then that I scan the hilltops far in the distance. I've learned to look for the quick flicker-glare of a camera's lens or a rifle's eye, yet I see nothing. I don't feel under surveillance—at least not like I did when the Trust was watching. I feel, instead, as if someone might have peeked in on us, ready to tuck in Michael and me for the night.

Today, I open the kitchen door and take my tea outside to the back yard, like I've been doing every morning. This time, I find something new.

Right outside our door and scratched into the surface of the dusty dirt, are four words—*Love You, Sister Girl.*

BOOK CLUB QUESTIONS

(Possible Spoiler Alert!)

1. Do you think organizations like the Trust exist in our country? If not, could they? What do you think of the Trust's initial mission statement and goals?

2. At some point in the book, Kate says that long distance relationships are the toughest breed. Do you agree? Can long distance relationships work? Do you think Michael and Kate moved too fast?

3. Before reading this book, did you know about the Phoenix Program? (The Phoenix Program was a real, CIA-initiated program that operated during the Vietnam War. Its existence was classified until 1980.) What did you think about what Michael had to do as part of the Phoenix Program?

4. Should Liza have been more careful about introducing Kate to a member of the Trust? Once Michael and Kate became close, should Liza have done something more to caution her, even though it violated Trust protocol?

5. Michael wanted to retire from the Trust, but he found it tougher to step away than he anticipated. Were his struggles specific to his work or is retirement universally difficult, no matter what your profession?